H

MW00811058

Dale Dye

"A singular achievement...vivid, terse, exceptionally moving...the tension builds and never lets up."

—*The New York Times*

"Dye fills this dialogue-driven thriller with plenty of action and lots of military detail—all of which (no surprise) rings completely true."

—*Marc Leepson, VVA Books in Review*

"Dale Dye has a flair for telling stories and evoking images. His details about Marine life are accurate...Dye has the ability to draw the reader far enough into the story that the reader sees with the author's eyes and feels with his emotions...Dye's ability to tell a story the way it really happens is rare, and one sincerely hopes this book will not be his last...."

—*Orlando Sentinel*

"Here, in prose that positively crackles, he takes us along on what has been one great ride."

—*Ed Ruggero: Veteran, Writer, Motivational Speaker*

Also by Dale Dye

HAVANA FILE

DALE DYE

WARRIORS PUBLISHING GROUP
NORTH HILLS, CALIFORNIA

HAVANA FILE

A Warriors Publishing Group book/published by arrangement with the author

PRINTING HISTORY
Warriors Publishing Group edition/May 2016

ISBN 978-1-944353-09-4

Library of Congress Control Number 2016900703

The name "Warriors Publishing Group" and the logo

are trademarks belonging to Warriors Publishing Group

PRINTED IN THE UNITED STATES OF AMERICA

10 9 8 7 6 5 4 3 2 1

For the often battered but never broken Buttplates of Rent-A-Battalion (2nd Battalion, 3rd Marines) Vietnam circa 1967-68. I was privileged to walk with you through some hard times. Semper Fidelis.

Washington, D.C.—Memorial Day

He inhaled a warm, wet breeze that swept up from the Tidal Basin in a northerly direction across West Potomac Park carrying the attar of dying cherry blossoms. It was pleasant here just a few hours after dawn and before the high tide of exhaust fumes crested over the National Mall. He paused on his route, squinting toward the east where rays from a rising sun caused the recently renovated Washington Monument to sparkle and shimmer. The big blond dog at his side pawed at something buried under a carpet of fading pink petals and then lifted his leg to mark the spot as previously explored terrain. To his left front along the curb of Henry Bacon Drive, a short radial that connects the Lincoln Memorial with Constitution Avenue, he saw crowds beginning to form as he knew they would in larger and larger numbers throughout the day.

There were some early rising bikers wearing leather vests festooned with military pins and patches, straddling Harleys spiked with so many American flags they looked more like porcupines than motorcycles. Some pop-up tents were being erected to accommodate various veterans' groups that had pledged to gather on this day for ceremonies at the Vietnam Veterans Memorial. Unit banners and the ever-present black POW-MIA flag moved sluggishly in the early morning air. He offered his dog a Milk Bone from the pocket of his jeans and squatted, watching little clusters of early arrivals, most in one form or another of ancient camouflage or olive-drab jungle uniforms. They hugged, postured, and popped high-fives. Many of them, he knew, were strangers to each other, but gatherings like this always goosed them beyond human territorial imperatives. Just having been in Vietnam at one point or another was enough to make them act like prodigal sons returning to the family fold.

And it was enough to make him decide that this, likely his last visit to the black chevron-shaped memorial nearby, would be quick, just a murmur with the spirits of a few really close friends that he'd long ago determined were somehow present behind the sterile names etched in various places along the 250-foot length of ebony stone. He'd always felt such moments were best savored or suffered in private. Crowds of somber veterans, searching for succor or surcease from the survivor guilt that drove them here to stand teary-eyed touching the wall bothered him. At gatherings for special occasions like Memorial Day the place took on the trappings of a noisy Irish wake and the little mementos visitors often left somehow seemed to trivialize the experience.

He tarried for a while near a wrought-iron fence that was designed to keep visitors to this patch of green south of Foggy Bottom moving in an orderly fashion past memorials that marked American sacrifice in modern military conflicts from World War I to Vietnam. Somewhere in here and fairly soon, he thought as he secured the dog's leash to a stanchion, they would have to find space for a memorial to those killed in Iraq and Afghanistan. He rose, wincing at the stiffness in a right knee that still housed a dime-sized hunk of shrapnel from an enemy landmine, and motioned for his dog to stay. The big animal settled into his sphinx posture and worried the treat between his paws. Bear would be fine during the short spell his human companion needed to commune with buddies who had gambled and lost during the Greater Southeast Asia War Games.

The memorial was deserted when he arrived at the cobblestone walkway fronting the wall except for a night-shift Park Service Ranger who gave him a quick eyeball followed by a weary nod and then turned to check the growing crowds near the Lincoln Memorial. As he turned right to begin his visit, he felt the strange power of the place. As it had on every other occasion when he visited, the wall seemed to exude an eerie miasma, an aura that wrapped him like an invisible cloak settling heavily on his shoulders and squeezing at his chest. His heart thumped a little more strongly as he began to walk along the ascending panels, and there was a catch in his throat as he breathed in the fragrant air. His destination on this visit was ahead of him, at the intersection where the two arms of the memorial joined at an obtuse angle. The 10-foot-tall sections in that area listed the dead from 1968-69, the bloodiest years of the long war. It was midway up on one of those panels that he found the man he'd come to see.

"Won't be visiting much anymore, Emmet." He whispered, focusing on images of a ruddy little beer-barrel Marine who stumbled, fumbled, and laughed through the tough times calling himself a "combat tourist," just visiting Vietnam on a little cultural exchange. "I sold the condo in Arlington. We're moving to Texas—a little town called Lockhart just south of Austin." He reached up and touched the cold surface of the stone, letting his fingertips glide lightly over the etched letters in the name of a man who died walking behind him on a shitty little meaningless patrol along the banks of the Cua Viet River. "You'd like it there, dude. They got ice-cold beer and the best barbecue in the Lone Star State."

The roar of motorcycle engines interrupted him and he turned to see a phalanx of veteran bikers pulling into the parking lot. "I gotta hit the road before it gets crazy around here, Emmet, but I wanted you to know that I'm really sorry I missed that mine. I was walking point and I should have seen it. I'll never know why I didn't. I know you'd tell me it wasn't my fault if you were here, but that's the point, Emmet. You're not here and I am. I'm sorry, that's all. I'm just really sorry—and I wanted to come by and let you know."

Having said the piece he'd come to say, he focused on his image reflected from the polished surface of the wall. There was something about seeing yourself reflected here—as if you were inside that wall with all the others—that gave cold comfort, but he'd long ago learned to take comfort where and when he could get it. He was about to leave when he caught sight of someone standing nearby, staring at the same panel and massaging a well-worn boonie hat in his hands. The man was balding and bearded, wearing faded jeans and a ratty OD jungle jacket with the big black and gold patch of the 1st Cavalry Division on the left shoulder. He nodded. The man nodded back and then fell into formation at his shoulder as he walked toward the end of the wall.

"What year?" The man asked without introduction or preamble in a voice that rumbled with the effect of too many cigarettes or too much whiskey or maybe both.

"Years," he corrected. "I went over in 67 and then just kept extending through the middle part of 70."

"Damn," the stranger said as he strapped the boonie hat back on his head and adjusted the brim into a forward rake. "I guess you were a glutton for punishment."

"I guess," he confirmed. "I was in it for the long haul and it seemed like the place to be at the time."

"Marine?"

"Guilty as charged. First Marine Division for the most part, up on the DMZ and west of there."

"I was Army, 67-68. First Air Cav."

"I noticed the horse blanket on your shoulder. We worked with you guys on Operation Pegasus. You there?"

"Most affirm. Clear Route Nine from LZ Stud to Khe Sanh and relieve the Marines." The stranger chuckled and shook his head. "Not that you guys needed any kind of re-lievin' but that's the word got passed to us doggies."

"Glad you were there. I never saw so many helicopters in one place at one time. Every time we looked up there came another Army Huey while our Marine birds always seemed to be grounded or busy elsewhere. You guys pulled a lot of our wounded out of it on that op."

"That's the Air Cav for you. Why walk when you can fly. Mind if I ask you a question?"

"If I can answer, I'll try."

"How come the Marines made a tour in Nam thirteen months? I always wondered about that. We had three-sixty-five straight up. How come you jarheads had to do an extra month?"

"Never really understood that myself. I heard some loud and long bitching about it but nobody ever really explained it to me. I read somewhere that the Corps wanted to be sure they got a full year in the field out of us so they added an extra thirty days to cover travel and training and stuff like that."

The stranger nodded and chewed on his lip for a moment. "Makes you wonder how many of them dudes on the wall got blown away in that extra month, don't it?"

"I guess." He stopped at the end of the wall and offered his hand to the stranger who took it in both of his. "I gotta get on the road. Hope you meet up with some of your buddies today."

The stranger squeezed his hand and nodded in the direction of the wall. "I already met up with the ones who count. Welcome home, Marine."

"Thanks," he said, "and same to you." The sentiment had always seemed off-putting but he'd learned to deal with it after hearing it so many times from other Vietnam Veterans. He really had no home during the two decades he served as a Marine. Home was where you stowed your seabag. Home was where you dug it in the field. Home was a concept, not a place. He smiled and walked away from the wall.

The stranger growled at his back. "Take care. See you at the last firebase."

He waved without turning back toward the wall, hoping Emmet and all the others memorialized there would understand why he couldn't stay any longer.

Squads of Memorial Day observers were descending on the wall by the time he retrieved the dog and made it to his bulk-loaded pick-up. When he had Bear comfortably settled in the backseat of the crew-cab, he fired the engine and powered up his voice-activated GPS. A breathy female greeted him through the speakers in the dashboard.

"Hello, Gunner Shake Davis. Where are we going today?"

"Select Option Bravo," he said as he pulled the truck into gear and waited for the device to display the route map he'd pre-programmed. "Let's go to Texas."

On the Road

Shake was stopped at a grassy turnout about 90 miles out of Atlanta by sundown and watching Bear carefully select a pooping spot. He was full of coffee and sandwiches, planning a route around the city, and keeping an eye on threatening weather to the west when his phone rang. Caller ID told him daughter Tracey was on the line. He'd been expecting to hear from her since she'd sent a text letting him know she started on her sabbatical from the regular gig at Woods Hole Oceanographic Institution. During her time off, Tracey was volunteering with a program called Xchange, run by Shake's friend Lynn Fulton, a retired Marine Gunnery Sergeant. The program, designed to help exploited females escape sex trafficking—a brutal and prevalent problem in Central America—had caught Tracey's interest during her visit with Shake and Chan in Belize.

Hey, girl. Where are you?"

"Belize City, Dad—got in day before yesterday. Gunny Fulton's got me hard at work already. Where are you?"

"Somewhere north of Atlanta, on my way to Texas." Shake paced away from the truck when he heard his dog barking furiously. "Bear is keeping me company on the road."

"Good Lord! Is that him I hear?"

"Yeah. He's got a squirrel treed out here and he's thinking snack. The squirrel seems to have other ideas. Can you hold on for a minute while I get him?"

Shake whistled for the dog to no avail and finally had to use the leash to get Bear out of hunter mode and into the truck. He poured fresh water into a travel bowl and got back on the line.

"OK; he's pouting in the truck. So how's the work?"

"It's all good, I think. Maybe I can help out down here but...you know, I've only got a couple of weeks before I need to get back to Woods Hole. Who knows? Anyway, I'm gonna give it a shot."

"Listen, Tracey. You saw the situation can get dicey last time we were all down there, so you be careful. Stick close to Gunny Fulton and follow her lead."

"It's instinctive, Dad. I've been following orders from Marines ever since I can remember."

"You could do a lot worse. Anyway, I want regular sitreps while you're down there. If you can't reach me, call Chan's cell number."

"How's she doing?"

"Good, I think. The DIA didn't much want to see her go and they've left the door open if she wants to come back, but I think she'll be happy with the thing at UT in Austin."

"I'd love to audit one of her Poly Sci courses. Chan is bound to warp a few young brains."

"Well, they wanted somebody with real-world experience and they damn sure got it with Chan. She's down at the house in Lockhart dealing with the movers. Give her a call."

"OK, but I wanted to ask you about this Cuba situation. We've got a few women down here—refugees mostly—that are plenty upset about this normalization plan, lifting the embargo and all that."

"They aren't the only ones, Tracey. I had a call the other day from an old Mustache Pete in Miami. Guy's a survivor from the Bay of Pigs deal back in '61. They're all old men now, but they've got good memories. It's fair to say most of the Cuban population in the U.S. is not happy with the President's proposals."

"What's your take on it?"

"Well, I'm not happy with this president or his proposals in general, but you know that. I'm worried about what's happening or is gonna happen down there behind the scenes. The Cubans are in the hip pocket of every anti-American country or organization there is and lifting an embargo, normalizing relations and all that stuff ain't gonna change the situation. I think we're opening ourselves up to a nest of snakes ninety miles offshore and that's stupid. Any real change for the better in Cuba has got to come from the grass-roots. The people have got to get rid of the Castro regime."

"Yeah, I thought that's what I'd hear from an old anti-communist warhorse."

"Don't take my word for it, girl. Call Chan. She'll tell you the same thing."

"Guess I better do that. Give me a call on this number when you hit Lockhart and send me some phone-snaps of the new place."

"I'll do it. Remember the sitreps."

"Copy all, Dad. Love you. Bye."

On the road again, driving through the gloom on a long northerly loop around Atlanta to rejoin US 20, it began to rain hard. An hour further on, a flashing highway alert just east of the state line said there were thunderstorm warnings and flood watches posted for most of central Alabama. Shake reduced the speed on his cruise control and switched the wipers to high rate. As the truck forged on through the driving rain, he found himself thinking about the administration's announced re-set of relations with long-time adversary Castro's Cuba. He popped the Willie Nelson CD out of the audio console and began to search for talk-radio stations.

There were more than a few high-powered blowtorches on the AM dial, but none seemed to be talking about Cuba other than brief mentions in concert with other criticisms of the sitting President and his policies.

Understandable, Shake supposed as he checked the fuel gauge and decided he could push on and fill up once he crossed into Alabama. Economic recovery in the country was somewhere between substandard and shitty. There was a major situation developing in several urban areas between police and minority populations that threatened regular outbreaks of violence. And the damn *jihadis* in the Middle East were rapidly regaining ground that had been paid for with American blood and treasure over the past decade. Americans had a lot more on the collective mind than relations with Cuba.

It was enough to send him searching for a bolt-hole which is a big part, he admitted, of why they decided to finally make a move away from the flagpole—to relocate someplace where the major concerns were more mundane things like cattle, crops, and high-school football. He was fairly frustrated with the radio by the time he started seeing signs for an approach to Birmingham and went back to riding with Willie. Bear was stretched out on the backseat and didn't seem to mind either way.

It was raining hard and the dark sky was periodically rent with vivid lightning spikes when he stopped for gas at a little country joint that featured a convenience store and a couple of pumps. Shake set the nozzle to run and then let Bear out to pee. The dog did his business in a hurry and then whined to get out of the rain and back to his nap. Shake topped off the tank and jogged into the store to empty his bladder and fill his snack sack. He hit the head and then broke out his plastic to pay for the gas, soda, and munchies. The kid at the

counter in a greasy John Deere cap had seen Bear watering
one of his outdoor display racks and wanted to know what
kind of dog that was.

"Golden Pyrenees," Shake told him. "Looks like a killer
but he's just a hundred-pound lapdog." The kid got a kick
out of that and noting out-of-state plates on the truck asked
where Shake and his dog were heading. When Shake told
him, the kid whistled softly and scratched at a patch of lank
hair under his cap.

"So, y'all plannin' on headin' south out of Birmingham?"

"Yeah, I guess. Map says 59 out of there, south to 20 and
then west across Mississippi."

"Reason I asked," said the kid, "is y'all might want to
look at another route. Radio says a big old stretch of 59 south
is washed out. State Troopers been advisin' alternate routes.
Ain't no tellin' when the road will be open again."

"Yeah? What would you do?"

"Well, sir, if it was me headin' for Texas, I might take
78 North toward Memphis. That old road is always good as
gold. You'd be cuttin' across Mississippi contrary to the way
you want to go but you'd pick up 55 near Tupelo, then turn
south to Jackson and pick up 20 West."

"That the best option?"

"I believe it is in this weather which ain't supposed to let
up anytime soon. Elsewise you'd be chasin' all kinds of
country roads to keep yourself going south and ain't no tellin' what condition they're in."

Back in the truck, Shake re-programmed his GPS to get
a look at the option suggested. In a minute or two the program confirmed that most major southbound routes out of
Birmingham were closed or heavily restricted due to
weather. The alternate route to the northwest was green all

the way to Memphis. He made a few scrolling adjustments and discovered the trek to Tupelo and then south to Jackson on the Natchez Parkway and I-55 would cost him about 190 miles, three hours or better depending on the speeds he could maintain in the wind and rain. A local station he dialed up on the radio said the weather front was expected to hang around for the next two or three days effecting Alabama, Mississippi, and Louisiana so there wasn't much chance of driving out of the storms in any kind of a hurry. He checked his watch, re-set for Central Daylight Time, and punched the speed-dial to check with Chan.

"How's the weather in Lockhart?"

"Light rain just started. The movers have been at it since ten this morning and they're just about finished. We've got a lot more house than we've got furniture."

"Yeah, and that's why I'm gonna build that woodworking shop out by the bunkhouse, Chan. I'll make us some new stuff."

"I'll believe that when I see it, Shake. Where are you?"

"I stopped for gas outside of Birmingham. It's raining like hell and most of the southbound roads are a mess. Kid I talked to here says I need to head north before I turn south. If I do that, I'll have to stop somewhere and sleep. Probably put me a day or so late getting into Lockhart."

"How'd it go with the closing?"

"Piece of cake. Realtor handled it like she knew what she was doing. I even met the new owners: Mr. and Mrs. Federal Bureaucrat and the two little Bureaucrats. They seemed thrilled with the place."

"Bear OK?"

"In his element, either asleep in the backseat or chasing squirrels when we stop. He's having a ball."

"Well, be safe. I've got this down here so you don't need to push too hard."

"When do they want you to start at UT?"

"Next week I'm supposed to go up for faculty orientation, meet the department head and like that. I don't start classes until September so there's time for us to get settled."

"Any regrets yet?"

"Not a one so far. Some people dropped by around lunchtime to welcome me to the town. Very nice folks and they made me feel, you know—very small town, very country girl."

"You tell 'em you're a former spook?"

"No, the subject didn't come up. I just said my husband was a very handsome retired Marine and I was going to start teaching at the university up in Austin. They liked the Marine connection. People down here are very patriotic."

"OK, go get a beer and some barbecue at Black's. I'll be home in a day or two. Call me if anything changes and I'll do the same. Love you."

He broke the connection and started the engine. Bear growled and rolled over on his back. "Get comfortable, boy. We're gonna head for Tupelo and RON." *Tupelo*, he thought as he wheeled the truck toward an intersection that was sign-posted for access to US 78. *Tupelo, Mississippi: where the hell have I heard that before?*

He was crossing the state line leaving the heaviest rain sheeting down in the truck's wake when it hit him. Tupelo was the birthplace of The King. Elvis Aaron Presley was born there in some little two-room shotgun squat back in 1935. Shake had always been an Elvis fan. In fact his fondest teenage memories all seemed to run with a soundtrack of Elvis tunes.

Dale Dye

He belted out the chorus loud enough to wake Bear. "Continue the march, boy! And then we remain overnight in the cradle of The King!"

U.S. Naval Base Guantanamo Bay

He'd been waiting too long for the hard-eyed men who shadowed him everywhere to relax their vigil. The pair of them—Tweedledee and Tweedledum—stuck to him like leeches at first, sitting outside his bedroom door at night, hanging around every other place he went on the base, and cruising along behind in a golf-cart when he went on his morning runs. After the first week, they got over-confident as he'd hoped they would. His mundane schedule—and the fact that the authorities at Camp Delta where he conducted classified interrogations wouldn't allow his personal security detail inside the compound—led them to split shifts and disappear completely every once in a while for short periods. The security men were especially bored on the evenings when Carlos Ruiz-Romero went to an on-base recreation center to play dominoes and gossip in Spanish with the ancient *Cubanos* who lived on the base.

It was there that Carolos made first contact with Ramon Munoz, the man he'd come to Guantanamo to see, the man his mother said might help him fulfill her deathbed wish. The old man was pushing 80, one of a dwindling number of Cuban refugees that escaped Castro's revolutionary pogroms to gain asylum at the U.S. Navy Base. All of them expected to immigrate to the States but for one bureaucratic reason or another, they wound up in permanent residence on the base, living in military family housing and working at menial jobs, essentially wards of the U.S. government for the past 50 years. Neither Munoz nor any of his *compadres* ever ventured outside the wire—that would mean instant arrest as

Castro's state security minions knew precisely who they were and where they were—but most of them maintained some contacts outside the wire.

And Ramon Munoz had a contact southeast of Havana that was very important to Carlos. The old man was a distant relative of the Ruiz-Romero clan. His cousin in Colon was Senora Carmen Martinez, *née* Carmen Ruiz-Romero, older sister of Carlos and the teenager who remained in Cuba when their mother fled with her brother. Carlos had never told anyone about his sibling living in Cuba and he'd begged his mother to keep that information secret. A man who worked with highly sensitive information in the U.S. Intelligence establishment was subject to serious background scrutiny, and a living relative in communist Cuba was not conducive to career enhancement.

His mother kept the faith through FBI background checks plus a number of other increasingly intense and intrusive investigations as Carlos advanced within the DIA but before she died, she extracted a solemn promise that he would do everything in his power to contact that long-lost sister. His mother knew how the game was played in Cuba and didn't really expect that Carlos could get a married woman with children to flee for the U.S., but she had some things that she wanted delivered to her daughter.

During a break in the boisterous domino game, while his security guard stood outside the recreation center whacking croquet balls around the lawn, Carlos cornered Ramon Munoz and told the old man his story. Munoz was saddened by news that Carlos' mother had died. He remembered her well from Colon. In fact, he remembered the entire Ruiz-Romero family with great affection. He'd worked in a cigar factory with Carlos' father before the revolution. When Carlos told the old man he wanted to try and see his sister,

Munoz just shook his head. "Impossible, my friend," he said. "You would be arrested immediately." Castro's goons were everywhere and knew everything, Munoz said. "Better to wait a few months. We hear they are planning to lift the restrictions."

Carlos decided not to press the matter at this first meeting and they went back to the dominoes table. As they played, Munoz was subdued, an unusual state of affairs among the regular players who shouted and laughed their way through the game. When they broke up late in the evening the old man caught Carlos at the door and hauled him into a corner. "You must keep this to yourself, *amigo*, but there may be a way I can help you make contact with your sister."

Carlos met Munoz at his home the next evening for dinner. The security guard on duty that night was not invited inside but seemed happy with a plate of spicy *arroz con pollo* that an old Cuban lady set before him on a little patio table. Inside the house, they sat down to a delicious Cuban meal prepared by that same woman. She was introduced as Senora Catalina Constanza, a widow and another of the resident refugees who worked part-time at the Base Exchange. The woman served them, made small talk about friends in Miami, and then left promising to return and clean up the mess in a few hours.

When they finished eating, the old man lit a cigar and led Carlos to his living room where he walked around in a cloud of aromatic smoke, peeking through the blinds to be sure there was no one else in the immediate area. Then he led Carlos to a credenza in the corner of his living room. It was littered with framed photos of what looked like the Munoz family in earlier, happier days. He pointed at one of the photos that depicted a pretty woman in a colorful Cuban frock. "Your sister," he said. "She still lives in Colon. Sometimes we talk." Carlos picked up the picture and stared it for a long moment. The only other pictures he'd seen of his sister were baby photos or one that his mother particularly treasured from her first communion. As an adult, Carmen looked very much like their mother and very much like her brother, the same eyes and facial structure he saw every morning when he shaved.

Munoz took an old fashioned brass key from his pocket, unlocked a drawer in the face of the credenza, and pulled out an old Motorola flip-phone. "This is a Cuban phone. We're not supposed to have these things, but there is really no other way to talk to friends or family outside the base. Catalina got it for me. Her brother works for telecommunications here on base and he can get civilian phones. We keep it quiet or everyone would pester us to make calls."

Munoz donned a pair of thick reading glasses, toyed with the keypad and then mashed the speed-dial button. When the call was answered he smiled and told the person on the other end there was someone she might want to meet—even if it was just by phone. "It's best not to talk too long," he said handing Carlos the phone. "It sometimes fades after a few minutes." The connection was fraught with line noise, odd clicks and pops, but the female voice Carlos heard when Munoz handed him the phone sounded strong if a little puzzled as they exchanged pleasantries. Her scream of delight came through clear and vibrant when Carlos finally identified himself. They talked in long strings of disjointed gabble until Munoz caught Carlos' eye and tapped his watch. Then they hung up with plans to speak again as soon as possible.

Carlos was thrilled with the contact and effusive in his thanks for the opportunity. He offered to pay Munoz for the cost of the call, but the old man just shrugged and carried the phone to a charging station. "There is no charge. Catalina's brother covers it for me," the old man said as Carlos headed for the door. "Come back anytime, but please don't tell anyone about the phone."

In his spare time over the next two days, Carlos scoured the news sources he could find for reports on the proposed normalization of relations between Cuba and the United States. It was a frustrating exercise. Internet service on the base was antiquated and slow. His smart phone was little help, but from what he could gather the dispute in Congress continued to rage. The administration seemed to consider it a done deal while opposition on Capitol Hill threatened to block their normalization efforts any way possible. Adding to his frustration was the approaching end of his time at Gitmo. He'd been given three weeks to conduct the interrogations and that was rapidly coming to an end with no extension of his time in Cuba likely. That evening after dinner, he found Ramon Munoz and made arrangements for another visit.

His bodyguard remained in the car parked in Munoz' driveway when Carlos arrived at the house the next night. They made small talk for a while, mostly about the proposed lifting of the American embargo. Munoz thought it was a bad idea but supposed it wouldn't make much difference to him at his age. He thought Raul Castro was running a scam that would backfire on the Americans. Carlos listened in nervous silence until Munoz finished his cigar and went to the credenza to retrieve the phone.

Trying to keep the call short as directed, he got to the point and told his sister that he had a package of things that their mother wanted her to have—an old collection of photos, some letters, and a few pieces of family heirloom jewelry. How could he deliver it? Was the mail reliable? Carmen didn't trust the mail, especially with something sent from the

American base, but she had an in-law living in Santiago de
Cuba, a town west of Guantanamo Bay that she was due to
visit. Was there a way her brother might meet her there? She
would bring his two nephews and they could have a family
reunion. Carlos said he'd look into it and get back to her after
he copied the cousin's address.

All that led to days of rapid planning and several more
calls on the illicit cell phone. Carmen's husband had a friend
in Santiago de Cuba, a man that owned a taxicab and owed
him a few big favors. If Carlos could provide payment in
U.S. dollars, this friend could meet him at a designated place
outside the base and drive Carlos to the rendezvous and back
the same night. It was quite safe, Carmen's husband promised, the kind of thing that happened all the time in Cuba.

The key was getting outside the base and Carlos thought
he might be able to pull that off safely. He did a lot of running along the 17 miles of base perimeter, early in the morning and at dusk after he'd finished with his interrogation
sessions. He ran slower than his usual pace, searching for a
place not too far from the main access road where he could
slither under or climb over the chain-link fence. While he
was on the road, he timed the security patrols that drove the
length of the perimeter in armed Humvees. At mid-week—
with only five days left on his mission at Guantanamo—he
found what he wanted: a stretch of fence that was being re-
paired by civilian contractors. Work vehicles were parked at
odd angles where the crews left them for the night and the
ground beneath the stretch under repair was freshly turned
where a drainage ditch was being dug. There was a stand of
wormwood trees close on the other side of the fence at that
point, and his pacing told Carlos that once in those trees he
had just over a half-mile to go after a right turn to reach the
base main access road. He made another call from Ramon

Munoz' phone and set up the meeting for the next night, an evening when he'd overheard his security detail making plans to pig-out on a special at the on-base Taco Bell.

When he finished at Camp Delta and filed his daily summary of the results he returned to the Visiting Officer's Quarters, he told the security guard on duty that he was exhausted by the day's interrogations and would be turning in early. The guard smiled at that news and wished him a pleasant evening. Carlos saw him heading for the Base Exchange area through his window and sat down to wait. When the guard had not returned by nine p.m., Carlos quickly dressed in the dark athletic outfit and sneakers he'd prepared, bundled the little package of keepsakes into a backpack, slipped out of BOQ, and started an easy lope toward the perimeter road.

He reached the selected stretch of fence, jogging easily and never drawing more than a glance and a wave from the two patrols that passed him traveling in opposite directions on the perimeter road. They were used to seeing him by now. Behind a parked Bobcat earth-mover he began to dig a trough in the loose dirt beneath the fence. A Marine he'd met at the detention center told him there used to be landmines planted on the other side of that fence, but they'd all been removed and replaced with motion sensors. He'd likely trip one or more of those, but the patrol that responded would be looking for someone trying to get in not out. If all went well, he'd be back in the BOQ before dawn.

He'd long since decided the risk was worth the reward. Talking to the only other living member of his immediate family—being so close to her after so many years of separation—set some long-suppressed Latino emotions raging. What was most important to him right now was seeing his sister, meeting his nephews, and carrying out his mother's last wish. And he couldn't deny there was a certain seductive thrill to it all.

If there were sensors on the other side of the fence, Carlos didn't see them, not that he'd recognize one anyway. He simply headed for the stand of trees, got his bearings, turned right and started to walk. Nothing happened. No sirens, no alarms, no problem. He hit the perimeter road after about 20 minutes and looked right toward the base gate. He saw nothing in that direction, and there were no vehicles in sight coming or going. Carlos turned left and started to walk away from the base through the shrubbery that lined the paved road.

After about 15 minutes, he saw what looked like a road-weary, 60s-era Chevy Bel Air parked in the dark facing toward the base. He could see the glow of the driver's cigarette and what looked like a taxi sign set at an odd angle on the car's roof. He stepped cautiously out onto the road and waved. The driver flashed his lights in the prearranged signal, then opened his door and waved for Carlos to approach.

When he was seated in the taxi with his backpack in his lap, he introduced himself. The driver shook his hand and assured him all was well. He knew a route that would take them around the Cuban military checkpoints surrounding the base, but he made no move to start the engine. They sat nervously eyeing each other until the driver finally held out his hand. Carlos got the message, dug in his backpack for five twenties, and handed them over. The driver tucked the wad into his shirt pocket, lit another smoke, and cranked the engine. He turned the car with a great grinding of gears and differential complaint and finally got them moving. They'd be on the road a little over an hour, the driver told Carlos, as he had to duck and dodge on the way to Santiago de Cuba, and he'd have to stop for gas about mid-way.

The fuel stop turned out to be a little shack with a corrugated tin roof where the driver negotiated for foul-smelling gas in one-liter glass bottles. Carlos was outside the car in the dark, stretching his back and legs when the men with guns showed up and bundled him like a trussed hog into the back of a black van. Fumes from a vial they broke beneath his nose made him groggy, but he was still aware enough to feel the prick of a needle at his right elbow. For some reason they were drawing his blood.

On The Road Again

Shake seemed to be outrunning the worst of the rainstorms as he pushed the truck through northern Mississippi. After a couple of hours, he began to follow road signs that took him off his track and onto a southbound road that promised to lead to downtown Tupelo. Blowing into the city center, he cruised the downtown area looking for a hotel or motel. There was only one whitewashed, pillared, and porch-fronted antebellum hotel that he could see along Front Street, and it looked like the kind of touristy, upscale joint that might be leery of sheltering a weary human with a wet dog. He passed several signs and billboards that heralded Tupelo's most famous native son and provided directions for pilgrims wanting to visit the actual shack in which The King had swiveled his way into this world. Maybe tomorrow, he decided. Right now he needed to consume something more substantial than Fritos and Dr. Pepper and get a little rest.

On the other side of town, near an intersection crowded with signage that offered travelers a variety of directions toward Memphis, Little, Rock, St. Louis, and a number of other destinations, he spotted something that looked promising. It was a ramshackle little spread of bungalows fronted by a fairly large parking area in which sat two semi rigs dripping muddy water. A flickering pink neon sign indicated the Crossroads Motor Court had vacancies, and it didn't look like the place was crowded enough to be picky about patrons with pets.

The lady at the desk demanded a fifty dollar deposit—refundable in the morning if Bear didn't chew up the furniture or pee on the carpets—swiped his credit card, and handed over an old-fashioned key with a plastic fob that guaranteed return postage should it be found anywhere in the Continental U.S. She also indicated it might be tough to find a good restaurant open this late, but there was a little juke-joint a half-mile south that was said to serve a good burger if he could catch the cook before they closed the kitchen.

The room was semi-shabby in a kitschy Down South décor and the shower had last been scrubbed with something that smelled like embalming fluid, but the double bed was reasonably clean and only slightly rump-sprung. It would do for an overnight and Bear seemed amenable once he'd thoroughly nosed his way through an area reconnaissance. Shake poured kibble into the dog's bowl and then headed back out to the truck.

It was near midnight when he finally found the place. There were three vehicles in the parking lot, all of them work-weary pick-ups with local tags. A sign bolted to a rusting corrugated metal awning that covered the entry said the joint was called The Buttplate Bar wherein, according to various hand-lettered announcements, a visitor could get ice-cold beer and Tupelo's Best Burgers. As he trudged through the drizzle toward a door that had been painted fairly recently in a familiar shade of olive-drab, Shake squinted at the sign on the awning. It seemed like an odd name for a honk in rural Mississippi unless it was some kind of inside joke. If so, the proprietor might be a veteran. He knew of at least one unit in Vietnam in which the grunts referred to themselves as Buttplates, the part of a service rifle that takes the most punishment. On the other hand, he decided as he pushed through the door, there were a lot hunters and gun-nuts in this part of the south who knew what a buttplate was.

It looked and smelled like a hundred other small-town dives he'd frequented. A gaudy jukebox in one corner war-bled a tune that let listeners know Garth Brooks had friends in low places. There was a burnished and stained wood bar complete with brass foot rails and mismatched stools that comprised the locus of activity for three or four serious drinkers nursing beer mugs. Booths tracked along one wall and five or six pedestal tables surrounded what might be a dance floor backed by a little raised platform that probably served as a stage on nights when the place featured live mu-sic. Muggy air, moved sluggishly by a couple of rattan-bladed ceiling fans, carried the musk of spilled beer and cig-arette smoke, but Shake caught the tang of burned grease and hoped for the best as he approached the bar.

"Gitcha sompin'?" The bartender was a rotund man with caramel-color skin who smiled to reveal a magnificent set of horse-teeth that reflected the colors of the neon beer signs hung haphazardly over his head.

"Too late to get something to eat?" Shake tossed a leg over an empty barstool and glanced hopefully at a service window that led to a kitchen. He could see a black man in an apron over a white t-shirt moving around back there.

"Kitchen's just closin'" The bartender studied his watch, sucked on his teeth for a while and then glanced up at the clock over the bar to confirm his declaration. "Lemme check with the boss. He's cookin' tonight and he might could fry you up a burger. That be OK?"

"I'll take a beer while you're at it, thanks. Whatever's on tap will be fine." Shake sipped foam from the top of a frosted mug as the bartender pushed through the kitchen door to con-sult with the cook. He saw the man in the apron glance through the service window and nod briefly before the bartender returned to announce that his boss could only offer a burger with fixings. No fries as the deep-fryer had just been emptied and cleaned. Would that suit?

"Suits me just fine. I appreciate the effort. I'll be over there when it's ready." Shake carried his beer to one of the booths where he might be able to stretch the driving cramps in his legs. He was halfway through a second beer when a tall, muscular black man arrived at his booth with a thick china platter bearing a burger about the size of a small wagon wheel and emanating a delightful aroma of fried meat and onion.

"Many thanks. That smells really good." Shake took a closer look at the man as the plate was proffered and decided there was something familiar about him. He couldn't quite get a grip on it but he was fairly sure he'd seen this guy somewhere. The jaw-line beard and grey hair didn't help, but there was something about that flat nose and high cheekbones that reminded him of someone. The man was slouched against the upright of the booth smiling at him, making no move to return to the kitchen. Shake decided he'd be bothered by it all night if he didn't ask.

He slapped the top of the bun on his burger and took a bite. It was delicious, so good he would have appreciated the quality and taste even if he wasn't starving. "This is really good, man. I appreciate you frying it up for me." The cook just crossed his arms and added another lumen to his smile. Shake chewed for a bit and then noticed the tattoo on the man's sinewy forearm. He'd missed it earlier in the dim light as it was nearly lost against the man's dark skin, but he knew an eagle, globe, and anchor when he saw one.

"This sounds nuts, I know." He pointed at the tattoo and swallowed. "But I think we might have served together—in the Marine Corps?"

"You don't recognize me, do you?" The man pushed himself upright and slid into the bench across from Shake. He signaled for the bartender to bring a couple of beers and leaned across the table to stare into Shake's eyes. "You'd think a Marine like Shake Davis would remember one of the old Buttplates from Echo Two-Three."

Shake paused in mid-bite and then dropped the burger onto the platter. The deep, drawl and hoarse timber of the man's voice was something he knew immediately. He'd heard it for months regularly over the rattle of gunfire or over a PRC-25 radio.

"Simmons?" The burger was forgotten and Shake reached for the new beer that landed on the table. "You've gotta be shitting me! Lance Corporal fucking Simmons?"

"Close." The man grinning back at him held up his beer for a toast. "It's more like *Master Sergeant* Henry Simmons, USMC, Retired."

"Christ! Now I get the name of this place. You own it?"

"Owner and operator since I retired out of Camp Swampy back in 84."

"This can't be happening, man. Shit like this only happens in the movies."

Simmons laughed in that familiar chesty chuckle that Shake remembered so well and cupped his beer mug. "Yeah, in the movies, like—what was that one with Bogart? You know—Casablanca, right?" Simmons affected a Bogey growl. "Of all the gin joints in all the towns, in all the world—Shake Davis walks into mine."

"I'd been wondering what ever happened to you, Henry. You were the best—maybe the only—Lance Corporal Platoon Sergeant in the Nam."

They let the bar close down around them and talked about lives and times. There was so much to say, so many memories, so many mutual friends to trace and so many seminal events to recall. Simmons had the bartender roust the remaining patrons and close up but leave the beer taps in place. They settled into a comfortable, disjointed back and forth, but around two a.m., Shake drifted to another time and place.

Rent-a-Battalion was milling around, stretched out in a defensive line along the southern banks of the Cua Viet River. In a shabby GP tent near the center of that line, the commander of 2nd Battalion, Third Marines was trying to determine who his outfit belonged to this week. If it was their parent 3rd Marine Division, they'd probably be moving west toward the Rockpile where there were reports of an NVA build-up south of the DMZ. If it was Task Force X-Ray of the 1st Marine Division, to which they'd been on loan for the past month, they'd likely be moving south toward Quang Tri where there were similar reports. Either way, the under-manned, war-weary outfit was headed for a fight. The only easy day for Rent-a-Battalion was yesterday.

About a klick west of their battalion headquarters, the Buttplates of Echo Company had a more pressing problem. "The way it stands right now," said the Company Gunnery Sergeant to the assembled leaders gathered around a little field-expedient lean-to that served as Echo's CP, "this lash-up would have a hard time mustering a ten-man working party."

"Word is we're gonna get five or six newbies and maybe a couple more coming back off medevacs," said Second Lieutenant Wild Bill Tehan, who ran what was left of Echo's third platoon. "They're supposed to be coming out either to-night or tomorrow."

"Drop in the bucket—but every warm body helps at this point," said the company's new CO as he spooned Tabasco

into a steaming can of pork slices. Tall, lanky First Lieutenant Jim Jones had been the XO until three days ago, when
the original Company Commander took a bad burst of shrapnel during one of the NVA's regular mortar attacks. "What's
got me worried most is leadership, gents."

"Ain't nothin' encouraging to report there, Skipper." The
Company Gunny leaned back, lit a c-ration cigarette and
looked up at the six-foot-five frame of his new CO, wondering what unlucky shitbird he would assign to hump the radio
for a target as big and inviting as Lieutenant Jones. "This
here company rates six officers and we only got three including yourself, Mister Tehan in the third herd, and Lieutenant
Devlin runnin' weapons. I ain't heard word one about any
new officers."

"Me and Kendrick are OK running first and second pla-
toons without adult supervision, Skipper." Staff Sergeant
Shake Davis waited for the expected chuckle before he continued. "We both got good three-stripers to handle platoon
sergeant chores."

"Maybe we should move one of the sergeants over to
third platoon." Jones glanced at Tehan who was scraping
mud off the sole of a well-worn jungle boot with a K-bar
knife. "You OK with that, Bill?"

"I'm OK with what I've got." Tehan looked directly at
the Company Gunny and shrugged. "Simmons is shit-hot
and my Marines do what he says with no argument."

"Goddammit, Lieutenant…" The Gunny shook his head
and shredded the butt of his smoke. "You can't run that outfit
with a fuckin' lance corporal as your platoon sergeant."

"Don't see why not, Gunny." This wasn't the first time
Tehan had been over the subject with the unit's senior NCO.

"Out here rank doesn't mean much. What counts is leadership ability, and Simmons has got that for damn sure. We ought to just promote him and…"

"Yeah, we tried that before, didn't we?" The Gunny retrieved a battered and badly stained pot from the middle of a small campfire and began to pour coffee into proffered canteen cups. "We got Simmons corporal stripes, and he wasn't wearin' 'em two weeks when he beat the shit out of some pogue at Dong Ha and got himself busted back down to lance-coolie."

"He's a shit-storm in the rear," Staff Sergeant Davis commented as he blew some of the heat off his coffee. "But he most definitely packs the gear in the field."

"Can't argue with that," added Staff Sergeant Kendrick, leader of Echo's first platoon. "He's got a Bronze Star and at least two Purple Hearts. More important, I ain't never seen anybody in the third herd give him any shit about orders. That right, Mister Tehan?"

"Simmons has the respect of my Marines. When he passes the word or gives an order, it's obeyed—no questions asked." Lt. Tehan was still staring at the Company Gunny. In the end, the decision on whether or not to leave Lance Corporal Henry Simmons serving as second-in-command of the third platoon, a billet that was normally filled by a Staff Sergeant, would be made by the CO with the advice and counsel of the Gunny.

"I ain't sayin' he don't pack the gear in combat." The Gunny stared back at Lt. Tehan over the rim of his canteen cup. "But he's still a loose cannon and I don't feel right about no lance corporal as a platoon sergeant. I don't care what kind of hard-ass he is."

"Looks to me like we're trying to fix something that ain't broke." The CO signaled the end of the meeting by calling for his radio operator. "Get the Jeep and a fireteam for security. We're gonna head over to battalion and see what's up." He shrugged into his fighting rig and looked around at the company leadership. "Keep 'em rested, fed, and watered until I get back. I'll stop by the S-1 and see about replacements." He grinned at the Gunny. "And maybe I'll even see if we can get Simmons promoted—again."

When the CO and his security guard walked down off the little hump of high ground occupied by the Echo Company Buttplates, the Gunny grabbed Staff Sergeant Davis by the elbow. "I know you got a lot on your plate with second platoon, Shake. But do me a favor and talk to Simmons. Maybe you can give him some tips from an NCO perspective or something. That dude gets to runnin' wild out here and we're gonna lose Marines we can't afford to lose."

On his way back to his own platoon, Shake stopped by Lt. Tehan's little field hooch and interrupted the officer's conference with Lance Corporal Simmons. They were going over the platoon's ammo requirements. "Hey, Sir, the Company Gunny asked me to talk to Simmons." Shake glanced at the big black Marine who was scribbling figures in a ratty notebook. Simmons just glanced up briefly and shrugged. "I don't feel right about doing that without you knowing about it," Shake continued and jabbed Simmons with an elbow. "And truth of the matter is I don't think Henry here needs much talking to anyway. With or without the chevrons, he seems to be doing just fine as a platoon sergeant."

"Tell that to the Gunny," Simmons lit a Kool from a ration four-pack and exhaled a cloud of smoke. "Maybe he'll climb off my case."

"I did tell the Gunny that, Simmons. So did Mister Tehan. I don't think you really need any advice but if you ever think you do, I'm your man. How's that?"

Shake stuck out his hand. Simmons stared at him for a moment and then took the hand. "I appreciate that, Sarn't Davis,"

Lieutenant Tehan smiled and nodded. "You're welcome in this platoon anytime."

Over the next few days as Echo Company resupplied, welcomed dribs and drabs of new or returning men, and got themselves set for the inevitable orders to initiate close contact with the NVA everyone knew were also milling around in the area. Shake kept a close but clandestine eye on Simmons and the third platoon. It wasn't hard to do most of the time. His own second platoon was tied into the third herd on the left flank.

Simmons was efficient without being officious. He seemed to know that he didn't have the rank to shout and strut like a Drill Instructor, so he gave orders and received responses quietly, often with not much more than a nod. He also seemed to understand from being on the other end of such bombastic behavior that it was too often a power play, a show without much substance, bound to foment resentment among hard-pressed grunts that had plenty of problems without the added indignity of being treated like unruly kindergarten kids.

The third herd's platoon sergeant had a sharp eye for the little details, attention to which was the hallmark of a good enlisted leader in Shake's experience. Simmons had a good working relationship with the platoon's senior Corpsman and wanted to know about any real or perceived injury, especially any problems with his men's feet. He was always checking on things like water levels in canteens, condition of unfired ammo in magazines, and the cleanliness of rifles and machineguns. And Simmons didn't just inquire. He looked to be sure.

While Lance Corporal Simmons didn't do much barking, he could bite when required. As the third platoon mounted up a patrol one morning, Shake watched Simmons inspect the squad that was going outside the wire. A portly Blooper Man carrying the M-79 grenade launcher obviously had a bandolier of ten ready rounds draped over his flak jacket, and he was supposed to have at least ten more in the satchel suspended from his shoulder.

"You got your extra rounds?" Simmons pointed at the satchel. "Yeah, yeah, I got 'em." The Blooper Man sucked on a smoke and walked away to join his squad waiting to move out but Simmons froze him. "Show me."

"What? I said I got 'em"

"Did I stutter? I said show me your extra rounds."

Turned out that instead of extra rounds, the Blooper Man had extra rations plus a stash of PX candy and snacks in his bag. Of spare HE rounds there was no sign. Simmons grabbed an entrenching tool left near a pile of half-filled sandbags and delivered the Blooper Man a resounding clout to the helmet. It knocked the kid to his knees but Simmons jerked him upright and sent him running to his hooch to return with the required spare ammo. Then he turned on the squad leader, another black Marine, and delivered a lecture at a level that was sure to be heard by everyone in the squad.

"That fat motherfucker could have got you killed out there. Ten blooper rounds ain't shit in a firefight and you been in the bush long enough to know that. Squad Leader's supposed to inspect his dudes before they leave the wire, my man. You didn't do that, did you? Nah, you fuckin' didn't. So, do it now—right fuckin' now—while I watch."

It took nearly an hour for the Squad Leader to do the inspection and make corrections to Simmons' satisfaction. Lt. Tehan stood leaning against a palm tree quietly watching and not very successfully hiding a smile. When the errant patrol completed their radio checks and departed, Shake walked over across the platoon lines and nodded at Simmons.

"That was some good platoon sergeant work, Henry, but you might have dispensed with cold-cocking the dude with an e-tool."

"What else am I gonna do? Don't feel right a lance corporal writing up another lance for fuckin' office hours."

"But you ain't just another lance corporal, Henry. You're the lance corporal *acting platoon sergeant*. Look, dude, I don't like writing people up either. They gotta face office hours for some bullshit and it just takes 'em out of the field where we need 'em most. Company punishment is usually better for little stuff." Shake pointed at the pile of unfilled sandbags where he was resting his foot. "Put that shitbird on sandbag detail until you get tired or put him to burning shitters. Whatever—Mister Tehan will back you on it. It's been my experience that manhandling or beating on Marines is not the way to go. One day you come across some tough bastard who fights back and kicks your ass. When that happens, you got no leadership left."

"Yeah, I copy that, Sarn't Davis, but I know that fat-ass. He used to be in my squad and he's always fuckin' off."

"So fix it, Henry—once and for all. Use peer pressure and let the other dudes in his squad do the dirty work of getting him squared away. You had it right with what you told that squad leader. You said the Blooper Man could have got 'em all killed out there. You hammer away with that message and before long you won't have to send it again. They'll unfuck him in a heartbeat."

On his way back to the second platoon, Shake ran into Lt. Tehan making perimeter rounds. "Heard what you said to Simmons, Sgt. Davis." Tehan bashed him on the shoulder and smiled. "Good advice. Thanks."

It was called Operation Ford for some reason no one in Rent-a-Battalion knew or questioned. What they'd been told before the operation kicked off was that another Marine battalion was waiting somewhere near the foot of a long, slim peninsula south of Hue. That outfit was the anvil and 2/3 was the hammer. As usual, Rent-a-Battalion's role in all this was in accordance with their unofficial motto: Why do it one-half when you can do it 2/3? So they got the shitty end of the stick which involved a push down the peninsula from north to south in hopes of crushing a battalion of NVA between the two Marine units. That was the plan and the only other thing the grunts in Rent-a-Battalion knew for sure was that no plan ever survives the first round fired.

Echo Company Buttplates were on the left flank of the sweep when that happened. Tehan's third platoon caught the worst of it when the NVA suddenly opened fire from a cluster of reinforced bunkers on their left. Third platoon was immediately pinned down in an open, sandy patch while enemy machinegun and B-40 rocket rounds cut through the rest of the company in a wicked hail of enfilading fire. The company radio net erupted with chatter and Shake heard Wild Bill Tehan calmly requesting fire support of any or all kinds so that he could pull his platoon back to a line of sand dunes that would provide some cover. He already had a couple killed and several more wounded.

Shake looked up from flat on his belly and saw those sand dunes off to the left of his platoon which put them between his unit and Tehan's. The Echo CO was calling for 81mm mortars from battalion as the quickest and easiest form of suppressing fire available, but Shake thought he might be able to help relieve the pressure while the mortarmen tried to find the range.

He reached to his right and his radioman slapped a handset into his palm. "Echo Two, this is Two Actual," he called on the platoon freq. "All elements turn ninety left, come on line and advance to the sand dunes. When you're set, pour it on those bunkers so Echo Three can pull back to join up."

As his squads began to maneuver, ducking and weaving across the seventy or so meters to the line of dunes, Shake held up a finger indicating he wanted his radioman to switch frequencies to the company net. When he got the nod, Shake depressed the switch and called for Tehan. "Echo Three, Echo Two Actual, be advised my elements are moving to the sand dunes now. When you hear us open fire, make your move and join up with us there."

"Echo Three rogers your last, Two Actual." The voice was Henry Simmons and he sounded relatively calm, but Shake could hear close rounds snapping and popping over the ambient hiss of the radio frequency. He was distracted by two or three of his own wounded as he dragged his radioman toward the sand dunes so the second platoon was in position and pouring fire into the treeline masking the NVA bunkers by the time he was able to observe the status of third platoon. It wasn't good.

Tehan and Simmons had pulled most of the casualties back to some sort of depression closer to the treeline than the sand dunes. Simmons was manning an M-60 machinegun dropped by one of the dead in that swale, pumping rounds and adding to the din of the second platoon's fire. Shake watched for a while and didn't notice much reduction in the incoming. The NVA gunners had both the trapped third herd and the supporting second platoon in their sights now.

Rounds were chewing into the dunes and showering every-one with fine white sand. Despite the incoming, Shake could see clumps of third platoon Marines successfully making their way out of the beaten zone. They were going to get hurt doing it, but the third herd would survive this flank ambush.

Shake and his Marines couldn't hear any of it over the roar of friendly and enemy fire, but there was another kind of fight going on out in that depression to their front. Lance Corporal Henry Simmons was arguing with Second Lieuten-ant Wild Bill Tehan about which one of them should stay with the wounded and which one should head back to the sand dunes to reorganize for a counterattack. "Simmons, this is a fucking order. You get back there and count heads. When you're ready, push me on the net and we'll make a flanking attack."

"Fuck that, Lieutenant. I'm just a lance corporal. I don't know nothin' about doin' that shit. That's your fuckin' job!"

"Simmons, I'm not gonna say this again…"

"Then don't," Simmons interrupted and hammered out the remaining M-60 rounds in the gun. "You just get back there and take care of the rest of 'em. I got this." He reached for his rifle to begin cranking rounds into the treeline.

Tehan probably had more to say but it was lost on Sim-mons and in the chaos of the fight. He thought about it for a moment and decided action trumped the principle of the thing in this case. He would argue it out with Simmons an-other time. Right then his obligation was to his disorganized Marines and they needed leadership. Tehan took off running toward the sand dunes.

Shake borrowed a pair of field glasses from a nearby FO who was trying to correct the first mortar rounds that had fallen well long and left of the intended target. He could see Henry Simmons gathering spare magazines and grenades

from the wounded and dead in the depression. He could also
see a unit of NVA sprinting through the treeline, running
parallel with available cover and trying to reach a position
opposite to where Simmons was holding out there in the kill-
ing ground. They had a gaggle of sitting ducks trapped in
that depression and it wouldn't take much effort or maneuvering to kill them all.

Shake reached for his radio and then changed his mind.
Simmons was too busy to talk, and he likely couldn't see the
maneuvering NVA unit. If he missed the movement they'd
be all over him and the surviving wounded. He looked to his
right where a machinegun team was triggering short bursts
at one of the bunkers. In Shake's platoon, all assistant ma-
chinegunners and all squad leaders carried one magazine of
tracers marked with tape, so it wouldn't be confused with
magazines loaded with standard ball ammo. In the chaos of
a firefight, a tracer was often the most effective way of marking a target. Marines might not hear or understand shouted
directions but they could damn sure follow the fiery finger
of a tracer aimed where they were meant to direct their fire.

"Gimme your tracers!" Shake shouted at the a-gunner
who nodded and tossed him a magazine. Shake took a quick
look and spotted the red-painted nose of the top round and
then dropped his own magazine, ejected the ready round and
clicked the tracer-filled magazine into the well of his rifle.
He chambered a round and took a quick look for the NVA
still maneuvering in the treeline. They were hard to spot but
he finally saw an RPG gunner doing the Groucho walk with
a B-40 on his shoulder. He shouldered his M-16 and began
to trigger tracers toward the enemy maneuver element. The
nearest squad leader got the picture and began yelling for his
people to fire on the tracers. That was the result of good

training but Shake was more concerned that Henry Simmons get the hint.

Simmons watched the bright lines of tracer lancing into the treeline. This wasn't just the one-in-five fireworks display of some machinegunner firing cover. This was concentrated fire designed to get everyone's attention. He recalled the briefing at Dong Ha that Staff Sergeant Davis had given the platoon sergeants and squad leaders about marking targets with tracers. Was someone sending him a message? And then he saw it. Just below where the tracers were impacting, he caught sight of an NVA aiming a B-40 rocket launcher in his direction. Simmons was down to just two remaining magazines of rifle ammo but he'd scavenged about six frag grenades from the dead and wounded. As the rocket round sizzled over his head and detonated to his rear, Lance Corporal Simmons began to arm and heave grenades into the treeline. It wasn't much and likely not very effective but it was all he could do to keep from being overrun.

Through the field glasses, Shake could see Simmons plucking grenades from a dwindling pile and heaving them like a machine. And he could see more NVA moving through the dense brush to reinforce their assault element near the depression where one frazzled Marine was putting up a last-stand fight. He looked to his right down the line occupied by his first squad, screaming for his Marines to increase the tempo of their suppressing fire. Strapped to the top of each pack on that line was an M-72 LAW or Light Antitank Weapon, the disposable, tube-launched 66mm rocket designed to kill armored vehicles. With no enemy tanks in the fight for the most part, the Marines in Vietnam had turned the LAW into an effective bunker-buster.

"Gerheim!" He screamed at his first squad leader. "Have all your people pass their LAWS to me."

In less than three minutes Shake had six of the LAWs piled by his side. They represented about 40 pounds of high-explosive weight he'd have to hump out to Simmons with no help. There was no way he was going to ask any of his guys to make the effort. It would be a long, potentially deadly open-field sprint and not the kind of thing he could order anyone to undertake without an option. In this situation, he was the available option.

Tossing his rifle to his radioman and grabbing the LAWs by their nylon straps, three in each hand, he rose to a crouch and shouted for covering fire. Dunes to his right and left exploded with outgoing rounds. Shake fixed his eyes on Simmons still chucking grenades in the distance and broke cover like an Olympic sprinter coming out of the blocks.

On the run, he felt two or three rounds rip through the flapping tails of his jungle shirt and winced at the really close ones that snapped and popped way too close to his head. Shake zigged and zagged over the sand until he reached the depression. He was at this point closer to the enemy in the treeline than he'd estimated when he started the run just a couple of nerve-jangling minutes past. He flopped down next to Simmons, marveling at how much bigger, more livid and loud the enemy AK fire looked and sounded at this range. They didn't have much time or space to keep these guys at bay.

"You're the Lawman," he screamed at Simmons, his adrenaline-soaked voice sounding somewhere between a macho bark and a ridiculous survivor's giggle. "I'll shuck 'em and you shoot 'em."

Shake rolled over to prep the first LAW and saw the look in Simmons' dark eyes. It was wild and weird with incandescent flecks of vivid red as if he'd been caught in an unexpected camera flash.

"Get some, mothahfuckah!" Simmons was on the same high—the same combat crest, the same sadistic wavelength. Shake barked and reached for another LAW as Simmons sent the first round into the NVA and hooted at the resulting explosion. They'd fired all but one of the LAWs and every remaining round of rifle ammo before a rocket round impacted the back wall of the crater and showered them both with hot shrapnel.

Tupelo

"**D**on't remember much after that, Shake." Simmons was sprawled on the bench seat of the booth and had to contort himself to add yet another empty beer mug to the pyramid they were building on the table. "Next thing I know, I'm on the Repose with some pecker-checker digging chunks out of my ass and legs."

"They finally got the mortars adjusted on target, but it was Tehan and the rest of the third herd that saved us." Shake walked over to the bar for refills and shouted over his shoulder. "When the eighty-ones busted up their plans, the gooks were crawling back toward their bunkers. Wild Bill and the rest of your guys hit 'em in the flank like a fuckin' bulldozer and killed most of 'em."

"Wish I could have seen that."

"Here's what you need to know, Henry." Shake plopped fresh beers on the table and slid into the booth. "Those dudes were chewed up, but they weren't about to leave their hot-shit lance corporal platoon sergeant out there to bleed to death. They came roaring out from behind those sand dunes like the cavalry riding to the rescue. You were out like a bad bulb, but I stayed conscious long enough to watch those crazy motherfuckers charge. It was something to see, my man."

"You know that was my third Purple. They fucked up and made me a sergeant when I got to Okinawa. Seems like Lieutenant Jones and Lieutenant Tehan sent a letter of commendation or something and they just skipped right over the corporal thing."

"That likely had more to do with the Silver Star you got than anything else."

"Maybe." Simmons drained his beer and checked his watch. "The miracle is that I even managed to keep them stripes until I rotated back to the States."

"And that's where you shipped over?"

"Yep—changed my MOS and got into supply, finished out my twenty running a bunch of box-kickers and label-lickers. It was mostly cruise-control. Rack full of medals covers a lot of sins, you know? I used to hear from Mister Tehan and Lieutenant Jones every once in a while. Old Wild Bill went to work for some spook outfit and finished as a light colonel. And Jones wound up as Commandant of the Marine Corps wearing four stars. Ain't that a bitch?"

"You know the Gunny got blown away, right? Tripped an old French mine buried somewhere along Route Nine about three weeks after we got hit. You probably won't believe it, but he was one of the guys that helped write up your citation."

"Never knew that." Simmons checked his watch again and yawned. "Listen, Shake, I got to get home. The old lady starts to frettin' if I don't show up before dawn. I'd like for you to meet her. You got someplace to stay tonight?"

"I got my dog waiting for me at that Crossroads Motor Court and I really need to get a few hours of sleep. How about we catch a late breakfast and you can show me where Elvis was born?"

"Hell yeah, Shake. We can even take a trip down to Itta Bena and Rolling Fork. That's the hometowns of B.B. King and Muddy Waters. You are in the cradle of the Delta Blues, brother."

"Breakfast and a quick peek at the Elvis shrine is gonna have to do it for this trip, Henry. I gotta get down to Texas without too much delay."

"Texas ain't that far from Tupelo." Simmons draped an arm around Shake's shoulders and steered him toward the door. "We gotta do this again real soon."

They had eggs and grits at a Huddle House in downtown Tupelo around mid-morning. Mara Simmons was a smiling, solid, raven-haired woman whose features reflected her Chickasaw tribal heritage. Mara was gracious enough to say she'd heard a few Shake-Davis-in-Vietnam stories from Henry over the years and was "just tickled" to meet him in person. "I feel like we've got a lot in common, Shake. You had to deal with this sinner in Vietnam—and I've had to handle him ever since."

Shake heard from her about a daughter holding down a municipal government job in Jackson. "And then there's Henry Junior." She smiled and glanced at her husband who picked up the narrative. "Did most everything I could besides breaking his fool neck, but he insisted on joining the Marine Corps right out of high school." Henry shook his head but he couldn't hide the proud parental grin. "He went grunts and then recon. Did pumps in Iraq and Afghanistan where he got himself wounded and decorated. These days he's with that MARSOC outfit down at Lejeune—not that he stays anywhere very long."

"They keep those guys busy," Shake nodded and smiled at the photo of a handsome Marine in dress blues with a rack of silver and gold on his left chest that Mara pulled out of her wallet. He looked amazingly like his father. He was posed with a striking Asian woman that Mara identified as her daughter-in-law and a frowning two-year-old that was the Simmons' first and only grandchild.

"Yeah, Shake—and it's just gonna get worse now that they're callin' 'em Marine Raiders again. You read about that? Junior says first rule in his battalion is never unpack your seabag."

"He'll be fine. I know that and so do you two. He comes from good stock."

It was still misting rain when they finished their meal. Shake let Bear out for a romp behind the restaurant, but that didn't last long. He sniffed the Simmons family, decided they were OK by his sensory reckoning, and then whined to get back in the truck. "Just follow us," Simmons said as he and Mara walked toward a muddy Jeep Wrangler. "Watch for me to flash my lights as we go through town. I'll point out the Citizen's State Bank. That's the last joint old Machine Gun Kelly robbed back in 1932. Nobody ever wants to see that, but I get a kick out of it."

They splashed through running water at several intersections heading for the east side of Tupelo where the house in which Elvis was born had been restored on a broad street now named Elvis Presley Drive. The portion of it that was the city's big tourist attraction had been called Pig Trot Trail back in the late 1930s when the little King was running up and down it in raggedy overalls. The area around the white-washed little homestead had been greened and expanded to include a park and an Elvis Presley museum. Despite the steady drizzle, Shake saw lines of faithful fans waiting to pay their money and take the tours.

Mara Simmons knew the chatty old lady who sat inside the birthplace. She was a Presley family friend, resident docent, and font of all esoteric knowledge about the King's earliest days in Tupelo. She waived the six-buck entrance fee for the Simmons party and guest then showed them around the little shack, an event that took only about 15 minutes and about that many steps from the front door to the back. "It was a sight more shabby when the Presley's were here," she said in a thick Mississippi drawl. "And they weren't here that long. Vernon and Gladys got evicted when they couldn't pay the rent. They stayed in a lot of places over about thirteen years in Tupelo, but this here is pretty much the way they lived wherever they could afford."

Shake reluctantly begged off a tour of the museum. This visit reinforced the rags-to-riches story he loved about Elvis Presley, and he didn't want that lingering image spoiled with the flashy, late-career glitz and extravagance of the King's Vegas days. He exchanged contact information with Henry and Mara Simmons, promised to stay in touch, and got back on the road bound for Texas.

Camp Mantanzas

Carlos Ruiz-Romero woke up naked, sprawled on a sweat-soaked mattress. He had a pounding headache and a very full bladder. Swinging his bare legs over the side of what appeared to be a standard military folding cot, he looked around the narrow cubicle. There were no windows in any of the walls painted a putrid shade of pale green, but there was a stainless steel commode in the far corner. He staggered over to it, relieved himself, and eyed a door at one end of the cubicle. There was no knob or handle on the inside. Two plastic bottles of water were on the floor near the cot, so he sat back down, opened one, and drained it.

As his head began to clear, Carlos assessed his situation. Likely he was in hands of either local thugs or Cuban Security Services. Given the look of his surroundings, it was likely the latter. You didn't work inside the Intelligence community for long before you understood such things happened. And it was no great mental leap to realize why the Cubans would want him. They had to know he was DIA and a high-value individual. Likely their signals intelligence people were monitoring the regular reports he sent from the detention facility. He'd warned his colleagues at NSA the system was full of holes and an easy hack for people who knew what they were doing.

Carlos opened the second bottle of water and glanced up at the shiny black eye of a surveillance camera mounted high on the opposite wall. If the Cubans monitored encrypted reports on a secure server out of Guantanamo, they could certainly monitor Ramon's little cell phone. Why hadn't he thought of that earlier? He was no trained field agent, but he'd screwed up and tried to act like one.

The problem now was how to let U.S. authorities know he'd been arrested or kidnapped or whatever term applied to this awful mess. He sat for a few minutes mentally whipping himself for being both stupid and sentimental. Very likely his sister and her family were also now in custody. He looked up at the camera again and realized there had to be someone watching and listening.

"I want to talk to someone in authority here, please." He spoke in Spanish and stood staring at the lens until he heard deadbolts clicking in the cubicle door.

Two men entered carrying folding chairs. One of them—an older man in Cuban military uniform—wore a small pistol in a leather holster on his hip. Carlos didn't recognize the insignia on the man's shoulder boards, but there was enough red and gold to indicate the guy was likely a senior officer. The other man was short and swarthy, dressed in shiny trousers and a well-pressed pastel shirt open about halfway down his chest.

"Have a seat," he said, motioning for Carlos to sit on the cot as the two men unfolded their chairs. "We need to discuss your situation." The man in civilian attire sat easily and crossed his legs. Carlos was surprised to see the man was wearing straw sandals and no socks. "We can talk in Spanish or English—or Arabic if you wish. It's your choice."

"English is fine. I'd like to have my clothes back." Carlos watched as the civilian got the nod from the military officer and turned back toward him with a smile that revealed a brace of stained teeth. "We will provide clothing shortly. Meanwhile, you should know that your sister and her family are now in state custody. They will not be harmed if you co-operate fully."

"Cooperate with what? Where am I—and who are you people?"

"We are your hosts. That is sufficient for our purposes, Carlos. You are in a very secure area near Havana, but you won't be here long. What happens while you are our guest is mainly up to you. We require your cooperation and good behavior. And we will get that, Carlos. What is it the Americans say—the easy way or the hard way?"

"I won't cooperate."

"Then your stay with us will be very unpleasant, Carlos, and things will be equally unpleasant for your family."

"I think you've made a very big mistake here. You know my country will exert every effort to get me released."

"I don't think we need to worry about that. You left the American base at Guantanamo voluntarily, did you not, by crawling under the perimeter fence? Who knows why? Right now you are simply missing, but very soon you will be declared dead. Why would the Americans come looking for a man they believe is dead? Think about your situation, Carlos, and that of your family." Both men stood, folded their chairs and left the room.

The Director General of Cuba's *Dirrecion de Inteligencia* and General Enrique Constanza, Chief of Cuban Military Intelligence, stood in a chilly room in the basement of a nondescript cinder-block building at Camp Mantanzas sipping strong black coffee. They were at a very delicate stage of a major coup, planned and launched just days earlier on an upper level of this building, the dark heart and ultra-secret soul of Cuban espionage operations.

At the center of the room, bathed in greenish light from low-hanging fluorescent fixtures, two surgeons labored over a body on an autopsy table. It wasn't much of a body now that the head and limbs had been removed, but it would do for their purposes. "Gruesome piece of business." The general winced as one of the medics tore at a leg stump with what looked like a small garden rake.

"Necessary to make it look like a shark attack." The other surgeon was wielding a similar tool around what was left of the corpse's neck.

"And you verified the blood type?" The Cuban spymaster shuffled through a series of pictures on his phone. They were all angled shots of Carlos Ruiz-Romero taken while he lay naked and unconscious on the folding cot in a room above the surgery.

"We typed and matched the sample you provided." The surgeon tossed his instrument into a pan of disinfectant and stood back to examine his work. "He's a match in every possible way."

The Cuban spymaster nodded and moved to another table where a technician was mutilating Carlos' clothing to reflect the damage done to the torso. The poor soul on the table, plucked from a Havana prison cell, resembled their captive almost exactly in height, weight, and coloring. With his head missing and no limbs left for fingerprint comparison, he would pass for Carlos Ruiz-Romero, a drowning victim who had been savaged by sharks in Guantanamo Bay.

"When they're done here, get the body down to the boat immediately. It's a long trip and I want him in the water around midnight. That's when the tide will carry him right into the bay. What about the old man?"

"Heart attack," the General said rubbing at the stubble on his chin. "My brother reported no trouble. He used the air embolism method and at eighty, no one is going to question his passing. Just to be safe, I'm ordering him and my sister to leave as soon as possible. The Americans might start sniffing around on the base, and I don't want any loose ends."

"It's their mystery to solve," said the spymaster with a smile. "We have bigger fish to fry. Did you check with the doctors?"

"Of course I did. Fidel is undergoing the kidney treatments again. He will not be able to move for at least three weeks, according to his personal physician."

"And Raul is on a swing through Central and South America," the spymaster said heading for the exit, "which leaves *Punto Cero* deserted except for the security guards and the boat crew. It's time to get our guest moved to nicer quarters."

Lockhart, Texas

Chan Davis sat on the screened back porch of her new homestead, sipping what the locals called sweet tea and staring out over the expanse of her lawn covered with a colorful profusion of Blue Bonnets and Indian Paintbrushes. The movers were gone and all the possessions she and Shake decided to carry from Virginia were scattered throughout the rooms of the solid old house built back in 1915. When Shake arrived in a couple of hours, they would do the detailed arranging and storing. At this point, she was just drifting, trying to assimilate the major changes in her life and absorbing the abiding charm of this new place and property.

She wandered into the kitchen, looking down to admire the ancient oak boards of the flooring throughout the two-story structure. A *Chicana* fine artist had owned the house and surrounding five acres of pecan trees and she'd cared for it beautifully, hand-painting the walls, ceilings, and fixtures in funky Tex-Mex colors and patterns. The whole place was rugged and reliable. Every square foot of it seemed to exude an air of permanence that Chan had always wanted in her life, an air polluted over the years she worked and traveled around the world as one of the Defense Intelligence Agency's top analysts. Now that she was about to settle into stable academe as a teacher, there would be time to absorb that warm glow of belonging to some place rather than some thing, to drift around the anchor of a real home.

Shake was just as excited about the new place and full of plans for planting deep roots in the Texas Hill Country which was yet another benefit to their monumental paradigm shift.

He'd be much more likely to stay home—now that the term had meaning for him—and out of the dangerous situations that had seemed to plague them once every few years since they'd become a couple. At least Chan hoped that would be the case. Shake had a very low tolerance for boredom and a nagging adrenaline addiction that always loomed in their background. At this point there didn't seem to be anything on the horizon that would interfere with domestic tranquility, so she pushed that concern back behind more practical and pressing matters. He'd be arriving soon with Bear so Chan rummaged in the cupboards among the stash of supplies laid in from Lockhart's HEB grocery store, wondering what she might fix for a first meal in what Shake had already taken to calling *la casa* Davis or *el ranchito*.

She stood staring out the front window over a slope of lush greenery intersected by a stream fed by the property's artesian well and caught site of two whitetail deer grazing not more than 50 yards from where she stood. The breeze wafting through the open kitchen windows carried the aroma of charred post-oak, and Chan decided their first meal together as new Lockhart residents should be some of the savory brisket they both loved from Black's Barbecue just down the block from the house.

That decision made, she stepped outside to a patch of grass between the two sprawling live oaks whose branches stretched like a livid green tarp over their circular driveway. A couple of long-time residents who visited yesterday swore that Sam Houston had given his infamous, long-winded anti-secession speech to an assembled mob of Texicans beneath those very trees back in September of 1860. She'd meant to do some internet research on that and now seemed like as good a time as any to test the wireless router installed that morning.

Inside at a desk jammed temporarily into a corner of the den, she fired up her laptop and logged into her account. Her email inbox was crammed with messages, most of them from friends wishing her and Shake the best with the move plus the standard assortment of advertising teasers. Nothing new there except that most of the junk was from Texas sources which made her smile. The Lone Star State internet hustlers were on the case and tracking potential new customers. She deleted most of it before she finally got down to something tagged DIA.us.gov that caught her attention. It was a short note from a fellow analyst in her old work section, a woman friend with whom she'd been very close in her Washington days. The friend wanted to be sure Chan knew that Carlos Ruiz-Romero was dead.

There weren't many details—at least none that Chan's friend felt comfortable including in an open-source email—but apparently Ruiz-Romero, one of the agency's top cryptographers, had been found dead, floating in Guantanamo Bay with no apparent explanation of what happened to him. Chan chewed on that for a while for two reasons. She'd become very friendly with Carlos shortly after she left the Army to take a position at DIA, a friendship that had blossomed into an intense but relatively short-term affair. She'd remained fond of Carlos even after their inevitable break-up and ran into him regularly at work. He was a nice guy—often a little weird and frequently distracted, but basically a nice guy that Chan just couldn't come to love in any lasting manner. As far as she knew, he had no one to mourn his passing and it made her sad. That was thing one.

Thing two piqued her spook instincts. She knew about Ruiz-Romero's last assignment and it was unlikely to provide much free time or opportunity for fishing or exploring anywhere in Cuba. He'd been sent by DIA to Guantanamo

Bay to interview some very high-value *jihadis*, mainly AQ heavy-hitters and affiliate detainees, about their clandestine worldwide communications methods. Carlos, fluent in Arabic, Spanish, and a couple of other languages, had to campaign hard for that assignment. He had a brain crammed with ultra-secret coding and comm information up to and including Yankee White, the nation's most sensitive and compartmentalized level of classification. A guy with that kind of clearance was at risk anytime he wandered outside the Beltway. She remembered that the agency had only agreed to the deal if Ruiz-Romero was restricted to the detention facilities at the Naval Base and guarded during his stay. It didn't make sense. What was he doing outside the wire? And in the water? As far as she knew Carlos had never been a swimmer or much interested in any kind of water-oriented activities.

Chan re-read the email looking for hints from her old friend but there was nothing more than bare-bones about the incident. Carlos had showed up missing one morning and a search throughout the base had proved fruitless. Two days later, with the DIA in a panic and the American command in Cuba at a loss to explain the disappearance, a patrol boat fished a body out of the bay near the Navy base. It was tentatively identified as Carlos Ruiz-Romero—end of story.

It was a puzzle she couldn't be expected to solve so Chan signed off, closed her laptop, and strolled back toward the kitchen to see if the deer were still at play in their front yard. They weren't, but it was such a pretty morning that she picked up a recently delivered catalog advertising a big sale on western work clothes and carried it out to the rustic old log bench beneath the live oaks. She should do a little shopping and maybe find some clothes to match the chores a rural Texas homeowner needed to handle. She'd marked a few items and located the local outlet that had them on offer when her mobile phone chirped to announce a text message.

"Howdy, y'all! Can we palaver for a spell?" The sender was the man who calls himself Bayer.

It must have been a strain for their old friend and frequent nemesis—an educated and erudite man whose vocabulary had never stretched to include terms like howdy and palaver—to compose that text. At last report Bayer was laboring somewhere in the labyrinthine bowels of the Department of Homeland Security. He was well aware that both she and Shake were declaredly out of the game, so it was likely safe to respond. She acknowledged the text and told him to call when he had time. Her phone rang in less than three minutes after she hit send.

"This better be a social call."

"Mostly it is, Chan. How're you doing? Got the new place in shape?"

"All is well, thanks. We'll have it squared away as soon as Shake gets here. He's due in about an hour."

"I hope you'll invite me down sometime. I'd like to get out of the rat-race for a few days and see your place."

"You're welcome to visit anytime, Bob, but I have a strict prohibition against anyone who arrives with an ulterior motive. You take my meaning?"

"I do indeed, Chan. And I promise not to burden you or Shake—unless under extraordinary circumstances."

"That brings two thoughts to mind. The first is that your definition of bother and mine have never matched. And the second is that every situation with you is extraordinary. Tell me this call is not about that kind of circumstance."

"I'm actually calling about a situation with a DIA employee down in Cuba."

109

101

59WS4H001LXX

Title	HAVANA FILE (THE SHAKE DAVIS SER
Condition	Good
Location	Aisle 10 Bay 9 Shelf 8 Item 109
Description	Book is in good condition, including the original dust jacket, with no markings or highlighting inside.
Source	GW
SKU	59WS4H001LXX
ASIN	1944353097
Code	9781944353094
Employee	shane
Date Added	1/6/2025 3:57:05 PM

||||||||||||||||||||||||||||||

"That would be Carlos Ruiz-Romero. I got an email about him this morning. A friend tells me the poor guy is dead."

"That's what we're told. At any rate, there are some nagging questions about the case and I'm trying to dig into his background a little. A friend of mine told me you and Ruiz-Romero were an item at one time. Is that right?"

"Do I have to go into this with you?"

"No, not at all, but I'd appreciate it if you'd answer a few questions. It might help with the inquiry I'm conducting."

"Go ahead—cautiously."

"I'm actually reaching out to you because the man apparently had no surviving parents or siblings. He had very few friends that we can find and none of them very intimate. Does that sound about right to you?"

"Yes, Carlos was definitely a loner. He never seemed to have very many friends outside of work. I'd be hard pressed to name more than three or four."

"And he was of Cuban parentage?"

"Also correct as far as I know. Dad died in a Cuban gulag for opposing the Castro regime and his Mom escaped, brought him to Florida when he was nine or ten, I think. They settled in Miami and Carlos went to school at Florida State. He did his graduate work at MIT on a full-ride and went to work for DIA shortly after he graduated. His Mom died about a year ago, I guess it was. That's really all I know about his background. He was never very outgoing with that kind of stuff."

"And how long did you and Carlos—what's the proper word? How long did you date?"

"We lived together at my place in Crystal City for about six months. Turns out we weren't very compatible."

"What I'm after here, Chan—and this is delicate so I apologize in advance—would you recognize intimate details about his physical appearance? Did he have tattoos, was he circumcised, things like that."

"You are really a piece of work. You know that? I'm gonna hang up now."

"Let me explain, Chan. The body they discovered at Guantanamo was ravaged by sharks—or torn up badly by something—presumably sharks given where it was found. Actually, it was just a hunk of bloody meat. No head or limbs so we can't really, positively identify the man."

"OK, two things: He *was* circumcised and he had no tattoos or scars that I ever saw anywhere on his body. He was really a kind of blank slate physically."

"Seems odd doesn't it? Not even an appendectomy or hernia scar?"

"Pure as the driven snow for the whole time I knew him. Carlos was not the kind of guy who got involved in anything that was likely to leave a mark. He was a runner, a health nut—took good care of his body."

"Thanks, Chan. You have my best wishes for happiness and success in your new life. Give Shake my regards and tell him I called."

Cayo Piedra, Republic of Cuba

As the sun was just beginning to creep up over the eastern horizon, a rattletrap Russian-made Mi-8 helicopter drilled lazy circles over a long strip of white sand beach near the Bay of Pigs. The pilots were waiting for permission to approach *El Supremo* Fidel Castro's very secure private island located about 10 miles off Cuba's southwest coast. The island was called *Cayo Piedra* by the few locals who knew of its existence but the trusted aviators allowed to fly into the heavily guarded complex called it *Punto Cero*, Ground Zero. The veteran pilots flying this classified mission for Military Intelligence knew the drill. You called for clearance from the standing guard force and then circled until it was given. Any aircraft—friendly or otherwise—that didn't was subject to instant attack by the air defense systems that dotted the island.

When they finally got permission to land on the southernmost of the two little islets that composed *Cayo Piedra* the pilot twisted in his seat and showed a thumbs-up to let his passengers know they would be descending. He wondered about the man in the back, sitting with hands manacled between two armed guards and General Enrique Constanza, Director of Cuban Military Intelligence, but he knew better than to ask. The pilot had transported *el Presidente* Raul Castro and a few select VIPs on this route plenty of times, but he'd never hauled a prisoner under guard. "Must be a big fish back there," he mumbled to his co-pilot as they set the helo on approach. The man in the seat to his right just shook his head and drew a finger across his throat. There were no questions and no speculations allowed about flights to *Punto Cero*.

Carlos Ruiz-Romero sat quietly in the back of the helicopter trying desperately to work out a plan of action. Nothing specific came to mind but he understood under the circumstances he would have to help himself if there was any hope for help at all. Much depended on what the Cubans intended to do with him, and so far they'd given him no hint about that. He was dressed in something that looked and smelled like hospital surgical scrubs and a pair of ill-fitting rubber-soled sandals. The shabby outfit and a plastic bag containing minimal toilet articles was all they provided when his captors hustled him out of the little cubicle in the early morning dark. He was cuffed at the door of the building where one armed guard covered him with a beach umbrella for some reason and another steered him toward a patch of asphalt where a helicopter sat idling with blades swishing slowly through the muggy air. The senior military officer he'd seen earlier was waiting in the door of the aircraft, but the civilian with the straw sandals was nowhere in sight. Carlos was quickly hauled aboard and strapped into a seat by one of the guards. The other guard sat opposite him fondling a small submachinegun.

The air was frigid at altitude and Carlos sat shaking, wondering where he was going and what would happen to him when he arrived at wherever it was. He'd been full of questions and demands for information when they came for him but he'd been told that he could either shut up or be gagged. Just before take-off he'd heard one of the guards mention something about *Punto Cero* to one of the pilots, but he'd never heard of a place in Cuba called that. Looking out the door of the helicopter as it descended he saw an island—actually two small verdant clumps in the ocean connected by a long bridge—and decided that must be Ground Zero.

The place looked relatively attractive from the air, like an under-developed beach resort with a long pier for visiting boats. There was only one vessel in sight: a huge, palatial yacht tied up alongside a jetty. Carlos didn't know much about boats, but he knew expensive when he saw it, and the big power boat was extremely well-appointed—likely to have cost its owner several million dollars.

The beach umbrella was popped back into place overhead as the guards hustled him toward an L-shaped concrete structure and through a set of gilded doors into a foyer that was composed of polished granite tiles. The air smelled of sandalwood and cigar smoke. He couldn't see much more but it looked like he had been brought to someone's well-appointed mansion or to the lobby of a Castaways resort. He was shoved toward an elevator at the other end of the foyer and a mirrored car carried Carlos and his escorts downward. When the doors opened they emerged into another long passageway, this one dimly lit and drab with two or three doors opening along its length.

He was marched to the nearest one on the right where the senior officer punched numbers into a keypad. When the door was opened and he was shoved inside, Carlos stood looking at what might have been an economy room in a cheap motel. He noted a bed, a small desk, a dresser with three open drawers, and a bathroom with no door. Camera lenses stared down at him from four corners where walls met ceiling.

"You will be comfortable here," the officer said as a guard removed the manacles. It was the first time Carlos had heard the man speak and it was in fairly unaccented English. "You will be fed shortly. I'd suggest you rest after that. Any attempt to escape, any act of defiance will be dealt with harshly."

Carlos Ruiz-Romero decided to ignore that. He was about to begin his resistance, shouting questions and demanding answers, but his escorts abruptly departed and the door to this much more comfortable prison cell slammed shut before he could begin. There was a narrow barred window on the wall near the little desk, and Carlos stood looking out over a field of tall tropical saw grass, wondering what he might do to get himself out of this mess.

As he stepped out of the elevator and into the tiled entryway of *El Supremo's* private estate, General Enrique Constanza was met by an aide waiting in the foyer and holding a satellite phone receiver. "I made the call to let Director General Panteros know our guest is safely in his new quarters. The helicopter is standing by to take us back whenever you are ready, General."

"Did Panteros contact the Russians?"

"He did, sir. We have a complete transcript of the call at headquarters. They are ready to negotiate. Two special representatives are on their way from Moscow."

General Constanza simply smiled and led the way out of the Castro mansion complex. If all went as planned over the next week or so, he would have the money to build a similar place for himself and his family. There was a lot at risk but Enrique Constanza had been living with risk since his days as a hard-pressed, half-starved guerilla in the mountains with Fidel. He knew more about risk and reward than a Moscow-trained puppet like Manuel Panteros would ever know.

"You never told me about this guy." Shake grabbed another slice of white bread and topped it with a hunk of Black's best brisket. "I think I'm jealous."

"Give me a break." Chan poked at her plate and portioned some meat they could carry back to Bear who was avidly exploring his new home. "I never complained about the ex-wife, skivvy girls, and other sordid flings in your past life."

"Yeah, well it sounds like the thing with you and old Carlos was pretty serious."

"It was never gonna be anything long-term, Shake. He was way too dedicated to his work. The guy could drift off anytime, anywhere. He had one of those weird brains, you know? Anything that wasn't a mathematical formula or some arcane code didn't hold his interest for long. When I began to bitch about it, he just packed his trash and disappeared one day. I saw him at work, of course, but we both knew it was over. No hard feelings."

"Seems weird the DIA would let a techie like that with burn-before-reading clearances out of the building much less send him down to Gitmo where Cuban intelligence might get a shot at him—especially a guy who had Cuban roots."

"There was a lot of argument about that. Carlos wanted to go badly, swore there was nobody in Cuba that he knew or that knew him anymore. And his argument about why he should go personally played right into DIA's frustration with the lack of actionable Intel we were getting from Gitmo. Carlos said what little we got from the interrogators at the detention camp was useless. He needed to hear it for himself from the detainees so he could interpret and dig around, ask the right questions, and let the jihadis know they were dealing with an expert—that kind of thing."

"And he was trying to find out how they communicate with cells or allies around the world?"

"Yeah, he was the leading guy in that effort for all the alphabet soup outfits. Carlos was convinced the AQ and ISIS leadership had developed a sophisticated communications net and an advanced code system. He was determined to get a handle on it so we could either disrupt the net or monitor it without letting the bad guys know they were compromised. He had some serious backing at very high levels. The NSA was pushing hard behind the effort."

"Makes sense that he'd want to do the interrogations himself, I guess. You know, once the subject realizes he can't bullshit a bullshitter all kinds of beans get spilled."

"What beats me is how he got outside the wire." Chan wrapped Bear's treat in a napkin and drank the last of her tea. "When they agreed to send him down there, they insisted on tight security. They even brought in a couple of gorillas to babysit him. So how does he just disappear and what was he doing out on the water?"

"That's likely what Bayer and a bunch of other panicky investigators are trying to find out. Maybe the guy was trying to defect."

"No way." Chan preceded her husband out of the BBQ joint into the warm evening air. "You've got to look at motives for a thing like that, right? Carlos had plenty of money. The guy never spent a dime he didn't have to and he was no kind of conspicuous consumer. I know for a fact that he had a solid, profitable investment portfolio. He used to give me advice and I saw his bottom-line—very healthy. And he damn sure hated the Castro regime for what it did to his family. He wasn't passionate about much, but if you ever wanted a lecture about the evils of communist Cuba, Carlos was your man."

Shake was silent for most of the short walk back to the house until they turned the corner onto Commerce Street. "I guess the real question that's got their skivvies in a twist is whether or not the Cubans had anything to do with it."

They sat on the log bench under the live oaks digesting and watching Bear romp in and out of the tall weeds that were springing up on either side of their little creek. "Either way," Chan said as she kissed his cheek and whispered in his ear, "it's no concern of ours—not anymore."

Shake called the dog and led Chan inside the house, up the stairs toward their new bedroom. She was right of course. As a practical matter and as a direct result of a deliberate disconnect from old concerns, the mysterious death of a high-level agent in Cuba was no skin off their noses. They no longer had any skin or any noses in that game.

Chan got to sleep quickly after a tender bout of welcome home lovemaking, but Shake lay awake for quite some time, staring at the profusion of puffy clouds painted on the bedroom ceiling, listening to the overhead fans and the lonesome whistle of a passing train. He couldn't erase fitful images of Cuba, floating like a dangerous naval mine out there in the Caribbean just 90 miles off the southern coast. Eventually he rolled over, punched the pillow, and tried to think about building a hobby shop.

While Lockhart was only 30 miles due south of the Texas capital city and an easy commute, Chan wanted to give him some uninterrupted exploring and planning time, so she took advantage of the university's generous offer to put her up for the week of faculty orientation. Shake had planned on using the time to get the riding mower they inherited from the previous owners into useful shape to attack the jungle of weeds sprouting on the lower part of the property. He tinkered around a little every morning and made a list of the parts he needed, but after an hour or two he always wandered away to sketch plans for his hobby shop.

Once he got the chores in hand and established a regular maintenance schedule for all the little things that needed doing around the house and on the spread, he intended to build that shop just the way he wanted it—equipped with all the little hand and machine tools that distract, delight, and entertain any bog-standard male human being. It would be a sanctuary of sorts, a place dedicated to creating things as opposed to destroying things, his primary pastime for way too many years. Although he hadn't discussed it with Chan very much, Shake had an idea about creating little gewgaws, mementos, and souvenirs with a military flavor—some handy and some simply decorative—made from natural woods, bamboo, and military surplus bits. He'd call it "Bushcraft by Davis" and the products would incorporate his latent creative bent, employing all the designs and skills he'd developed over long years of living and surviving in a field environment. Some of it he planned to give away to old friends and some of it he might even sell for a few bucks if anyone was interested.

It was well past noon when he decided it was time to test the Shiner Bock that he'd bought on recommendation from some old cowboy standing behind him at a local branch of the Texas Department of Public Safety where he'd gone to register his truck and obtain a set of Purple Heart tags. The guy was an Air Force vet who struck up a conversation when he saw Shake proffer a copy of his DD-214 discharge papers. They talked for a while, waiting on the clerk to do the necessary business and Shake mentioned the local weather which was heating up as summer approached. The cowboy said it usually got "chili-pepper hot" around mid-afternoon and the best remedy was an ice-cold Shiner. "Never mind that old Lone Star or Pearl," the cowboy advised. "You want you a good Texas beer to beat the heat, you get you a Shiner."

He was halfway to the house when he heard tires crunching gravel. A shiny green Audi with Avis stickers on the front bumper was turning into the driveway. He stood watching as the car nosed under the low-hanging branches of the live oaks. Tinted windows kept Shake from seeing much of the driver. When he heard the grind of a parking brake, he walked toward the car wondering if it was a salesman hawking something or maybe a neighbor wanting to meet the new folks in town. The driver who unfolded from behind the wheel was neither of those things. The driver was the man who calls himself Bayer.

"Hello, Shake." Bayer pulled a pair of sunglasses off his nose and stood looking around with his hands on his hips. "Very nice place you've got here." He was dressed more casually than Shake was used to seeing. He'd taken a turn or two on the cuffs of an oxford cloth dress shirt and there was no tie knotted at his collar. As they shook hands, Shake noticed a roller-bag in the backseat and Bayer's blazer draped over the passenger seat.

"Just got into Austin and I'm on my way to a meeting in San Antonio. Thought I'd stop off enroute and say hello."

"You missed Chan." Shake pointed at the house and led the way. "She's up in Austin for some faculty mixers. Won't be home until tomorrow sometime."

"I know that, Shake. It's one of the reasons I decided to take this detour. I wanted to talk to you in private for a little while."

Shake chewed on that while he opened a couple of beers and got Bayer settled under the ceiling fan on the breezy little back porch. "You ought to know by now we don't keep secrets," he said as he settled into a cane-back chair across the table. "Whatever you've got to say, she'll find out about it because I'll tell her. If you don't want that, let's just drink beer and catch up."

"Inevitable, I suppose. She seemed a little upset with my call, so I didn't want to add any irritation." Bayer sipped his beer. "This is good, Shake. I used to drink a lot of Shiner when I was working the Central America desk out of Houston. Very Texas—very refreshing."

"We've got about ten more on ice. Think that's enough for you to tell me why you're here?"

"I wanted to talk about Cuba. I'm headed down there as part of an exploratory task force next week. It has to do with this normalization nonsense."

"Nonsense is a good word for it. I've got no idea what the Administration thinks they're gonna achieve messing around down there."

"They don't either, Shake. Believe me." The man who calls himself Bayer drained his beer and belched politely. "May I trouble you for another one of these?"

"You know much about Castro's Cuba?" Bayer asked when Shake returned with refills. "I mean other than the Kennedy-Khrushchev missile stand-off and that gutless performance we pulled off in the Bay of Pigs. That was well before our time and not very relevant these days except as context."

"I know what I read. That's about it. I was only in Cuba once, long time ago on Marine Corps business. If you ask me, nothing's ever gonna change in that country until they get rid of the Castro regime and that's not gonna happen anytime soon. Cuba is just one of those hard-core commie states that won't give it up, won't admit that the system has failed regardless of the evidence."

"Cuba is a lot more than that, Shake." Bayer stared up at the ceiling fan for a moment, folded his hands across his stomach and began to talk. "The CIA calls Cuba the 'Intelligence Trafficker to the World' and that's not hyperbole. Espionage is their most lucrative national export. When the Soviet Union caved, Havana lost a three billion dollar annual subsidy. You can't make that up by selling sugar cane and cigars. So the Cubans started dealing in classified information, a lot of it serious stuff that's pulled down by their Russian-designed signals intelligence facility at Bejucal. Selling secrets to the highest bidder is Cuba's key revenue stream. And here we are about to lift the economic sanctions and establish normal diplomatic relations. Do you know what that means for this country?"

The man who calls himself Bayer didn't wait for a response. "Take the travel restrictions, for instance. Opening Cuba to American tourists is going to make the Castro regime rich in a hurry. More accurately, it's going to pour millions of U.S. dollars into the Cuban intelligence and security services, and they run everything in that country using the military as their private police force. A flood of ignorant, naïve Jimmy Buffet fans looking for the new Caribbean hot spot just gives Cuban spymasters an unprecedented opportunity to recruit American agents and potential traitors in the same way ISIS is doing right now around the world.

"And there are more serious pitfalls. Normalization includes unrestricted access to foreign technology as part of the package. But the Cubans aren't interested in flat-screen TVs and smart phones. What they want—and what they will have the cash to buy—is the kind of stuff that allows Havana to make significant upgrades in espionage technology. And that technology will be directed against their number one and only target, namely the United States. We hear arguments from some of the idiots on Capitol Hill who say Cuba is no threat to this country. That's about as wrong-headed as it can get. Think about it, Shake. We decree that Cuba is no threat and we're playing right into their hands. Spying against an enemy that thinks you're no threat is a hell of a lot easier than working against a nation that's got its guard up. Bottom line: we relax about those bastards and everyone smiles while Cuba's three foreign intelligence services jut bleed us dry."

"So how come a guy like you that sees all the dangers is going down to Havana with a team that's setting up to open all those doors?"

"I'm a self-assigned strap-hanger, Shake. I pack enough clout at various levels that the State Department dupes couldn't say no. I'm supposed to be looking into Homeland Security concerns, and I'll do that. But the truth is, I'm looking for solid evidence I can present to make a case for putting this whole thing on semi-permanent hold, or better yet, dumping the idea entirely."

"Good luck with that." Shake retrieved two more beers and decided he'd better offer the man who calls himself Bayer a bed for the night. "It's a done deal, right? We got a guy in the White House who's looking to justify his Nobel Peace Prize even if it destroys the country he's sworn to preserve."

"He's vulnerable, Shake. More importantly, his cock-eyed schemes can be stalled or reversed with support of a Congressional majority. All it will take to deep-six this deal is a bombshell that proves the Cubans are conducting an active, undeclared, and very dangerous intelligence war against the United States."

"Maybe it's the beer, but I'm starting to think that the bombshell is somehow related to the DIA guy who turned up dead at Gitmo. You know the dude was once my wife's lover which is likely the real reason you dropped by while she's not here. Any of that hit near the mark?"

The man who calls himself Bayer straightened in his chair and leaned over the table. "I don't think the hunk of bloody meat they found in the bay down there is Carlos Ruiz-Romero. I think it's a deception plain and simple. I think somehow Cuban Intelligence got hold of Carlos Ruiz-Romero, and they planted this corpse to keep us from looking for him."

Shake saw muscles bunching in Bayer's jaw and watched the flush crawling across his cheeks. The old clandestine warrior was serious as cardiac arrest, but did he have a case? Or was it just a die-hard commie-buster suffering paranoid delusions? "Granted the Cuban spooks are serious players, but that's a stretch, isn't it?"

"Is it, Shake? Deception and illusion, smoke and mirrors, right? We've been doing stuff like that in the game for eons. Remember the poor sap the Brits floated in the English Channel for the Nazis to find before D-Day? They planted papers on that corpse that said the invasion was coming at one place when they knew it was going someplace else. That was a classic deception, and so is this deal down in Cuba."

"What makes you so sure?"

"I don't like it when things add up too neatly, Shake. When everyone else was ready to shrug it off as a tragic accident, I began to dig. Think about this." The man who calls himself Bayer held up a hand and began to tick off points. "Ruiz-Romero goes missing one day for no discernible reason and despite assigned bodyguards. Search indicates he likely left the base by crawling under the perimeter fence. No indications that anyone came in that way or any other way during the time. So he ducks security and leaves on his own hook for some reason. Why? Did he defect? Unlikely— the guy reportedly hates the Castro regime. Next, we get a report of a body found floating offshore in Guantanamo Bay. No reports of any other missing persons, so the assumption is that it must be what's left of our DIA guy. The corpse is missing a head, both arms and both lower legs, supposedly lost to sharks, so no fingerprints to match. The forensics people go to work with what they've got but it's not much. Same blood type as Ruiz-Romero but that's where the verifiable similarities end. We don't have a family member available to sample for a DNA test so everybody's ready to call it a day."

"But not you."

"Definitely not me, Shake. Medical records showed Ruiz-Romero had no scars or tattoos to help with identifying him, and I confirmed that with Chan. She also told me something that sealed the deal. Whoever the guy was that they found down there, it was not Carlos Ruiz-Romero."

"What did she tell you?"

"That Ruiz-Romero was circumcised. The torso they fished out of the bay was not."

Shake got up to walk around the porch, sipping his beer and trying connect the dots Bayer was laying out for inspection. It was silly and immature, but he was having a hard time focusing beyond images of Chan making love to another man. He finally got a grip on it, shook his head and resumed pacing. "Supposing you're right, Carlos might still be alive, maybe somewhere in Cuba. If he's no threat to defect and takes off voluntarily, there's got to be a reason. Maybe something or someone lured him off base. I'd start looking at that aspect."

"OK, he gets lured off base for reasons unknown. What if the Cubans grabbed him? They've got checkpoints and roving patrols all around Gitmo and you know they'd love to get their hands on a guy with his knowledge—maybe hand him off to the Russians or sell him to the highest bidder. So, say that's the case here. They'd go to long lengths to avoid any kind of full-press search for him or any suspicion that they were involved in his disappearance. Something like that would do significant damage to the normalization process, and that's the last thing they want right now."

"So what are you gonna do about it?"

"I'm going to find out what really happened to Ruiz-Romero, Shake. And if it's what I believe it is, I'm going to let Congress and the press know what kind of people we are about to blindly jump into bed with."

"Well, you need to start at Gitmo. Start poking around inside the wire. Talk to his so-called bodyguards. They still down there?"

"One of them is—the guy who was off duty when Carlos disappeared. FBI's got the other guy under wraps at the Miami field office. Claims he left Ruiz-Romero sleeping in his BOQ room and decided it was safe for him to go for a late dinner. Claims he was gone for about an hour and then resumed his post outside the door. When Carlos didn't show the next morning, the guy checked and found an empty room. He's got no idea what happened and he's got no reason to lie. His career is over, and he knows it. I talked to him personally. He's a knuckle-dragger, no Mensa candidate by a long-shot, but I don't see him as on the take or involved in any way other than screwing up an important assignment."

"You need to get started on this in a hurry. If the Cubans have got Ruiz-Romero they'll be moving him as soon as possible."

"That's a problem for me, Shake. This State Department task force I'm part of is going to be working out of Havana. I'll do what I can in the capital, but I don't want them to know I'm a fox in their hen-house. I can't just leave for Gitmo and start running an investigation on something that might jeopardize their precious normalization program. They'd dial up the White House and have me on a plane out of there in very short order."

"And you can't use your influence with Homeland Security or the CIA or the FBI and get some undercover support for this thing? I mean they've got to understand that if Ruiz-Romero was somehow abducted by Cuban Intel, they are facing one of the most serious potential compromises since WikiLeaks."

"I'll get all the support in the world, Shake—but not until I can show some evidence that Ruiz-Romero is alive and the Cubans are involved in this thing. This administration has got everyone running scared "

"You know I can't do this for you."

"Shake, believe me, I wouldn't be down here asking you to get back in the game if I had another viable option or if it wasn't so damn vital. You said it yourself. This could be worse than WikiLeaks—much worse and much more damaging to national security."

"That's a familiar tune. You know Chan will probably leave me and shoot you—or both—the minute I mention this."

"I'll talk to her personally." The man who calls himself Bayer checked his watch. "I can drive back up to Austin and give her a call."

"You're not driving anywhere tonight. And you're sure as hell not going to talk with Chan about something like this without me there to filter the bullshit. She said she'd be home tomorrow around noon. I'm gonna make up a spare bed for you."

A flashing sign above the breezeway at Miami International said departure of his American Airlines flight to Key West would be delayed by an hour. Shake checked his watch, stashed the thick dossier on Carlos Ruiz-Romero he'd been reading, and headed for the bar across from the gate area. Seated on a stool with his bulging backpack on his lap, he held up a finger for the bartender and pointed at the stand of taps.

Waving away a menu, he focused on the tall pilsner in front of him and then dug for his phone. There was a text from Chan asking him to be sure and call when he got into Guantanamo. Neither of them was sure about cellular service in Cuba, and she said she would feel better if she could talk to him regularly while he dug around down there. Shake glanced up at his image reflected by the mirror behind the bar. Garish pink and green neon from a nearby beer sign made his shock of white hair look like a clown wig and the hard light deepened the creases around his eyes and mouth. He reached for his beer glass and saw a spray of liver spots that highlighted the scars, calluses and dings on his mistreated hands. He was an ugly old warhorse and not aging very well. Chan could do a lot better. Thank God she didn't want to, but she damn sure could and he didn't want to ever forget that.

Her attitude when they'd discussed the Cuba mission with the man who calls himself Bayer was both stoic and surprising. Maybe she'd agreed with so little argument because she loved him for who he was and what he was with no caveats. Maybe she understood the crucial nature of what he was being asked to do. Or maybe she wanted to discover what really happened to her former lover. Whatever it was that made her accept what was happening, Chan didn't seem anxious to discuss it after the decision was made.

"I'm just a little hurt that something like this comes up so soon after we started a new life," she told him as Bayer worked the phones in another room to set up Shake's trip and his cover. "I'll get over it."

Shake gathered her in his arms. "And I'm just a little surprised that you aren't upstairs packing your bags."

"I knew something like this was bound to happen, Shake. It's who you are and what you do is a reflection of that. For better and for worse, right? I can't live life angry and resentful and I won't. Just don't get yourself killed and leave me all alone in this big house."

"It's just a fact-finding deal, Chan. What Bayer does with those facts is his business. I'll be home in a week or two—promise."

Shake finished his beer, checked his watch, and decided he had time for another before they started to call his flight. He broke out his cell phone and began to tap out a text message for the operations officer at Marine Medium Tiltrotor Squadron 263 at Beaufort, South Carolina to let him know he might be a little late arriving in Key West. The squadron headquartered in Beaufort ran a detachment of MV-22 Osprey aircraft that made regular runs from NAS Key West to the Naval Base at Guantanamo Bay, and if Bayer had the clout he claimed, there would be space for Shake on the next flight.

He was halfway through the second beer when his phone chirped. "Tracking your inbound domestic," the ops officer wrote. "Plenty of time to make our outbound for Gitmo. Call this number when at gate for transpo to flightline. Check in with ops there." Shake saved the text and then scrolled through his email to see if there was any word from Crazy Earl. There wasn't, but that was no surprise. Gerheim promised to meet the flight and the man had always been true to his word.

Retired Chief Warrant Officer Earl Gerheim, an old and flamboyant Marine buddy who had been one of Shake's Buttplate squad leaders in Vietnam, was serving as the Marine Corps Criminal Investigative Division chief at Gitmo. He was also the only one down there that knew what Shake was really up to during his visit. Shake had been in semiregular contact with Gerheim over the years, and when he agreed to nose around the Ruiz-Romero case, he got in touch. A buddy working for CID, who was also an old Cuba hand, would be a tremendous asset. Crazy Earl was just the type of non-regulation, mission-focused old operator that thrived on undercover investigations.

A letter of introduction to the command, the required area clearances and cobbled up credentials that identified Shake as a government contract HVAC consultant on an inspection visit would get him only so far and so deep at Gitmo. Shake knew approximately zip-point-shit about heating, ventilation, and air-conditioning and the cover Bayer provided was really only designed to get him on the base where a visiting contractor would be provided quarters and logistical support during his stay. When he really needed to dig or had to get around restricted access, he would depend on Crazy Earl to slap on the grease and provide the necessary leverage with his CID credentials.

When the taxi from Key West airport dumped him at the gate of the Naval Station, Shake made his way to the Master-at-Arms desk and showed his retired Marine ID card and his phony consultant credentials and asked to use the base phone. The lanky, tattooed Chief on duty picked up a receiver, punched in the number Shake dictated, and handed over the phone. A Marine corporal answered with a rapid-fire greeting that was so clipped and conjoined that all Shake heard for sure was 2-6-3 and may I help you, sir. He identified himself, discovered he was expected, and got orders from the corporal to stand by for a vehicle that would bring him to the flightline.

A Marine crew chief with a nametag on her flightsuit that indicated she was Sergeant Della McCarty gave Shake and two other strap-hangers a perfunctory safety brief and then fitted them all with cranial helmets and life preservers. Sergeant McCarty was obviously very proud of her aircraft and her position on the flight crew. Once she found out Shake was a Marine about to embark on his first Osprey ride, she made time to give him a walk-around tour of the bird.

"I guess it's like everything new and revolutionary that comes down the pike," she said after explaining how the tilt-rotor system worked. "We had some teething problems. We pranged a couple into the deck before we got the bugs out of the system and learned to fly the Osprey, but I don't think there's a better bird going today for what the Marine Corps needs to do."

"Teething problems are nothing unusual." Shake noted the age of the pilots as they sat in the cockpit running a pre-flight checklist. They looked like a couple of teenagers getting a hot-rod ready for a drag race. "I remember when the Corps committed to the Harrier VSTOL back in the seventies. Seemed like we dumped one every other week, but it was just a matter of getting used to something new. Once we got the system working and the pilots trained up, the Harrier turned out to be a real barn-burner in combat."

"Well, this baby sure burned some barns in The Big Sandbox, that's for sure."

"Did you fly in the Osprey's over there?"

"I did," Sergeant McCarty responded as she led Shakes up the cargo ramp at the rear of the aircraft. "And my squadron is about to go out on a float next month. I reenlisted for it."

"Doesn't anybody in the Corps ever say ship over anymore?" Shake fumbled with his seat belt and decided Sergeant Della McCarty had likely enlisted in the Marines about ten years after he retired. "I thought reenlist was an Army term."

"That's old-school, Gunner. Everything is *Joint* these days, you know? Gotta try and speak the same language as the other services. Can't have a good military acronym unless it's got a J as the first letter."

"Joint used to be something we got busted for smoking back in Vietnam, Sergeant McCarty. I don't want to say that joint concept sucks—but it certainly inhales deeply."

McCarty laughed and patted Shake on the shoulder like he was an old dog that needed comforting. "Not to fret, Gunner. We're still Marines and we always will be. You can take that to the bank."

By the time the Osprey's two big turbo-fans were spinning, the passengers were strapped into uncomfortable nylon sling-seats on either side of a stash of boxed cargo marked for delivery to the Marine Security Guard Detachment, USNB Guantanamo Bay. Shake had heard and read a lot about the Marine Corps' relatively new Vertical Short Take-Off and Landing or VSTOL aircraft based on sophisticated tilt-rotor technology. Sergeant McCarty's briefing had filled in some of the blanks with things he didn't know. The Osprey was designed and adopted to replace the aging fleet of

Vietnam-era CH-46 Sea Knight helos—commonly called Phrogs—and featured significant improvements in speed, range, and lift. The Corps was supposedly working on a way to arm the Ospreys with rockets and mini-guns, but the one rolling down the runway at Key West was slick as far as an old grunt could tell.

They lifted off much like a conventional aircraft and Shake was a little disappointed. He'd been looking forward to the experience of transitioning from vertical take-off to horizontal flight. When Sgt. McCarty came aft to check on her passengers, he shouted a question about it over the roar of the engines and the rattle of machinery. "Standard take-off saves fuel and wear on the gear," she said with a smile. "We'll probably make a standard approach and then go into helo-mode for landing at Gitmo. You'll get a kick out of it."

He certainly did. Waking from a nap when he felt the Osprey bank hard, Shake looked out one of the ports on his side of the aircraft and saw Cuba sprawling like a long green gash in the cobalt-blue Caribbean. As the pilots carved high circles in a cloudless sky, waiting for landing instructions, he identified the long jagged ridge of high ground running most of the length of the island as the Sierra Maestra range, Fidel Castro's old revolutionary hang-out. He could make out the sprawl of Havana near the north end of the island and when the Osprey descended, banking south to pick up the approach leg for landing at Gitmo, he saw the Navy base at the opposite end. There were some fleet auxiliaries nested by the piers. Farther out in the bay a warship was anchored like a haze-grey weed in Castro's Cuban rose bed.

The Osprey swooped toward the runway at the base's little airstrip but turned quickly after crossing the threshold numbers. He heard a nerve-rattling whine as the pilots transitioned the engine nacelles from facing forward to facing upward and it felt like someone had just jammed on a speed-brake. He was pitched forward against his lap-belt momentarily and when he straightened up to look out the port, they were in a hover. Below them he spotted a Marine in digital-camouflage utilities wearing a cranial helmet and waving wands at them to guide the Osprey toward a landing spot. Shake grinned back at Sgt. McCarty who was showing him a thumbs-up and thought about all the hairy combat insertions and extractions he'd made aboard Marine Corps helicopters. Something like the Osprey would have been a God-send.

"Excuse me, sir." The chunky man, wearing a pair of rimless spectacles perched on a nose flattened and fattened by opponents over years of competition in Fleet Marine boxing tournaments, stood beside an unmarked white cargo van. "Maybe you can help." He was dressed in pressed khaki trousers and one of those lightweight safari shirts that featured epaulets and way too many pockets. "I'm looking for some grizzled old Recon turd that claims he was a hero in our U.S. Marine Corps?"

Crazy Earl Gerheim hit a fighter's stance and tossed a few jabs past Shake's ears before he offered a hand followed by a hug. "Toss your gear in the van. We'll swing by the VOQ where I've got you set up in tropical style. You can grab a shower and then we'll go by the Facilities Management office and get you started."

The shower in the relatively Spartan VOQ room was refreshing and Shake put on a freshly laundered shirt, but shortly after he walked outside the building into Gitmo's muggy air, he was sweating and the shirt was wilting. Crazy Early arrived in just a few minutes and asked about documents, letters, and credentials. Shake patted his pocket and asked about cell phone coverage aboard the base.

"Might as well shit-can your phone or leave it in the room," Gerheim said. "I've got what you need in the van." When they were rolling down the pristine, palm-lined streets of the base, he handed over two phones, one smaller than the other. "The big one is a sat-phone. You'll need to use that for calling the states. The other one is logged into the base

cellular network. You can use it to call anyplace on Gitmo. I
plugged my number and some of the basic contacts into the
memory. When you've got to do email or internet research,
you're gonna have to use my machine at the office. Service
down here is terrible but I'm set up on the government server
and you can use that when you need it."

On the way to check in with the Naval Base Facilities
Management Office, Shake played with the satellite phone
and got it figured out sufficiently to call Chan in Lockhart.
She answered tentatively. "It's me," he said. "I'm at Gitmo.
Better put this number in your contact list. It's a satellite
phone and apparently the only thing that works down here."

"Are you OK?"

"I'm fine. Crazy Earl's got me in hand and he swears
there's no way we can get into any trouble."

"Then Earl really is crazy—or he doesn't know you very
well."

"I'm fine, Chan. Plan is to relax tonight and start work
tomorrow. I'll call you after dinner when we can talk a little
longer. Love you."

The Navy Civil Engineer Corps three-striper who ran the
base facilities and maintenance program was expecting him.
He was a little chilly at first, suspecting that Shake was on
some kind of witch-hunt but that didn't last long. The Commander had done due diligence and called the number on the
letterhead where he spoke to a representative—likely Bayer
himself Shake thought with a smile—but there wasn't much
information provided about just what Mr. Davis would be
doing during his stay. He warmed up to downright cheeri-
ness when Shake explained that his company had simply
sent him down to look things over and recommend what they
might do to improve things at Gitmo. It was a matter of some
surplus money that needed spending, Shake said with a

wink, and the company thought some unsolicited expenditure might help grease the skids for an upcoming contract renewal. The Commander understood completely, gave Shake his personal contact number, asked him to check in regularly and call if he ran into any problems. After a quick dinner at the Navy Exchange complex, Shake returned to his room in the Visiting Officers' Quarters where he sat at the rickety little desk and tried to make a plan of action. He had a few scribbled notes on a yellow legal pad but nothing coherent or very helpful emerged from the effort. He took another shower, spoke to his wife in Texas for a few minutes, and then crawled into bed. Hopefully, his instincts would guide him in the morning.

Gerheim arrived with coffee at 0730 and drove Shake to a sandy little outdoor recreation area near the bay where there were a couple of picnic benches shaded by a stand of palms. It was deserted and a good place to talk. "Here's what we know so far," Gerheim said when they were settled, surrounded by seagulls looking for scraps. "Your guy was in his Q room at approximately 2030—last time his security detail saw him. Next he's observed by one of our patrols." Gerheim checked his notebook and flipped a few pages. "At approximately 2140, running on the perimeter road, something he does regularly so no alert there. He's dressed in athletic attire and wearing a backpack.

"OK, so we get a motion sensor hit shortly after 2200 and a unit is dispatched to check it out. They poke around and discover someone has been digging under the fence near a construction site on a northwest sector of the perimeter. Base goes into full lock-down and search mode—SOP. Nothing turns up anywhere so the watch commander writes it off as an animal alert. Happens all the time with the sensor array on the other side of the fence."

"Nobody connects it with the guy running on the road?" Shake clipped one of the cigars Gerheim offered from a leather case and stared out at Guantanamo Bay.

"No reason to do that. When there's a perimeter breach, it's generally people trying to get in, not out. Anyway, things settled down to a dull roar by the next morning. That's when one of Ruiz-Romero's security guards drops by the NCIS Detachment down here. It's really a one-man shop, so I get a call and open a missing person case. Heat's on from Washington because this Carlos Ruiz-Romero is a heavy-hitter from DIA. I'm starting to work the case, thinking maybe a defection attempt or something, when one of the Navy patrol boats brings in that bloody hunk of meat. Your guy is the only missing person. We put two and two together and ask for Ruiz-Romero's medical records. Forensics people at the hospital go to work and list cause of death as shark attack. They determine the hunk has the same blood type as the missing man. We report a tentative ID and I'm ready to close the case. That's when you call."

"That hunk of meat is definitely not Carlos Ruiz-Romero, Craze." Shake explained why they were sure that was the case and outlined everything else he knew about the missing man. "This thing is not likely to be a defection, Could it have something to do with the work he was doing at Camp Delta?"

"I don't see a connection there, Shake. As far as we know, Castro's Intel guys have no interest in Al Qaeda or any of the other dipshits we've got locked up down here. They love the hell out of the Russians who have been keeping them in business over the years, and maybe the Russians have some interest in one or two of the HVI's at the detention facility. But it's a long stretch to tie that up with your guy. There's gotta be something else."

"Yeah, I think so too. Something prompted this guy to leave the base. If he's not lying dead on the other side of the wire, he's somewhere else and that might mean the Cubans got him, either intentionally or accidentally."

"We've swept the trace on the other side of the perimeter fence, Shake—all seventeen miles of it. There are no dead bodies out there. Assuming he's still alive, he's somewhere else, either holed up or the Cubans have got him. I'm checking what few cooperative sources I've got in Cuban law enforcement—such as that is—but no dice so far."

"We've got a serious player with the normalization task force in Havana. He's pressing to find out if the Cubans have got Carlos Ruiz-Romero."

Crazy Early Gerheim snorted and tucked his notebook back in a pocket. "There ain't a player in the world serious enough to make the Cubans spill anything they don't want us to know, Shake. If they've got your guy, they won't be advertising or admitting it. What they want us to think right now is that they are no threat and they play well with others."

"Can we take a look at that stretch of perimeter fence? And then I want to talk to the bodyguard."

They cruised past the Navy Exchange complex and through the military family housing area on the windward side of the base before Gerheim finally wheeled onto the perimeter road heading northeast in the general direction of the main gate. Gerheim pointed off to the right where a boxy building was tucked into the foot of a large hill. The crest of that hill was spiked with aerials, antennae, and relay towers. "Remember that place?"

He reduced speed running past the old Marine Barracks, a camouflage-painted two-story structure set amid a well-manicured patch of green grass. "The Marines assigned to the Security Guard Detachment don't stay there regular anymore, but they keep the place in good shape. Some of the relief that stands post at the North East Gate sleep there during their trick, and they still take good care of the emblem."

"Is that still here?" Shake grinned and remembered the story of how a gaudy scarlet-and-gold U.S. Marine Corps eagle, globe, and anchor wound up on the hill near the barracks in a conspicuous place facing the Cubans on the other side of the fence like a big middle finger. "Can we take a quick look?"

Gerheim wheeled off onto the approach road to the old barracks building and swung around to the base of the hill. There it was on the north face, still vivid with fresh paint, amid a field of scrub brush carefully trimmed back so that the 20-foot diameter concrete slab showcasing the Corps' most revered symbol would stand out proudly. "Marines put that thing up there back in the seventies sometime." Gerheim stood looking uphill with a huge grin on his face. "I woulda give a couple paychecks to be in on that deal."

"Yeah, it was a Crazy Earl kind of stunt." Shake tried to remember what he'd heard of the legendary coup pulled off by the Marines at Guantanamo Bay during the height of the Cold War. "Those dudes have got a special chapter in Marine Corps history. They floated a huge turd in Castro's punchbowl."

"You ever meet anybody was in on it?"

"Hard tellin'. I've met a lot of Marines who claimed they were. It was back in the day when Castro's revolutionary army was just on the other side of the fence." Shake turned toward the barracks and pointed at the roof. "They used to throw rocks and coat hangers and other crap onto the roof to keep the Marines awake at night. When that didn't work to their satisfaction, they mounted one of those big xenon searchlights and took to shining it in the windows of the barracks.

"That got irritating, so the Marines at the barracks decided enough was enough. They pitched a big sheet of canvas up on the hill there and made it look like it was covering a secret weapon or something. Naturally, the Cubans got curious and began sweeping the area every night with their searchlights. Meanwhile, behind that canvas, the Marines and Seabees were putting in that concrete slab and painting the emblem on it. When it was ready, they waited for Castro's goons to sweep the area with the searchlight and then dropped the canvas. The emblem lit up like a Hollywood marquee on opening night, like the bat signal over Gotham City! That was the end of the Cuban searchlight gag."

There was yellow crime-scene tape stretched between pylons on the suspect stretch of Guantanamo's outer perimeter fence. The construction vehicles had been moved elsewhere and Gerheim reported that any more digging or maintenance had been suspended until further notice. Shake took a look at the rapidly crusting dirt piled around what was obviously a crater deep enough for a small man to burrow under headed either way. There were no obvious tool marks so Carlos must have used his hands, easy enough in the soft loam under the fence.

"We've got extra security in this area right now," Gerheim said squatting next to Shake by the fence. "I've been all over it and so has the PMO. When you think you've seen what you want, let me know. They'd like to get it buttoned up."

Shake nodded and stood looking through the fence at the wormwood trees on the other side. "I don't think there's anything much to see here, Craze. He obviously had this place selected because of the ongoing excavation—probably spotted it on one of his runs. Can we take a look on the other side?"

"Yeah, we can do that." Gerheim pulled a portable radio out of his pocket and fiddled with the channel selector. "Probably take an hour or so to get clearance and muster a security detail. The Cuban perimeter is out about a hundred meters in most places, but we've got to go through the North East Gate to get on the other side of the fence and they've got a checkpoint right there facing ours. It might be quicker if I go see the Detachment Commander in person."

"You go ahead," Shake said. "I'm gonna walk the perimeter for a bit." He watched Gerheim wheel the van around to disappear down the road and then began to walk in what the compass on his watchband indicated was a northwesterly direction. He'd covered about 200 meters, sticking close to the fence line, when he saw it. Stretching beyond the fence in this area was a thick green carpet of *opuntia* cactus, what people in semi-arid parts of the U.S. called prickly pears. After all the years, it was still there and still as ugly as he remembered.

The Cactus Curtain—1965

"Listen up, Davis." Corporal Fred Tucker of the 2nd Reconnaissance Battalion detachment on temporary duty at Gitmo nearly blinded PFC Davis with a thumb he was using to apply camouflage war paint to the rookie's face. "Play time is over. You read me?"

"Lima Charlie, Corporal Tucker." Private First Class Sheldon (No Middle Initial) Davis jabbed his own thumb perilously close to his patrol leader's eye as he returned the favor with a streak of greasepaint. "Swift—Silent—Deadly."

"Focus on the first two, boot." Tucker pointed at the loaded M-3 Greasegun in Shake's lap. "Any shooting gets done tonight, I'll do it. Weapon on safe at all times unless I pass the word otherwise. This is snoop-and-poop. We ain't out there to get into no firefight with the fuckin' Cubans."

Shake fell in at slack position behind his NCO as the four-man recon team headed for a prepared cut in the perimeter wire. They carried a minimum of gear besides their personal weapons. Helmets were discarded in favor of OD kerchiefs worn on the head and knotted at the nape of the neck in what would years later become a common style among outlaw bikers. Even canteens had been left behind at the barracks to ensure there would be no noise from sloshing water as they moved. They were all dressed in utilities died black with scraps of canvas tied around arms and legs to reduce drag and prevent snags. And there were lots of snags where they were headed.

The Recon Detachment Gunnery Sergeant was waiting for them at the wire in the pitch-black moonless night that had been selected for their mission. He'd been against sending an untested, barely trained new guy along with the three veterans on this risky mission but the Detachment Commander, a grizzled Mustang officer who'd been a Recon Marine in Korea, overruled him. "We were all boots once," he said when the Gunny complained about the Marines selected for the mission. "I like Davis. The kid's got potential. He goes."

The Gunny was crouched by the fence holding open a flap of wire when they trundled across the perimeter road. Shake could barely see him in the dark but he heard that familiar growl in a rare whisper as he followed Tucker through the cut. "Two hours, no more, and then you beat feet back here." Shake felt the Gunny's punch on his shoulder. "Don't fuck it up, boot!" And then they slipped silently into the Cactus Curtain.

As rehearsed in a similar cactus patch on the windward side of the base, they moved slowly and cautiously among the prickly-pears, easing their weight down at each step, searching for the clear ground between the plants. Thick canvas gaiters strapped onto their lower legs kept the cactus needles from penetrating, but anyone who slipped and fell out here was in for some serious pain. Castro had planted the expanse of cactus as a stop-gap measure until he could get an adequate supply of landmines from his Soviet benefactors. Shake thought it was pretty shrewd of the old bearded bastard. It worked something like the spiky caltrops early infantry formations dropped to keep from being chased by horse cavalry.

Ahead of him, Tucker stopped to check the luminous dial of his compass and signaled for a pace count from the last

man in the formation. Shake passed the count forward in a
whisper and stood, dripping sweat, trying to remember everything he'd been taught in the Recon Indoctrination Program back at Camp Pendleton. Despite the anxiety of his
first real-world mission and the strain of trying to move
noiselessly, he decided what the Detachment Commander
told him in the pre-mission brief was true. The mission is
always easier than the training. It's supposed to be that way.

Prior to the mission, designed to pilfer one of the new
Soviet anti-personnel mines the Cubans were reportedly
planting along the edge of their territory, Corporal Tucker
and the other team members had put PFC Davis through a
grueling rehearsal period. All night, every night, they infil-
trated and exfiltrated what had to be most of the buildings
and structures on the base from the Navy enlisted barracks
to the mainside mess hall. No minor error, misstep or mental
lapse was tolerated. When Shake farted loudly during a long,
painful low crawl through a sugar cane field, he spent the
rest of the night doing push-ups and sit-ups until Corporal
Tucker got bored sometime around dawn.

Sweat more in training and bleed less in war, Shake remembered reading somewhere as he looked up to see Tucker
giving the freeze signal. He carefully took a knee and wondered if falling face down in the Cactus Curtain would be as
painful as incentive PT brought on by an errant fart. He
shook his head and tried to re-focus on Tucker who was doing a low and slow approach to a stand of palms. A long
thread of scrub brush ran off to the right and left of the grove
and it was recognizable from their map study. They were
about 100 meters into Cuban territory. Just past that stand of
palms were the minefields.

According to their mission brief, the Cuban sappers had
a little shack somewhere around here where they stored the

mines they were salting throughout the area to stop any invasion of their territory from the American base. Every PFC in the rear ranks with a rusty rifle knew the U.S. was not about to try something like that. Not after an embarrassing fiasco like the Bay of Pigs invasion, but Castro was nothing if not paranoid. And Fidel wasn't the only sweat-hog in the stand-off. The Americans also planted a broad belt of landmines around the Gitmo base perimeter. It was the danger of navigating that U.S. minefield that prompted Option Alpha for the Recon mission, an approach to the Cuban lines through the Cactus Curtain.

The three patrol members stuck out in the prickly pears waited on a knee, staring at the dark expanse of bush, looking for Tucker's signal to proceed and take up their over-watch positions. Shake saw it first and pointed. About 30 meters to their front inside the palm grove, Tucker was blinking a recognition signal with his red-lens flashlight. Lance Corporal Renaldo Keene, the pace-counter at the rear of the patrol, slid up beside Shake and flashed his own light to acknowledge the come-ahead signal. Then he took point and led the way to the grove.

When they were all bunched around the patrol leader with their heads touching so whispers could be heard clearly, Tucker passed the word. "There's a shack marked *peligro* about twenty meters to our right front. It's plastered with HE symbols. That's gotta be where they're storing the mines. Looks like there's a clear path right up to it that they use for access, so me and Keene are gonna go up there and have a look." He grabbed Keene's collar and pulled him closer. "Renaldo, you know what the new mines are supposed to look like, right? OZM bounding mine, OD color, weighs about six pounds, should have Russian markings, that's the one we want. You see one grab it. I'll do the same. We get a mine, we beat feet back here and exfil."

Tucker and Keene were gone about 20 minutes when it all turned to shit. Something happened in that little shack to their right front, something very noisy. Shake and Lance Corporal Sid Atwood, waiting in the palm grove tensed immediately when they heard what sounded like wood cracking under pressure followed by a loud thump. In the dead still of the night, it sounded like a rifle shot. The next thing they heard was an amplified voice shouting in Spanish for someone to halt. That was followed by a loud electronic buzz and then the entire area was lit by a searchlight. In a futile effort to preserve their night vision, Shake and Atwood shut one eye and tried to see what was happening with the other.

Tucker and Keene flopped into the grove breathing hard. There was little time for explanations as another searchlight clicked on and the Cubans began to sweep the area with crossing beams of blinding white light. "Had to break open a box and it shifted on me," Tucker panted and pointed at something Keene was holding. "We got a mine but we couldn't find the fuses."

They looked out at the Cactus Curtain that was now being flooded with light from somewhere along the Cuban lines. They could hear vehicle engines cranking up in the distance. It wouldn't be long before there were foot patrols combing the area. "Can't go back the way we came." Keene was stuffing the pilfered mine into an empty gasmask bag he'd carried along for just that purpose. He looked at Tucker and shrugged, "Option Bravo?"

"All we got." Tucker looked back and forth between the light sweeping the Cactus Curtain and the Cuban minefield to their rear where they could hear shouts in Spanish. The foot patrols were starting to fan out and time was tight. "We head direct west and stay in the scrub for sixty paces by my count. That puts us clear of the cactus. Then we look for the engineer tape, turn left through the minefield, and head for the fence. Order of march is me, Atwood, Davis, and then Keene."

They were in a hurry moving toward the western edge of the Cactus Curtain where the American minefield—a treacherous spread of anti-personnel mines laid out in clusters that could be triggered individually or in groups by sympathetic detonation—stretched for nearly 80 meters into a sort of no-man's land between the Gitmo perimeter fence and Cuban territory. Marine combat engineers had been dispatched the day before their mission launched to mark a clear path through the minefield with white tape that could be seen even on a dark night. That was Option Bravo.

It was not a preferred option by any stretch. Everyone who knew anything at all about mines understood that a map was a temporary guide at best. Mines left in the ground for any length of time tended to be mobile. After a while and for a variety of reasons, mines could wander from where they were originally buried. That's another reason why exfil through the minefield was second choice for the Recon patrol that was about to undertake it as a matter of survival.

When Corporal Tucker held them up at the entrance to the cleared channel through the American minefield, they were all breathing hard. The run westward from the palm grove was nothing for men in top physical condition, but adrenaline was surging through their bodies and demanding extra oxygen. To the east of them the Cactus Curtain was lit like the stage at a rock concert. There were some scattered rifle shots from that direction, but no rounds impacted near them. Likely the Cubans were shooting at shadows which suited PFC Davis just fine.

"File from here," Tucker said pointing to the narrow channel in the American minefield marked with two curving stretches of engineer tape. "Don't bunch up. Twenty meters between men." He held out a hand and snapped his fingers, "Gimme the wire-cutters." Shake dug the tool out of a pouch on his cartridge belt and handed it to the Patrol Leader. "Soon as I get through, I'll start cutting us another hole in the fence." He stepped off cautiously into the minefield. Atwood followed at the designated distance. Shake counted to 30 just to be sure, nodded at Keene, and stepped off himself, trying to see where Atwood put his feet and match his pace.

It was useless in the dark, but Shake couldn't help looking down at his feet, searching for any of the little three-prong detonator forks the engineers might have missed when they swept the path with their metallic mine detectors. Up ahead he heard Tucker talking to the Gunny. There was no need to whisper at this point, and they were being anything but quiet in hacking away at the fence to cut an access. Shake thought they had it made. They were compromised, but the Cubans could never prove it once they were back inside the wire. And they had the mine they were sent to steal. He was about 30 meters out, picking up the pace, as Tucker and Atwood waved him on from the base side of the fence when it happened.

He heard a hollow thump, the kind of sound a small mortar makes when firing, immediately followed by a blinding flash of light to his rear. The detonation was loud and sharp. Concussion drove him staggering forward and he felt like fire-ants were attacking the back of his legs. The stinging was intense, making his eyes water as he reflexively hit the deck. To his left and right he heard two more thumps and two more loud detonations. Shrapnel whined over his head, but Shake managed to get an angle and look back over his shoulder to check on Keene.

All he could make out was the sole of one boot. Keene was also prone but it looked like he was lying on his back. "Keene, you good?" The only response was a muted groan. Lance Corporal Keene was down hard. *He must have kicked a mine*, Shake realized, and that set off a couple of others nearby. "Hang on." He began to scoot around carefully on his belly to get a better look at the situation. The move hurt—badly. Shake realized that he'd caught shrapnel from the airburst when the mine detonated, but he was still mobile and likely in much better shape than Keene. "I'm coming to get you, Keene. Just hang on, man."

"Stay where you are, Davis!" The Gunny shouted from the other side of the wire. "Don't move. I'm getting some engineers and a Corpsman up here."

Shake froze in mid-turn. From this angle he could see that Keene had lost all or part of his left leg. Even in the inky black, he could see a darker stain spreading beneath the wounded man's body. Likely the femoral artery was torn up and Keene would bleed out in just a few minutes if he didn't get a tourniquet on that leg. Shake reached for his K-bar knife, pulled it out of the sheath and began to probe the stretch of earth between him and Keene. He'd been taught the technique as battlefield emergency only. Mines were touchy things and best destroyed by blowing them in place using a grenade or other explosive device to cause a sympathetic detonation. But that method was only handy when you weren't actually in the middle of the fucking minefield. If you were—as PFC Davis and Lance Corporal Keene were at the moment—the recommended procedure was to freeze and wait for the engineers with their minesweepers to clear a safe escape route. It didn't look like Keene would last that long.

Probing ahead of him, inching forward on his belly, Shake ignored the Gunny and Tucker who were shouting orders for him to stay put. They'd likely shut up if he took time to let them know how badly Keene was hit, but Shake didn't want to get engaged in a conversation. He was focused on the remaining 10 meters between him and Keene, and he wanted to ensure he'd hear it as well as feel it if his knife encountered buried metal.

He made it to Keene and saw what he'd suspected was accurate. The coppery smell of fresh blood and the steady pulse of warm liquid from Keene's thigh confirmed damage to a large artery. There wasn't much left of the leg. Keene would probably lose that, but Shake might be able to keep him alive if he hadn't already lost too much blood. Ripping the bandana off his head, Shake rolled it and tied it around Keene's mangled thigh up near the crotch. He pulled the collapsible wire stock out of his Greasegun, slipped it under the field-expedient tourniquet, and twisted hard. With his other hand he tried to assess the flow of blood from the wound. It was hard to tell in the goo and fleshy mess, but Shake thought he'd at least reduced the flow.

At his back, the Gunny was still yelling for him to freeze, that help was on the way. In the other direction, he could hear the Cubans in the distance shouting orders over a bullhorn. What started as snoop-and-poop had turned into scream-and-shout. Shake decided then and there to ignore it—all of it. What mattered now was saving Keene's life. The night sky was suddenly rent by a shower of pop-up flares launched from Cuban territory. The burning magnesium cast eerie shadows and gave Shake a quick look at Keene's condition. It was bad. He was in shock and gasping to breathe. If blood loss didn't kill him, shock would shut down his body before much longer. Shake rose to his knees and reached around Keene to get a solid grip that might allow him to lift the wounded man onto his shoulders in a fireman's carry. His fingers brushed something metallic and he froze. Carefully reaching across Keene's body he retrieved the flashlight hooked onto his suspender straps. In the red-glow of the lens he saw the little prongs sticking up through the blood-soaked dirt.

The AP mine was one of what the engineers who taught demo called a "Bouncing Betty," designed to launch itself a meter or two out of the ground before it detonated scattering shrapnel in a lethal fan. The fuse was what the instructors called a pressure-tilt type, and it only took two or three pounds of push or pull to set it off. Keene damn sure weighed more than two or three pounds, and the mine was resting just inches from his butt. If Shake tried to lift the man, there was a good chance he might stagger or miss his grip. He could just lay out here waiting for help while Keene died, but Shake didn't see that as an option. The mine had to be moved.

While he dug around carefully with his K-bar, Shake remembered he'd been told that sappers often rigged mines with boobytraps, a second anti-tamper fuse buried underneath that would detonate if the mine was lifted. Would the guys who buried this one have it rigged that way? No telling without feeling, so he slipped his fingers carefully down the sides of the device toward the bottom edge. He probed carefully for a few seconds without feeling anything but cold steel. There was no boobytrap in evidence, but that didn't make Shake feel much more confident about moving the mine. There was still that touchy detonator fork on the top of the thing. He was afraid to try unscrewing it from the mine body. One slip when he applied pressure and he'd be the next casualty.

Shake dug more dirt from around the mine and was just set to lift it with both hands when Keene groaned loudly and tossed his left arm right at the detonator. Shake caught it just in time only inches from the fuse. Gently setting the mine back in its hole, he grabbed Keene's forearm and secured it under the man's cartridge belt. Then he went back to work and got the mine safely out of the ground. He set it arm's length on the other side of the engineer tape and decided that was all he could do for the time being. Shake would have to trust to luck that there were no more mines that had some-how wandered into the supposedly clear channel.

As he maneuvered himself around to get a grip on the wounded man for a dead-lift onto his shoulders, another flare popped over the minefield and Shake noticed the gasmask bag containing the pilfered mine hanging from Keene's gear. The mission had been all about getting that mine. If he screwed up what he was about to try, the trophy would likely be lost. He looked back toward the fence. With a little wind-up using the strap of the bag as a fulcrum he could probably heave a six-pound hunk of steel that far and high enough to clear a six-foot fence.

"Heads up for incoming!" He stood with the gasmask bag in hand and began to swing it around his head like a cowboy about to rope an errant calf. "I'm gonna throw you the mine!" Shake let go of the bag and in the light of another pop-up flare watched it sail well over the Gitmo fence line. In the fading glow he could see dark figures scrambling to retrieve it, but he had other concerns.

Getting a guy off the ground and onto your shoulders in training for casualty evacuation usually involved a little cheat where the victim provides some subtle help for the benefit of the exercise. When Shake tried it for real, it was a different story. Keene was a solid 175 even with most of one leg nearly gone, and all of it was uncooperative weight. When he stood from a crouch with Keene's torso on one side of his head and his mangled legs on the other side, it was an unbalanced load. Shake staggered dangerously. Corporal Tucker was shouting for him to give it up: the Corpsman had just arrived.

That didn't seem like an advisable course of action. He'd likely kill Keene if he dropped him at this point—or the Corpsman might kick a mine on his way out to administer medical treatment. Best for all concerned to just get the hell out of this minefield. Shake began to stagger carefully ahead, reeling from side to side with each step, and trying to ignore both the encouraging shouts from the fence line and Keene's agonized groans.

It was a matter of minutes that seemed like hours before Shake bashed into the fence and leaned on it trying to catch his breath. The weight was lifted off his shoulders and he was dragged through the opening to safety inside the base perimeter. He was shoved inside an ambulance beside Keene's stretcher and the last thing he heard before the door slammed was the Gunny's growl. "Nice work, boot—A for effort—F for judgment!"

The next morning with a small bucket of mine shrapnel plucked painfully from his legs and butt, PFC Shake Davis was flown back for recovery at Camp Lejeune. Keene was in no shape for evacuation, so he stayed at the Guantanamo Naval Hospital where surgeons removed what was left of his leg. He survived to attend the ceremony during which meritoriously promoted Corporal Shake Davis was presented the Navy and Marine Corps Medal for his lifesaving efforts out in the Guantanamo Bay minefield. That ribbon was the first of many that Shake added to a growing stack on his left breast over a long and colorful career.

Gitmo

*I*t was right out there that I learned courage is not the absence of fear. It's the willingness to face fear for just a few minutes more. Shake took a last look at what remained of Gitmo's infamous Cactus Curtain and walked back in the other direction.

There was a fireteam of cammie-clad Marines wearing body armor and Kevlar helmets and carrying M-4 carbines surrounding Crazy Earl Gerheim when he got back to the burrow under the perimeter fence. They were standing around watching construction contractors working to fill the hole and complete work on the drainage system. "These guys were on the original search party," Gerheim said jerking a thumb at the Marines. "How do you want to handle this?"

"We'll just wander around a bit, Craze." Shake followed one of the Marines into a white government van. "Let's start with the stand of trees opposite where he came through the fence. I want to get a feel for what he might have done—and you can show me the motion sensors."

They drove the perimeter for a half-mile and turned onto the access road for the North East Gate and Shake noticed a pair of large, solid concrete pillars wrapped in barbed wire. They were painted with a typically bold and brash Marine Corps message for all concerned on the other side of the wire: Enter if you dare. Leave if you can. The North East Gate was the point in the Gitmo perimeter where the Cubans maintained their closest contact, a checkpoint housed in an old structure that used to be an American bank where Cuban workers who commuted to jobs on the base cashed their paychecks. "Back in the days following the revolution, there used to be a couple thousand commuters employed on the base," Gerheim explained as they walked toward the gate following the Marines. "That's long gone. Now we got exactly three old guys who are still authorized to commute. They come and go through the walking gate over there."

A sign on the American side identified their location as the North East Gate of the U.S. Naval Base Guantanamo Bay, Cuba. A larger sign on the other side where the Americans could see it easily every day read *Republica de Cuba. Territorio Libre de America.*" Shake grinned and translated. "Territory free of America—they might be taking that shit down before long."

"Yep," Gerheim agreed as he escorted Shake through the walking gate. "That's what the Navy guys hear every day at the liaison meetings. Both sides open the gates twice a day—0530 and 1630—for meetings. Supposedly no politics are discussed, just logistics and stuff like that, but you know the Cubans can't help bragging about what they consider a major change in their international status."

"There used to be big minefields out here, sir." The senior Marine, a sergeant with at least three radios strapped to his gear, led the party into the scrub of no-man's land on the other side of the fence. "They supposedly policed them all up in the 90s, but I'd watch your step. Once a minefield, always a minefield, if you know what I mean."

"I know what you mean, Sergeant. I've had some experience with mines."

"Mr. Gerheim said you were in the Corps," the NCO said. "Did time in Vietnam and Beirut? I'd be glad to buy you a beer sometime if you want to meet some of our Marines."

"My pleasure," Shake said as they turned left and began to walk along the long line of shrubbery headed in the direction of the fence breech. "Let me get my bearings and I'll come by the barracks in a day or two."

The sergeant held out an arm to stop Shake and pointed at the ground. Amid the bramble bushes was a small yucca plant that was a bit too uniform and shiny to be natural. "Motion sensor," the Sergeant said. "We got them planted about every 20 to 30 meters out here. Signal feeds to the guard shack. Most of the hits we get are wind or some little animal. Pain in the ass because we have to check them every time." The Sergeant shrugged. "But I guess we gotta do something since the mines are gone."

"There's still mines on the Cuban side of this area, right?"

"Yessir," the Sergeant nodded and looked off to his right toward Cuban territory. "And they don't even have the damn things mapped. We had some wildfires down here last year and about a hundred of 'em cooked off. You couldn't pay me enough to go wandering around over there."

Gerheim was stopped ahead in a stand of wormwood trees and pointed to the fence where the construction workers were running a Bobcat. "This is likely where he made his turn," he said when Shake arrived. "We know he headed toward the main road because the sensors that tripped were off in that direction."

"It's what—about a half mile to the gate from here?" Shake stood looking in that direction. "You've gotta figure he didn't go in a straight line or he'd have run into the sentries on our side or their side."

"Gotta be, Shake. He goes the other way toward the water and he's got ten miles or more to cover."

"And we know he didn't do that. So figure he cuts an angle to get behind the Cubans and out of sight of our people. He winds up somewhere on the main access road between the gate and the Cuban perimeter. What then?"

"Then he disappears. Maybe he gets captured."

"Yeah, but I still think someone or something convinced him to pull this sneaky-pete deal and leave the base. That's the key. What I need is a way to poke around out there." Shake swept his arm to indicate the rest of Cuba to the north.

"Well, you ain't gonna do that without Raul Castro's permission and you ain't gonna get that."

"You confident he's not out here somewhere lying dead in the weeds?"

"Not a chance, Shake. The Marines scoured the entire seventeen-mile perimeter on this side of the wire. They even had dogs working. They don't miss stuff like a dead body."

"OK. Let's talk to the bodyguard."

"All set up for tomorrow at zero-eight. You can grill him for as long as it takes in my office."

After a Taco Bell dinner, Shake and Gerheim retired to the little park beside the water to smoke cigars and polish off a six-pack of beer. Shake faced a cool breeze coming off the bay and watched a few small sailboats skipping over the whitecaps. "I read on line that the Cubans are still policing up people trying to escape by sea. That right?"

"All the time," Gerheim joined him and pointed toward the mouth of the bay out beyond the Arleigh Burke class guided missile destroyer swinging at anchor. "When they first started talking about this normalization deal, the Cubans picked up seventy or eighty of 'em trying to make a break for Miami."

"They claim the standard deal here—twelve miles off-shore as territorial waters?"

"Yeah, but some high-roller deep-sea fishermen and some guys with more boat and money than sense can get waivers, I'm told. There's some kind of big deal billfish tournament going on next week. All kind of rich playboys with big boats are gonna be in Cuba trying to make out like Ernest Hemingway. That's what they call the deal: the Ernest Hemingway International Billfish Tournament. You gotta have big bucks to enter, but if you've got the money, you get the clearances. It's like everything else in Castro's Cuba. You know the right people and you pay the right bribes, you get what you want." Gerheim walked back toward the picnic table where the last two beers sat sweating in the late afternoon heat. "You want another brew?"

"Pass, Craze. Take me back to the Q. I need to make a couple of calls."

Back in his room at the VOQ, Shake made a few notes on a yellow legal pad and then reached for the satellite phone. He spoke with Chan who let him listen to Bear barking at squirrels in their pecan trees and reported all was well in Texas. And then he called the man who calls himself Bayer in Havana.

"I'm fairly certain your estimate of the situation is correct," he said after being assured that the connection was scrambled and secure. "You got anything on your end?"

"Nothing concrete, Shake, but I'm watching a contingent of Russians who arrived last night. My agency contacts know these people. Two high-level GRU goons and just the kind of guys Moscow might send to make a deal."

"OK—stay on that. I'm fairly certain we won't get much more milling around down here on the base at Gitmo. We need to start looking elsewhere, which means we need a more mobile base of operations." Shake scrolled through the contact list on his phone. "There's this retired sailor we worked with on the Korea deal with Stokey." Shake dictated a name and number in Key West, Florida. "Give him a call and see what he's doing these days."

Punto Cero (Ground Zero)

Carlos Ruiz-Romero had been a captive at Ground Zero—wherever that was—for what he believed was three days. His wristwatch was confiscated and never returned, but the barred window of his room faced east so he could get a general feel for time by watching the sun. He was fed and watered regularly, surprisingly good food always served on china and a teak tray. He was definitely detained and isolated, but there had been no torture, not even an interrogation session. He'd tried to question the little waiter in a white coat who brought his food, but the old man simply waved off any conversation.

The only other humans he'd seen were soldiers when he was escorted outside for exercise in a field of saw grass between the legs of the L-shaped building. They were either in defensive positions with what looked like portable missile launchers close at hand or walking around the building, carrying guns and occasionally probing the dark with powerful flashlights. His exercise sessions were always at night for some reason.

He tried to ask the guard about that on the second trip outside, but the man merely pointed at the open field of grass. *"Silencio...ejerciccio."* Then he lit a cigarette and leaned against a wall. Just to kill time on the first night, Carlos did sets of standard exercises, jumping-jacks, squat-thrusts, and push-ups. On the second night, he trotted around the edge of the field. After an initial start that had him reaching for his weapon, the guard decided that jogging in a circle surrounded by armed sentries was not an escape attempt. He settled back to smoke and watch while Carlos jogged in an effort to burn off tension.

The Cubans were treating him well, he thought as he ran first in one direction and then in the other, so maybe he was more of a hostage than a prisoner. Maybe the Cubans were conducting negotiations with the Americans to get something special for his safe return. No, he'd been told the Americans thought he was dead. So why wasn't he being interrogated? Why weren't they trying to get what information they could from him? There was something missing from the picture. *They are probably just softening me up*, he decided when the guard motioned for him to stop running.

Likely the interrogations will start soon, Carlos thought as he wiped the sweat from his body with a paper-thin towel back in his room. They'll break me—physically or chemically—and then they'll kill me. Why not? If they've somehow already convinced the American authorities that I'm dead, keeping me alive any longer than they must to get what they want is a risk.

The question, he decided while trying to focus on anything but the articles he'd read about Americans being tortured in captivity, is whether or not the U.S. authorities believe I'm really dead. A dead DIA employee is one thing. A captive DIA agent with top security clearances is another thing entirely. Maybe they wouldn't buy it immediately. Maybe they'd be suspicious and come looking for him. But how can you do that in Castro's Cuba? Maybe satellite imagery—or drones?

Carlos Ruiz-Romero went to sleep on his third night at *Punto Cero* thinking about the high-value prisoners he interrogated at Camp Delta, about Bowe Bergdahl, the American soldier held by the Taliban in Afghanistan—and about an old

movie he'd seen with Gene Hackman as an American intelligence officer shot down in Vietnam, and Danny Glover as
the pilot who spotted him on the ground being chased by the
VC.

"The price is not negotiable." Manuel Panteros poured 11-year-old Santiago de Cuba dark rum for his visitors and then sat back in a lounge chair. "When the transfer of funds is confirmed, I will transport Ruiz-Romero to a place of your choosing."

"It's the cash that presents the problem." The senior GRU man sipped his drink, smiled his compliments at their host, and crossed his legs. "My country would prefer an arrangement involving an exchange of military hardware or technology."

"Of course you would." Panteros offered cigars from a teak humidor and waited until the two Russians had stoked their smokes into life. "But you must understand and convey to your leadership that this is not a deal between Russia and Cuba. This is a deal between Russia and Manuel Panteros. I have no need for weapons or technology personally, and my country will very soon have all the cash required to buy such things on the open markets worldwide."

"And you can make such a deal personally? Raul Castro or someone in your government will not interfere? What if you wind up in prison, unable to deliver?"

Panteros learned forward in his chair and placed his cigar in a crystal ashtray. "Raul is merely a figurehead these days. The man is eighty-four and he won't last much longer. He doesn't interfere with the military which is the real power in Cuba. And as Director of Intelligence, I have collected information that gives me a great deal of influence with our military leaders. I can—and I will—deliver on my end of the bargain. You may rest assured."

"This is a delicate situation. If you will not negotiate on the price…"

"Gentlemen, please." Panteros retrieved his cigar and pulled a Zippo lighter from his shirt pocket. "I read reports every day of your country's activities in Eastern Europe, the counter-moves in response to the build-up of American and NATO forces along your borders. What's on offer here is something that would give your country a huge strategic advantage over the Americans and their allies. You realize that and so does your President or we would not be having this conversation."

Manuel Panteros toyed with his cigar, letting his recitation of the obvious sink in for a few moments. "Carlos Ruiz-Romero is one of the world's top cryptographers and intelligence communications specialists. He was one of designers of the Joint Worldwide Intelligence Communications System, the system on which American intelligence agencies share their most sensitive information. When you have obtained the necessary information from him—a task that should be relatively easy with enhanced interrogation—your nation stands to gain unrestricted access to that network. And this would not be some easily detectable hack, you understand. With Ruiz-Romero's guidance Russia would be on the network and no one the wiser."

"And you are certain the Americans believe he is dead?"

"Nothing is certain in this world, my friends. I have taken steps—very detailed and convincing steps—to make it appear that way. There have been a few questions asked by a member of the American contingent here in Havana, some traffic we monitored from Guantanamo Bay to Washington

expressing concern with the loss. What we hear is concen—
not suspicion."

"Obviously, we will have to discuss all this with Moscow."

"Of course, my friends." Panteros stood and retrieved the
gift packages of rum and cigars he'd prepared for his guests.
"He is in a very secure location and in good health. You have
what time you require as long as our deal is completed inside
three weeks' time."

In the backseat of a black BMW, the senior GRU officials
sat in silence contemplating what they would say in a call on
the secure line to Moscow. The deal was expensive but the
prize was worth it for the invaluable intelligence edge it
would provide in rebuilding their nation's worldwide power.
A man with Vladimir Putin's ego and global aims couldn't
resist. His cronies and the oligarchs depending on him to re-
tain power would pony up the required cash. They certainly
had plenty of experience in secretly moving huge sums in
several solid currencies around the world.

The driver turned into Playa Miramar heading for the
Russian Embassy and had to stop at a police barricade where
local cops were directing traffic around a large section of
roadway under repair. The trucks parked around the work
site all bore Cuban government markings and none of the
workers visible around them seemed to be laboring with enthusiasm.

"That won't last long." The senior Russian said.

"No," his partner agreed. "It will all be privatized as soon
as the U.S. lifts the embargos, and that's when the power-
plays start. With the death of Cuban communism comes the
rise of Cuban oligarchs. We saw it at home in the Nineties."

"Yes, and with thirty million as a start-up fund, Manuel Panteros intends to be among those oligarchs."

"He intends to be first among them, I think. He's smart enough to remain in the shadows. That's his element. But the real power in a new Cuba—regardless of who claims to be President after Castro—will be the man in the shadows with the most money. Panteros wants to be that man."

The senior Russian Intelligence operative yawned and stretched in the vehicle's cool interior. "Panteros and Putin," he chuckled, "cut from the same cloth. They'll get along famously."

Gitmo

Tom Ellis was a former Army Staff Sergeant who left the 2nd Battalion, 75th Ranger Regiment at Fort Lewis three years earlier to hook up as a contract security man in a pool of former special operators maintained by the Pentagon. He had special FBI training in Executive Protection work to qualify him for detached duty with American Embassies in a number of worldwide hot-spots. That background was the reason Ellis and his partner with similar experience were selected to form a special security detail for Carlos Ruiz-Romero during his stay at Guantanamo Bay.

Shake knew all about that from the file Gerheim provided before they went into the interview room. According to Gerheim who had interrogated the man twice already, Ellis was cooperative at first but was now complaining that he'd done nothing wrong and should be released for return to his regular employment.

"I was off duty that night, for Christ's sake. Either charge me and let me get lawyered up or let me go."

"Yeah, we're just about through with you, Tom." Gerheim pulled up a chair, hit a button to start a recorder, and pointed at Shake. "But first this gent needs you to answer a few questions."

Ellis eyed Shake suspiciously. "OK, so first tell me who this gent is."

"Name's Shake Davis, Tom." He offered his hand and got a tentative response. "I'm just doing some follow-up on the disappearance of your principal."

"You FBI or what?"

"Let's just say I'm an interested party with backing at very high levels in the government."

Ellis turned to Gerheim. "Am I under obligation to answer his questions?"

"You're under no obligations at all, Tom." Gerheim leaned back in his chair and smiled. "But if you want to get out of here and if you want any chance at all of continued employment with DOD, you'll answer Mr. Davis' questions—quickly, completely and truthfully. How's that?"

"OK, shoot." He turned back toward Shake and shrugged. "I got nothin' to hide."

"Give me an idea of what Carlos Ruiz-Romero did on an average day down here."

"He was a runner, you know. First thing he usually did was go for a run on the perimeter road. One of us, sometimes both of us, followed in a golf cart. Then he'd get chow and head on over to Camp Delta. They wouldn't let us go with him inside, so we waited around until he finished and then escorted him back to the VOQ. Sometimes he'd stay there doing paperwork and other times he'd go places on the base, visit some people. He spoke good Spanish, you know, being Cuban and all."

"Tell me a little more about what he did at night—off-duty activities."

"He did all sorts of exploring when we first got down here. Then he started to go by the rec center fairly regular. He played dominoes or checkers or something with a bunch of old Cuban dudes. He did that a lot. We usually just waited outside screwing around until he was done."

"Remember anything special from those evenings?"

"Not much. Like I said, we mostly just waited for him outside the rec center, you know, just look in and check on him every once in a while. I don't remember anything about the guys he met—except maybe one old dude who invited him over for dinner a couple of times. We took him to a house on base where he said he was gonna get some real Cuban chow. I remember that. We got fed but we had to eat out on the patio. I didn't see anything harmful in it. He usually only stayed a couple of hours."

"You remember the old guy's name?"

"I think it was Munoz—something like that. It's in my statement." Ellis looked over at Gerheim. "I told you about that."

"Did he have any contact with any other Cubans or anyone else on base— anything you'd consider other than routine?"

"Nope; just the one old guy that invited him for dinner a few times. There was an old lady that cooked, I guess. She served us the chow out on the patio."

Shake sat across the desk in Gerheim's office reading a casualty report concerning the death of a Cuban national and long-time base resident named Ramon Munoz. "So this guy that he plays dominoes with and has dinner with a few times, keels over of a heart attack the day after Ruiz-Romero goes missing. Anything there?"

Gerheim shrugged and scanned the autopsy report prepared by the Naval Hospital staff. "The guy was eighty, too fat, and smoked way too many cigars, Shake. He had a bunch of medical complaints, old man stuff mostly. Cause of death listed as heart failure—natural causes."

"What else do you know about him?"

"Not much to know. He was one of the refugees that got stuck aboard Gitmo after the revolution. Been living here in base housing for nearly fifty years along with about two dozen others. There's a file on him same as there is on the other resident refugees. It's got background, personal details and like that." Gerheim hauled an old, crinkled pile of folders out of a drawer and shoved it across the desk. "I pulled the files but I don't think anyone has looked at them for years. No telling how accurate they are."

Shake picked up the file marked Munoz, Ramon and began to page through it as Gerheim re-hashed details from the casualty report. "Apparently, his lady friend, another resident refugee by the name of Catalina Constanza—she's the one Ellis mentions in his statement—found him when she went over to check on him after she got off work at the exchange. She called the PMO, they went out to check and medics figured he'd been dead for about twelve hours—probably his ticker gave out sometime during the night. You thinkin' there might be some kind of connection with the Ruiz-Romero disappearance?"

"I don't know what I'm thinking, Craze." Shake scanned a few pages of the old personnel file. "Says here he's anti-Castro and was a reliable worker at the golf course until he retired. He had a few relations still living in his home town but no known contact with them. That sound right?"

"Probably. The resident refugees write letters and they used to keep track of where they were sending mail, but I don't know if that's still done. We know there's probably an illegal Cuban phone or two floating around somewhere among them, but so what? I don't know what the hell kind of information they'd have that would do the opposition any good, so it's not a priority for the command down here. They're kind of like fixtures at Gitmo, old folks caught in the middle, you know? They've lived here a long time and there's a lot of sympathy for them. When they made it inside the wire years ago, the command told them they could live here until Cuba is free."

"What about Catalina Constanza? Same story with her?"

Gerheim pulled another file from the dusty stack and scanned it. "Just about. Been here since Sixty-One—widow woman originally from Colon same as Munoz. She's got two brothers, one works in the telecommunications office here on base and the other…whoa…I didn't know about this!" Gerheim bent some stays, pulled a sheaf of handwritten notes from the file and handed it to Shake. "That's from ONI, dated 1975…apparently Senora Constanza has another brother who is—or was—an upwardly mobile guy in Cuban Military Intelligence. You keep reading." Gerheim grabbed for his phone. "I need to make a call."

Shake scanned the notes from the Office of Naval Intelligence and discovered that Catalina Constanza and her brother Eduardo had been interviewed a number of times by agents when it was discovered that their brother Enrique was an officer in Castro's Military Intelligence division. Apparently, the man was one of Fidel's most trusted *revoluci-anarios* who was rewarded for his efforts in the anti-Batista putsch. At the time of the report, Enrique Constanza was reported as a junior officer assigned to the Cuban Intelligence training center at Camp Mantanzas outside Havana. The ONI report said his sister Catalina and his brother Eduardo had volunteered information freely about their brother and expressed strong anti-Castro sentiments. The interview reports were 40 years old. There was nothing more recent from Naval Intelligence on the brother or the sister.

"Here's news." Gerheim scribbled a note and hung up his phone. "I just talked to my guy at ONI. Enrique Constanza remains one of the Castro apparatchiks. Catalina's other brother is now *General* Constanza, and Director of Military Intelligence." He checked his watch. "She should be getting off work pretty soon. I'll call PMO and have her picked up."

"Good." Shake dropped the file back on the pile and stood. "Have you got Munoz' personal effects?"

"They should be in storage over at the Base Housing office."

"Let's take a look while we wait for Senora Constanza."

Eduardo Constanza pried at the lock in Ramon Munoz' credenza while his sister stood nearby fretting and pacing between her brother and the living room window where she constantly peeked through the venetian blinds. "Sixty-five years old, *hermano,* I just wanted to live a quiet life until the country is free again."

"It won't be long now, sister." Eduardo finally broke the old lock and jerked the drawer open. "It's time for us to move on to a new life. Enrique will take care of everything." He pulled a Motorola flip phone out of the drawer, checked the screen, and handed it to his sister. "Don't lose that. We may need it soon."

"Is the boat ready?" Catalina dropped the phone into her wicker purse and looked around her old friend's house one last time. She would go to her grave wishing her brother had not killed Ramon Munoz. It was orders from Enrique, Eduardo said, absolutely necessary if they were to escape. The old man would feel no pain and there would be no link to the gringo. Still, she would miss him.

"It's fueled and waiting at the docks," Eduardo reported as he headed for the door. "Just another fishing trip like all the other ones, except this time I'm taking my sister along. The man at the rental desk even gave me some seasick pills for you."

She sighed, picked up the satchel she'd packed with all the little personal things that would be important to her in a new life outside the fences at Guantanamo Bay. She crossed herself and said a silent prayer for Ramon Munoz who would never see a free Cuba. Then she followed Eduardo out of the house and into the maintenance van borrowed from the tele-communications office.

There wasn't much to show for the life Ramon Munoz lived at Gitmo over the 50 years since he escaped from the Cuban revolutionary pogroms. It amounted to four cardboard boxes, two of which contained clothing, books and some cheap jewelry. A third box was crammed with yellowing papers including some personal letters, citations attesting to his long and faithful service as a grounds-keeper at the base golf course, and a thick sheaf of medical records. Apparently, Munoz suffered from an enlarged prostate, irritable bowel syndrome, and high blood pressure among other minor ailments.

The fourth carton held Shake's attention. It was crammed with framed photos. Many of them showed Munoz posing with various dignitaries who visited to play a round at Gitmo's golf course. The remainder was shots of people, young and old, in group snaps or in single portraits, presumably Ramon's family or close friends. Shake pulled one of those individual portraits out of the stack and looked at it closely. It was a studio shot, obviously posed and retouched in vivid colors, of a pretty young woman wearing a low-cut dress with a frilly bodice. A small signature in one corner identified the portrait as the work of a photographer at Menendez Studios, Colon. It was undated but the women looked to be in her late teens or early twenties.

Clearly the camera loved her. She was one of those stunning Latin beauties with flashing dark eyes and pouty lips painted a livid shade of red. Her skin was clear and a caramel shade that contrasted beautifully with raven black hair, parted in the middle and pulled back tightly into a bun. She was smiling coyly to reveal even white teeth and the photographer's flash had caused a sparkle on the bangles hanging from her earlobes. She was a stunner, but Shake was looking at more than all that. The girl in the picture reminded him of someone.

He studied the portrait for a few minutes trying to place the resemblance and then he reached for his backpack where he kept the background files he'd been given in Texas by the man who calls himself Bayer. He set the photo aside and flipped through the file until he got to the DIA's official portrait of Carlos Ruiz-Romero. The likeness was staggering. The girl in the picture looked like a female version of Carlos.

"Craze, come look at this." Gerheim put the top back on a box he was searching and joined Shake to look at the two photos. "Damn, Shake. She's a spitting image, ain't she?" He picked up the photo to look more closely. "Same eyes, cheekbones, jaw line and every other facial feature. That could easily be Carlos' mother."

"Yeah. So what's a picture of Carlos Ruiz-Romero's mom doing in Ramon's personal effects?" Shake fiddled with some prongs and slid the portrait out of the frame. There was a pencil scrawl on the back of the photo paper: Carmen Ruiz-Romero, Colon, 1975. Shake handed the photo to Gerheim and began to dig through the background file. "It ain't his mother, Craze. Her name was Estella and she was not in Colon in 75. She escaped with Carlos to the States in 1971."

"Well, it's the family name, so I'm guessing a sister. That's a blood relative if I've ever seen one."

"Yep." Shake put the picture and the file in his backpack and zipped it closed. "So if our guy has an undisclosed sister in Cuba, he might want to try for a family reunion, right? And it looks like Munoz must have been a friend of the family. He's from Colon. Maybe he was trying to hook Carlos up with his sister. Maybe he had one of those Cuban phones you mentioned or some other way of getting in touch with her. We need to ask Senora Constanza about that."

Gerheim's phone rang and he checked the ID on the screen. "That's PMO now. I'll have them bring her to the office." Gerheim connected, listened for a few minutes and then punched off the call. "She called in sick at the exchange. Nobody home at her house, so they went to check with her brother over at the telecomm office—and he's off for the day. They found his van parked down by the marina. Guy at MWR down there says they left about twenty minutes ago in one of the rental skiffs for a fishing trip out on the bay."

"That's too many coincidences, Craze."

"Roger that. I'll call the Harbor Master. We need to interrupt that fishing trip."

Eduardo Constanza showed his sister how to handle the steering gear on the outboard engine to keep their rental skiff headed seaward while he maneuvered forward to dig around in the fishing tackle. They passed a few Navy yard boats lumbering around closer to the docks, but no one paid them much attention. The waters in and around the bay were still rife with tarpon, bonefish, and snapper and base residents often took the Navy Moral, Welfare, and Recreation Department's rental boats out on fishing excursions.

"How much longer?" Catalina was nervous and distracted by the breeze that kept crushing the brim of her sun hat against her face. She had been complaining since they left the docks that the seasick pills were making her ill.

"Will you relax?" Her brother dug around in one of the large plastic tackle boxes and extended the antenna on something that looked like a small portable radio. "We haven't even reached the mouth of the bay yet. Just keep the boat pointed like I showed you." He nodded toward the Navy destroyer coming up on their starboard quarter. "Once we're past the ship we can add some speed." He pulled an old Webley revolver out of the box, broke it open to check for rounds in the cylinder, and then shoved the gun into his waistband.

"A gun?" There was a tremble in his sister's voice as he moved up to replace her on the tiller. "Where did you get a gun, Eduardo?"

"Same place I got the phones, *hermana.*" Eduardo smiled and waved at a gang of sailors in coveralls and hardhats laboring on the bow of the destroyer as they motored past.

"But why do you have it? Why do you need a gun? You said there would be no trouble."

"And there will be no trouble, Catalina. Just relax." Eduardo moved the throttle forward a couple of notches and the little boat began to plane, headed for the mouth of Guantanamo Bay. Somewhere out there on the horizon there was a commercial fishing boat, flying a recognition pennant—a leaping game fish on a blue field—that would take them aboard. All they had to do was hold a course straight out into the Caribbean. The vessel that Enrique sent to carry them north had the necessary equipment to home in on the beacon in his tackle box.

Shake and Crazy Earl had to wait anxious minutes on the docks for the boat Gerheim finally obtained from the Navy after a lengthy explanation of their proposed chase. In one of his most impressive tirades, waving his CID credentials at a bewildered lieutenant j.g. serving as officer of the day at the Harbor Master's office, Gerheim finally convinced the man to muster the stand-by Visit Board Search and Seizure crew for a "mission imperative to national security." They could see the 35-foot Rigid Inflatable Boat rounding the pier in the distance carrying a crew of three sailors and three Marines in full battle rattle, but the Coxswain didn't seem in any particular hurry to pick up his passengers. Shake checked his watch and stared out at the sunlight glaring on the horizon. "That thing is rated for forty knots," he said, "and we might need it. They've got a good hour on us already."

"It's finding them that's gonna be the problem, Shake. There's a lot of open water out there and they're in a little fishing boat—hard to see." He zipped open a bag and handed Shake a pistol in a clip-on kydex holster. "I remember you used to be a hand with old slab-sides, but this is gonna have to do."

Shake checked the chamber on a mini-Glock and saw the little pistol was loaded with .40 S&W hollow points. "You think we're gonna need the firepower, Craze? We're chasing a couple of old farts in a fishing boat. That RIB has a 240 Golf mounted up forward and the Marines are carrying M-4s. That should do it."

"Better safe than sorry, Shake. If those two are in escape mode, they've got to be meeting someone or something out there, right? They ain't gonna drive a little outboard all the way to Havana. No tellin' what we might run into."

When the RIB nosed into the dock, a Marine Staff Sergeant hopped ashore. "Mr. Gerheim?" The lanky Marine stuck out a gloved hand and Crazy Earl shook it. "I'm Staff Sergeant Dennis Lindsey, sir." He jerked a thumb over his shoulder toward the RIB. "We're the duty VBSS team. They didn't give me much brief—just said to get the hell over here and report to you."

"We need to find and stop a little MWR skiff that's headed out to sea, Sergeant Lindsey. There are two old Cuban resident refugees aboard. They're wanted in connection with a felony aboard the base. We're gonna find 'em and take 'em into custody. I'll give you some more details once we're underway but we gotta get a move on. They're at least an hour ahead of us."

Lindsey nodded and looked at Shake. His eyes drifted to the holstered pistol and then he looked back at Gerheim. "This is Mr. Davis. He's a retired Marine Gunner, got more time in combat than most of us have in the chow line. He packs the gear and the credentials. He'll be running the show. We take our orders from him."

"Good enough for me, sir." The Marine shook hands and then jumped back in the boat. Shake caught Crazy Earl by the elbow. "So, now I'm the officer in charge?"

"I meant what I said, Shake. You've done more of this stuff than I have by a damn sight. Let's go."

When they were all aboard, the Navy Coxswain, a Hispanic-looking First Class Boatswain's Mate, swung the RIB smartly away from the dock and goosed the throttles to send the boat bounding toward the mouth of the bay. Shake scrambled forward next to the conning station and eyed the sailor manning the machinegun forward. It looked like a good boat and a capable crew. Now all they had to do was find Eduardo and Catalina Constanza.

"Course, sir?" the coxswain checked his instruments and glanced at Shake for orders. "Straight out through the bay, Cox. We're looking for a little fishing skiff and it's got about an hour head start."

"No problem, sir. We're full of fuel and speed. "You and the other man…" he nodded toward Gerheim, "need to put on life-jackets. They're stowed in that locker aft." He hammered the throttles forward and the RIB's stern dug into the waters of Guantanamo Bay. Shake glanced at the hooded radar repeater screen on the cockpit dash and then up at the mast above them. "Is this surface search?"

"Yessir," the Coxswain said. "But I don't know how much good it will do looking for a little skiff riding low in the water."

"Can't hurt." Shake smiled at the sailor and staggered aft to get a life-jacket. As the RIB bounded over the whitecaps, the Coxswain flipped a series of switches and the football-shaped emitter atop the mast began to rotate.

They were well clear of the bay and holding a steady course due south into deeper Caribbean waters when the phone in Catalina's purse rang. "Answer it." Eduardo nodded at his sister and then returned his gaze to the open water around them.

"Si…?" Catalina listened for a moment. *"Si, si…momentito."* She leaned forward and held the phone out to her brother. "Someone wants to talk to you, *hermano.*" Eduardo grabbed the phone and held it to his ear.

"Where are you?"

Eduardo checked the sun overhead and the watch on his wrist. "About thirty minutes outside the bay," he said. "We are heading south as directed."

"Are there any other boats in the area?"

He scanned the horizon and the empty waters around them. "No, nothing I can see."

"We have a contact on the radar—must be you. We are about a kilometer northeast of you. Turn to the right and continue at best speed. You should see us shortly."

There was no more conversation. Eduardo handed the phone back to his sister, pushed the outboard tiller to the left, and advanced the throttle. "A man from the boat Enrique sent." He smiled at his sister. "It won't be long now."

"Contact!" The Navy Coxswain nudged Shake and pointed at the radar repeater. "I've got it set to short-scan." He bent to see better under the glare screen and did a quick calculation. "Range is just over a thousand yards northeast."

"Gotta be them, right?" Shake pulled a set of binoculars out of the dashboard rack and scanned the horizon to their right front.

"Maybe." The Coxswain turned the wheel to bring them onto a new course. "Or maybe something bigger—the return is fairly strong." He shoved the throttles forward and put the RIB up on a high-speed plane. "We should see something before too long."

Shake maneuvered himself aft on the bounding RIB and motioned for Gerheim and the Marines to gather around him amidships. "We got a radar contact," he shouted over the wind and engine noise. "Once we come alongside, you guys show them your weapons and we'll order them to stop. They can't outrun the RIB and they aren't likely to put up any kind of fight. We get them aboard and Mr. Gerheim makes an arrest. Then we take the skiff in tow and motor back to Gitmo."

"Rules of engagement, sir?" Staff Sergeant Lindsey motioned for his Marines to take up stations along the gunwales of the RIB.

"I don't think that's gonna be a concern," Shake said and then decided it was a legitimate question that deserved a better answer. "If there's any kind of resistance, you and your guys put an end to it in a hurry." He pointed at the bundle of zip-ties on Lindsey's gear. "Hog-tie them if you need to, but they're older folks, so go easy with it."

Catalina Constanza spotted the 40-foot fishing boat on the horizon while her brother was scanning in the opposite direction. "There it is!" She sounded stronger and happier than she had since they left the docks at the Navy Base.

Eduardo turned to look where she was pointing and saw the fisherman churning toward them with deep-sea outriggers sparkling in the sun. The boat looked like any one of the hundreds of fishing charters that plied offshore waters all along the Cuban coast. There was a Republic of Cuba national flag whipping in the breeze at the boat's stern, and he could see a bright blue banner flying from one of the masts over the pilot house. "It's our ride!" he shouted and turned the little skiff onto a course heading directly for the bigger boat. They were about 300 meters from their designated contact when Eduardo heard the snarl of big diesel to the rear.

"There they are!" Gerheim pointed at the skiff with the two older Cubans aboard. It was an unnecessary announcement. Everyone's eyes were riveted on the stretch of water where the little boat and the bigger one would likely merge. "That Cuban fisherman has got to be their contact. No other boats in the area."

"How you want to handle it, sir?" The Coxswain maneuvered at high speed setting up an approach to the skiff on the left. They were only about 50 meters away from coming alongside.

"Swing around and get us between the two boats," he said, "and tell your gunner up forward to aim in on the fisherman. They'll probably get one look at the gun and sheer off."

As the Coxswain maneuvered and shouted instructions at the crewman manning the forward machinegun, Shake pulled a loud-hailer out of a rack and motioned for Gerheim to join him at the conning station. "It's cop time, Craze. Take this and warn that boat off."

"Better if we had somebody that speaks Spanish."

"I do, sir. It's a requirement for the VBSS crews down here. Let me do it." The Coxswain took the loud-hailer and nodded for his second crewman to take the wheel. He braced himself against the windscreen as his gunner traversed to take a bead on the approaching fisherman. When the RIB was positioned directly in the path of the two converging vessels, he aimed the loud-hailer at the bigger boat and hit the switch.

"Cuban vessel approaching, this is the U.S. Navy. We are recovering a boat stolen from the American base. Sheer off to starboard immediately and do not interfere."

There was no response from the fishing boat, but the bow wake it was pushing got noticeably smaller as it lost speed. An eerie quiet descended on the water. All anyone heard was the lap of waves on hulls and the throb of engines making just enough turns to hold position. The Coxswain repeated the command in fluent, distinctly authoritarian Spanish while Gerheim shouted unamplified at Eduardo and Catalina Constanza in the skiff puttering along off the RIB's opposite beam. "Shut down the motor—right now! Keep your hands in sight. You are both under arrest!"

It looked like a stand-off for a few long minutes. The Cuban fisherman was barely making way and the little skiff was idling. Eduardo and Catalina were glancing wide-eyed between the RIB and fishing boat. Shake spotted a coil of manila line on the deck forward of the conning station with a monkey's fist tied at the end to make a heaving line. He was maneuvering forward to get at it when the shooting started.

He turned to see a muzzle flashing on the weather deck of the Cuban fishing boat and heard the familiar crack of an AK-47 echo over the water. He ducked instinctively and saw the bullets splash very close to the RIB's bow. If the shooter corrected the next burst would chew into their hull. Apparently the sailor at the wheel came to the same conclusion. He rammed the throttles forward and spun the wheel. The RIB responded like a jack-rabbit, heeling hard to port and dumping Shake into the Caribbean.

He surfaced blowing saltwater and looked around over the chop trying to get his bearings. Sensors kicked in and he felt the pressure on his neck and chest as his life-jacket inflated automatically. Buoyed a bit higher, Shake could see the RIB and the fishing vessel in a high-speed water ballet in the distance. He could hear the crack of the AK pumping rounds, but the machinegunner on the RIB had yet to fire. He didn't know the Navy rules of engagement for this kind of thing—if there were any—but he suspected that the Coxswain was likely calling the base to report the encounter and ask for instructions. He'd probably wind up bobbing around in the Caribbean until those instructions came and the RIB had time to pick him up. There wasn't much else he could do for the moment.

Shake kicked and paddled around to scan the horizon and saw the little skiff heading in his direction. It looked like Eduardo and Catalina were going to fish him out of the water, so he waved to be sure they could see him. The boat corrected course in his direction and he was about to grab onto the gunwale when he saw Eduardo scrambling forward with a revolver in hand. The first shot cracked over his head and Shake porpoised down, fighting the life-jacket to disappear under the waves. He rolled over on his back letting the jacket scrape against the keel as he clawed under the boat.

When he surfaced on the other side, Eduardo was forward of him, facing in the opposite direction and sweeping the water with the muzzle of his revolver. Catalina screamed when Shake surged up out of the water and heaved himself into the boat, reaching for the pistol at his hip and hoping the saltwater immersion hadn't put it out of action. Fighting to stay on his feet in the rocking boat, Eduardo spun and fired. It was close but the bullet hit a plastic tackle-box that exploded in a shower of line and lures. Lying on his back amid a pile of tackle and life-preservers, Shake got the Glock in hand and shouted for Eduardo to drop his weapon.

The response was another round from the Webley. This one was better aimed and the bullet creased Shake's right thigh. Catalina was still screaming when Shake put two .40 caliber rounds into Eduardo's chest. He was crawling forward to see if Eduardo might have survived when he heard the distinctive roar of a 240 Golf in the distance interspersed with the pop of M-4 carbines. Apparently, the crew of the RIB had been cleared to engage. He looked to see the Cuban fisherman turning hard to the north. There was no further fire from the vessel as it churned away, chased by rounds from the RIB that sent a wall of water spouts rising in its wake.

With the fisherman summarily dispatched, the RIB maneuvered alongside the skiff. Fenders went over the side and one of the sailors tossed Shake a heaving line. When the two boats were securely lashed together, Gerheim vaulted into the skiff. He took one look at Eduardo lying in a pool of blood up near the bow, pulled a set of cuffs from his belt, and began to read Catalina Constanza her rights.

A Navy surgeon was putting the last of 18 stitches in Shake's right thigh. The bullet dug a neat little channel in the flesh but did no other harm. "From the looks of it," the doctor said pointing at several puckered white scars in other places on his patient's legs, "you've been hit a lot worse than this."

Shake just shrugged, watching the doc prepare a tetanus booster. "Sometimes you eat the bear and sometimes the bear eats you." As the doctor laughed and swabbed his shoulder, Gerheim arrived, took a look at the newly-sutured wound and smiled. "Cheap Heart…"

"Damn sure could have been worse," Shake said, wincing as the doctor hit him with the injection. "You get anything out of Catalina?"

Gerheim shook his head. "Let's do this elsewhere." He glanced at the surgeon. "Is he OK to go, Doc?"

The surgeon picked up a chart and made a few notations. "He's good to go." He watched Shake pull up his trousers and buckle his belt. "I'd take it easy for a few days to keep from ripping out the sutures. Your own doctor can remove them in about a week or ten days. I'll be glad to send him— or her—a copy of the paperwork."

"Just let me have it, Doc. I'll pass it along." Shake had been on the phone with Chan shortly after they returned to Gitmo with the dead man and the prisoner, just to check in and let her know he'd probably be returning soon. He made no mention of the incident at sea and wasn't looking forward to explaining it all when she got a look at the newly acquired wound.

"Once again the U.S. Navy Medical Corps saves the day." He smiled at the surgeon and pocketed the paperwork he'd been handed. "Many thanks, Doctor."

Gerheim wheeled his van into a parking space at the VOQ but left the engine running. "I've got to get back to the office. You can't believe the kind of paperwork something like this generates. I'll fill you in completely tonight at dinner, but here's the short version. Catalina Constanza is an emotional train-wreck. Just about collapsed under initial interrogation. We've still got a long way to go with her, but right now we've got enough to charge her with accessory to murder one. When the JAG weenies get her status determined, there's likely to be a bunch of other charges, but we've got enough to hold her and continue to dig."

"The accessory thing—is that about Munoz' death?"

"Yeah, apparently she set the old man up. She used her key to let Eduardo into the house. Eduardo gagged the guy and hit him with a hypo to inject an air-shot into his veins— instant heart attack. The why of it all is the interesting part: Munoz had a Cuban phone, provided by Eduardo, and he used it to put Ruiz-Romero in contact with his sister in Colon. Eduardo was monitoring the phone from the telecomm office and he passed the information on the proposed meet to his brother Enrique who set up a snatch on your guy. You can't believe the twists and turns on this one. It's gonna read like one of them fuckin' Jack Reacher thrillers by the time we're done."

"So brother Enrique is running the whole deal? That probably means Carlos Ruiz-Romero is in hands of Cuban Military Intelligence, right?"

"Probably—anyway, that would be my guess. I'd tell your man in Havana to start raising hell and looking into that rat's nest."

"I think everybody's gonna be raising hell when word about this deal gets out." Shake was anxious to talk to the man who calls himself Bayer and pass along the information obtained from Catalina Constanza. His job was likely finished now that they had solid information about what really happened to Carlos Ruiz-Romero.

"That's not gonna happen, Shake, at least not anytime soon. We sent a spot-report up through ONI to SecNav and DOD. The Secretary of Defense got on the case personally and immediately. They've slapped a hard classification on any and all paperwork we generate and everyone concerned is effectively under a gag order. If there are any questions asked, the PAO down here has been briefed to spin it as another encounter with Cuban refugees trying to escape by sea."

"That gag order include me?"

"They said anyone and everyone involved, Shake. But you've got friends in high places, right? I figure you'll do what you gotta do."

"No trouble with the shooting?"

"I'm calling it self-defense all the way. It's justifiable homicide with a bunch of witnesses. We'll have to do a full interview for the record and jump through a few legal hoops, but there's no way they can charge you with anything."

The man who calls himself Bayer had been listening to the satellite phone call from Guantanamo mostly in silence for the past 20 minutes. He'd interrupted Shake's narrative only once or twice to ask for clarification while he made quick, copious notes.

"OK," he said when Shake finally finished relating all the details he knew, "you stay where you are until you get your personal legal situation squared away. I'm gonna see what kind of heat I can put on the Cubans without getting myself arrested or sent home in disgrace."

"You're gonna need Catalina Constanza's testimony, right? My CID guy down here says they've slapped a national security lid on the whole thing. He says SecDef is involved personally."

"Yeah, I heard that." The man who calls himself Bayer scanned his notes and threw his pen across the hotel room. "Probably means the White House is informed and involved at this point. If anything gets done officially, it will be well below the radar so nothing leaks that could jeopardize the negotiations."

"Fuck 'em—just leak it. That'll generate the heat you need."

"And it would probably get Ruiz-Romero tossed in the Caribbean wearing cement shoes. We need to find that guy and produce the physical evidence that they can't bury or deny. Did your CID guy ask if the woman knew anything about where they took him?"

"I just got back from dinner with him and he had her on the grill for four hours until she finally fainted and the docs put a stop to it. He kept hammering for information on Carlos' location, but she claimed she had no idea. My guy has a lot of experience with this kind of thing and he thinks she's telling the truth. She was a patsy for her brothers and that's about it."

"All right, Shake. Let me digest this and go to work up here. I'm still watching those two Russians but who knows where that's gonna lead. Call me tomorrow—same time."

"So I stay on the case?"

"I really need a maneuver element while I'm stuck up here, Shake. The State Department people don't like my attitude, and they're watching me like hawks. If the Pentagon and the White House are keeping this thing sewed up under a gag order, I'm not gonna get any help in finding Ruiz-Romero from any other quarter. You know and I know the longer we wait the less likely it is we'll ever find him."

"So what you'd really like is to find the guy, rescue him, and then plop him down in front of the TV cameras where he tells his story and the resulting shit-storm puts the kibosh on lifting the Cuban embargo."

"In a perfect world, Shake, that's precisely what I'd like to see happen."

"OK. I've been working on a sketchy plan. If I can pull it off, you're gonna have to throw some weight around in a couple of critical places. Did you get hold of Commander Bartlett in Key West?"

"Yeah, we had a nice chat about the Korea thing. I didn't tell him much except that you were involved in something to do with Cuba and that he might be needed to lend a hand. He seemed anxious to help—thinks a lot of you and Stokey."

"Has he still got the boat?" Shake was scrolling through the contact list on his iPhone hoping he'd remembered to save a number he needed.

"Couldn't get him to shut up about it. He and his wife live on it apparently. It's tied up at some place called Oceanside Marina. He said to tell you ask anybody in Key West where the marina is and ask for The Steamer."

"Copy that." Shake jotted the address and then consulted his notes. "You've got the only secure phone, so I need you to make a couple of important calls. You still hooked in solid with The Company? Good. Get hold of the best Cuba man the CIA's got and ask him where they might stash a really high-value individual—just have him spit-ball it. Speculate and give us his best guess. I need someplace to start."

He picked up his phone and tapped a name on the contact list. "Then call Aeryon Labs in Ontario—yeah, Canada— here's the number. There's a guy named Jim Wiatt runs that outfit. Served with me in the Marine Corps. Tell him Shake Davis needs one of his Scouts—just tell him that—and tell him I'll call tomorrow around noon his time with details. And one last thing. I need you to look into a thing called the Ernest Hemingway International Billfish Tournament going on down here. Yeah, just do it and call me back."

When Shake disconnected, the man who calls himself Bayer flipped to a new page on his notepad and composed a bare-bones plan of action. He had the phone calls to make for Shake, and he needed to get an update from the non-official cover agent on loan from another old CIA crony. That asset was about the only real stroke of luck he'd had in Cuba so far. The NOC was an unsponsored, deniable CIA subcontractor in Havana working deep under cover doing intelligence collection work for both the Canadian and U.S. governments. Her handler was reluctant to commit the asset unless she was a volunteer. That required a meeting between Carla Koehler and the man who calls himself Bayer. As it turned out when he met the woman, Carla was connected and therefore motivated. More to the immediate point, she was an old friend of Shake Davis.

Chatting over coffee during their first meeting, Bayer discovered that Carla was nominally a travel writer working throughout the Caribbean from a base in Cuba. She was also a former soldier. She'd served as a liaison officer between the Canadian MOD and Princess Patricia's Canadian Light Infantry, and during that assignment she'd met a lot of Americans either visiting or doing exchange tours with Canadian forces. That led to name-dropping and a search for common acquaintances. When Bayer mentioned Shake Davis, her eyes lit up. She'd met Shake while he was in Canada for winter warfare training with the "Picklies," and he was one Yank that made a special impression on Carla Koehler. "He was really something," she said with a wistful look in her eyes that told Bayer all he needed to know. "If he'd stayed around much longer we might have made it work."

Once Carla Koehler discovered that what she was being asked to do for this American spook was connected to something Shake was doing in Cuba, she was all in. The man who calls himself Bayer set her to work watching and documenting everything the visiting Russian GRU men were doing while in Havana.

He ordered coffee from room service and doodled while he waited, trying to decide who he knew and trusted with the necessary insight on Cuban intelligence operations. He needed someone who knew the gut-level stuff, someone who could provide some worthwhile speculation about where the Cubans might stash a purloined American DIA asset. He'd worked for the Company a long time before he began free-lancing throughout the national security establishment. There were still plenty of people who owed him big time.

Room Service was slow and unmotivated as were most services in Castro's Cuba, so he had plenty of time to make his decision by the time the coffee arrived. Dave Martinez was no longer active in the business, but there was no one anywhere who knew more about the Castros, their revolution, and the current state of affairs in Cuba. Before he finally accepted a desk job with the CIA, Martinez had been the primary contact with the expatriate 2506 Brigade of old *Cubano* Bay of Pigs veterans. He lived somewhere in Miami, floating around Little Havana and keeping his oar in Cuban waters.

Martinez answered with a tentative greeting. Not many people had his private cell phone number, and he didn't recognize the number that came up on his caller ID screen. Bayer figured Martinez would recognize his voice and launched right into his pitch.

"Marty, I'm in Havana right now, working on something hot." The man who calls himself Bayer assured the old agent-analyst they were speaking on a secure connection. "If anybody's got an answer for me, it's probably you."

"What else are old friends for? Ask away."

"So, suppose Cuban MI grabbed an American high-value individual—make that very high-value individual—and they needed to stash him somewhere ultra-secret, ultra-secure. Where would that be?"

"Well, *amigo…*" Bayer could hear Martinez puffing on a cigar on the other end of the call. "If it's General Enrique Constanza and his boys that grabbed your HVI, they'd likely take him to Camp Mantanzas south of Havana as a first stop. Then if they really need to keep him out of sight, they'd likely find some hole up in the Sierra Maestra, probably in one of Fidel's old mountain hideouts. Several of them are still in use for training. If you give me a couple of hours, I can mark up a map and email it to you."

"Why would you say *if* it's Cuban MI, Marty?"

Martinez chuckled and Bayer heard ice tinkling in a glass somewhere in Miami. "Cuban Military Intel is really just a bunch of low-level goons, mostly used to collect dirt on opposition elements and cobble up order of battle estimates. The real power-brokers, the high-rollers who play the game internationally, are the shadow-spooks from the *Dirrecion de Inteligencia.* That outfit is run by a very aggressive and very ruthless sonofabitch by the name of Manuel Panteros. This guy is a friend of no one and trusts no one—except maybe the Russians. It seems to me if anyone packs the gear to set up a snatch on an American HVI, it would be him."

"OK, so would he use the same hidey-holes as MI?"

"Not a chance. Like I said, Panteros trusts no one."

"Best guess, Marty—and this is really important. Where would *Dirrecion de Inteligencia* hide an American HVI?"

"Assuming he's still alive and still in Cuba, *amigo*, there are very few places that a man like Panteros would trust as safe storage for such a valuable asset. It's not gonna be easy, but if I were you, I'd start looking at a little island off the northwest coast that Fidel built as his private playground. Very few even know it exists. It's called *Cayo Piedra…*"

General Enrique Constanza sat uncomfortably across the desk from Manuel Panteros and absorbed the man's glare of contempt. Usually, they conferred comfortably over coffee or rum on the couches, but there was little hospitality on offer today. The little bastard had power and he was displaying it. Enrique Constanza would never respect a man who came to that power primarily through foreign influence and not through revolutionary struggle.

"It didn't seem like a very difficult mission," Panteros said tapping his Zippo lighter on his desk blotter to emphasize how disappointed he was in his colleague, "which is why I thought even Military Intelligence could handle it."

"It was not something we could have foreseen, Manuel." General Constanza squirmed to get a bit more comfortable in the cane chair and kept his voice under control. "The American Navy boat showed up unexpectedly just before they made the pick-up."

"And you authorized them to get into a gunfight with the American Navy? You didn't think that might raise their suspicions?"

"I did not authorize any such thing!" Enrique Constanza took a deep breath, reached for his cigarettes and then changed his mind. "As you required, we used a civilian boat rather than one of our *Guarda Frontera* vessels as I recommended. Apparently, one of the hired hands decided on his own to open fire on the Navy boat. I have dealt with the situation."

"And these idiots report that your brother and sister are in custody?"

"They reported that the little boat was taken. I must assume that Eduardo and Catalina were also taken."

"It's all very awkward, Enrique. The Americans now have our long-time sleeper agents in custody. How long do you think it will take them to break a couple of untrained old people? They will know very shortly that your command was involved in Ruiz-Romero's disappearance."

"But they will assume the worst given the deception, will they not? They have what they believe to be Ruiz-Romero's corpse, so the logical conclusion is that we either took him and killed him—or that he was killed in an escape attempt. We simply deny anything and everything when they start to ask questions."

Manuel Panteros kept tapping the lighter on his desk blotter in a slow, steady rhythm. The general was likely correct in his assessment of the American reaction, but it was always hard to be sure about them. This glitch made him nervous. If questions were asked at high diplomatic levels, Raul might cut short his mission and rush home. Or perhaps Fidel might struggle from his sickbed and get involved. He was more than a little surprised that there had been no formal inquiry. For some reason—likely to save face and avoid giving ammunition to political elements opposing the normalization process—the Americans were playing it close to the vest.

"Fortunately for all concerned," Panteros said as he straightened in his chair and reached for his cigar humidor, "the Americans are making no official noise about this situation. They will investigate thoroughly as they always do, but as long as they believe Ruiz-Romero is dead, it will simply be a matter of stonewalling on our part. You may assume your money will be paid as soon as mine is—one third—as we agreed."

"I'd like to know what is happening with my brother and sister." The General stood and tried to maintain his dignity under Panteros' glare. "Can you make inquiries?"

Manuel Panteros slammed the lid on his humidor and pointed a finger at his visitor. "General Constanza, sometimes your stupidity amazes me! You want me to inquire with the Americans about your brother and sister? And let them know that we are officially aware of this entire incident? That just might make stonewalling a bit difficult, don't you think?"

When the MI officer made no reply beyond a subtle nod, Panteros slumped back in his chair and took a deep breath. "What you'll do now is tie up any loose ends. Have the family moved immediately. Put them somewhere up in the mountains and be ready to eliminate them from the picture if it becomes necessary."

Manuel Panteros waited for several moments after the MI general left and contemplated his next moves in a cloud of cigar smoke. This development was nowhere near fatal to his plan, but it did shorten the time-frame for action. Nothing could be allowed to interrupt the course of normalization. That was crucial. And that meant that Carlos Ruiz-Romero had to be gone before the Americans started snooping and possibly discovered that he was not as dead as advertised.

He reached for the phone and got his aide on the line. "Set up a meeting with the Russians as soon as possible. No, tell them I will come to them—details to be provided later today."

Las Vegas

Mike Stokey was skimming wind-blown leaves from his backyard pool when Linda brought him a phone. "It's Shake," she said, "and you won't believe where he's calling from."

"I take it you're not in Texas where you're supposed to be." Stokey took the phone into the shade and plopped down in a lawn chair. "Linda says I won't believe it, so lay it on me."

"I'm down at the Guantanamo Navy Base, Mike. Can't give you much on this line, but suffice to say I'm doing a little job for a friend of ours that you know and love."

"Oh, shit. What's he got you involved with now?"

"Details forthcoming soonest but I need you to lend a hand. Can you travel?"

"Depends, I guess—mostly on whether or not I can take Linda along. Ever since the deal in Beirut, she's kind of addicted to our brand of fun and games."

"Might be good cover. Think she'd like Key West, Florida?"

"I think she'll like anywhere but Vegas in the middle of summer. What do you need me to do?"

"Couple of things: You remember Commander Ralph Bartlett—the guy who was in command of the Reuben James, picked us up out of the drink on the Korea deal?"

"Yeah, very capable naval officer as I recall. He's the one they call The Steamer, right? Big liberty risk and everything he does is forty knots, no smoke. He's retired now, I thought."

"Yeah, that's The Steamer. He's retired in Key West and he's got a big yacht moored at a place called the Oceanside Marina on the east side of *Cayo Oeste*. We're gonna use his boat as a base of operations. I already called and got it set up, so you and Linda head for Key West to meet up with him. I'll give you my credit card numbers and you can pick up a couple of tickets on me. Make it one-way. I don't know how long this is gonna take."

"Copy that. I can probably close up the house and get us out of here no later than tomorrow some time."

"That'll work. I've still got to clear post at Gitmo and get myself to Key West. You guys just get reacquainted and wait for me. Be sure and bring your passports. I shouldn't be more than a day or two and I'll fill you in on the rest of it."

"I'm on it. Anything else you need me to do?"

"You still got that brace of Marine Corps CQB .45s that Morty P gave us when we left Belize?"

"Yeah, finest custom version of a 1911 I've ever handled. I've been giving mine a workout at the range. Yours is still in cosmoline."

"I know the paperwork is gonna be a hassle at the airport, but bring 'em along."

"Shouldn't be too bad, Shake. I've got all the documents and a couple of lock-boxes. You think we're gonna need pistols?"

"I don't know what the hell we're gonna need, Mike. Just bring 'em. Call it a security blanket."

"You're the boss. Anything else?"

"I'm having a package sent to Bartlett from Canada. When it arrives, you guys unpack it and read the instruction manual very carefully."

Ground Zero

There had been no change in his routine for days. Carlos Ruiz-Romero got his meals at the same time and his nightly exercise periods like clockwork. Beyond a stack of month-old magazines and little portable radio one of the guards provided one morning, his time was boring. No one bothered him or visited to ask questions and that made him increasingly nervous. The magazines were apolitical and filled with stories about Cuban society for the most part. The radio picked up just two local stations and they were broadcasting only salsa music interspersed with government announcements. When they occasionally broke for news, it was all local stuff layered around the big story which was that the Americans were correcting the long-standing error of their ways and the embargos cruelly levied on the Cuban people would soon be lifted.

As night fell, he walked with his escort outside into the little courtyard that he'd come to think of as his gym. The soldiers were still in place, still staring stoically at him, occasionally smiling and shaking their heads at the crazy gringo and his exercise efforts. Carlos ignored them and proceeded with what he usually did during his outdoor periods. First he launched into a series of floor exercises. When he was through with the push-ups, lunges, squat-thrusts, and jumping jacks, when the guards had become thoroughly bored with watching him thrash and sweat, he moved out into the field of tall saw grass and began to run what looked like wind-sprints or some sort of agility exercise.

This was the second night of his maneuvers out in the open field. At first the knee-high saw grass merely sprang back into place as he trampled back and forth. By now he was beginning to see a little progress. There had been relatively little rain, just a few passing showers, so the saw grass was turning yellow and the stalks were getting brittle. That made things a bit easier. He would finish the S tonight and begin on the O tomorrow.

While he was running and weaving out in the open field, Carlos Ruiz-Romero looked up to see the lights of a passing aircraft. The guards were tracking it as he was, but it was just a commercial flight heading into or out of Havana. The pilots would not be looking down for a distress signal on the ground at some tiny island, but that didn't deter him from making the effort.

Gitmo

Crazy Earl Gerheim took Shake to dinner after a grueling day with Navy JAG officers and endless repetitions of the events out in the Caribbean. There was nothing useful to report from the Catalina Constanza interrogations. They were beating a dead horse, Gerheim said over steak and beer, Catalina had told all she knew for the record and it wasn't much. ONI and NCIS were about to quit and turn her over to the legal affairs folks who would determine her status and then decide what kind of court she might face.

Shake's flakey cover as a visiting government contractor was blown sky high shortly after his interrogations began. There were some initial threats of detention and prosecution until Shake finally got the man who calls himself Bayer on the line. The JAG officers did a lot of listening, grunting, and nodding as Bayer made what sounded a lot like dire threats. That was followed by an hour-long recess during which the lawyers contacted Washington for instructions.

Apparently during that time, Bayer had worked his bureaucratic magic with influential contacts in high places. When the lawyers returned, they were much more civil and primarily interested in the shooting. All agreed by the end of the day that Eduardo Constanza's death was indeed justifiable homicide, a matter of self-defense. They also agreed that Shake Davis should catch the first thing smoking out of Gitmo.

"Suits me," Shake said to Gerheim as they walked off a few calories and chased the meal with cigars. "I need to get to Key West soonest."

"I got you a seat on the Osprey flight in the morning. I'll keep you apprised of anything that develops down here, Shake, but I don't think I'm gonna be much more help."

"You've been a huge help, Craze. Hadn't been for you, we'd still be running in circles."

They walked in silence for a while, feeling the tropical breeze blowing in across the bay and admiring a sky full of bright stars. "You think he's still alive?"

"I think he most likely is, Craze. The Cubans can be ham-handed, but they took Carlos for a reason. Either they want to squeeze him for secret information or they want to sell him off to someone else that wants that information. Either way, they won't whack him. The only thing that could make them do something like that is a full-blown international incident and a public outcry that threatens their international situation. We both know that's not gonna happen and likely so do they. They've got us just where they want us, odds all running in their favor. As long as the Administration insists on proceeding with the normalization no matter what, the Cubans don't have to worry about getting caught dirty on this thing."

"For what my opinion is worth," Gerheim said, "I think you ought to be looking at option two. The Cubans will go the least risky route. They don't pack the gear to exploit the stuff that Carlos could reveal, but they know a bunch of people in the opposition camp who do."

"So you'd bet they're holding him someplace until they can make a deal?"

"That would be my guess, yeah."

"Well, I'm gonna proceed on that course anyway. Thanks again for all you've done, Craze. I'll call you from Key West."

A staff car dropped Manuel Panteros half a block away from the restaurant where he was to meet the Russian GRU representatives. It was as close as the car could get to his destination. The through street fronting the restaurant was under repair. Irritated but resigned, Panteros slipped on a pair of Ray Bans and started to walk. His two bodyguards split up immediately and without command. One went ahead of his principal checking the sparse pedestrian crowds for potential threats while the other man walked at Panteros' shoulder and scanned for closer risks.

Panteros didn't circulate in public much, so his security men were slightly out of practice. That's likely why they both ignored the attractive middle-age woman wearing a t-shirt emblazoned with a Canadian flag who sat at an outdoor coffee shop across the street from the restaurant. She casually raised a cellphone and pointed it in their direction, but there was nothing unusual about a tourist in Havana taking snapshots. By the time they opened the door for Manuel Panteros and had a last look around the area, Carla Koehler had dropped the phone in her big straw purse and gone back to reading a paperback novel.

The advance man led Panteros to the back of the place, confirming that the Russians had already arrived and the private room looked clean and secure. Panteros paused outside the door and gathered his thoughts. He needed to do some acting here. The stage he'd selected for the meeting should help. It was neutral ground where neither he nor his guests would appear to have the home-field advantage. He was about to re-cut his deal, but he didn't want the Russians to think it was anything more than a matter of impatience: a strong desire on his part to get paid. A meeting like this in a public place should assure them that there was nothing wrong, no pressure that demanded speed over secrecy.

He entered the room late as planned, leaving his body-guards posted outside the door. He'd asked the two GRU men not to delay their luncheon for him and the Russians were picking at nearly empty plates when he shook hands and took a seat on the other side of the only table in the small space. He opened a string bag and exposed a bottle of Cuban rum, the brand he knew they favored.

"Gentlemen, thank you for coming on such short notice. I hope you enjoyed your meal." He gathered glasses and poured drinks for them. The Russians merely nodded and sipped for a while, talking about local cuisine and trying to get a feel for the real subject of this unexpected meeting. Panteros smiled and added a comment or two as he swept his gaze around the room. There was only one small window, but it was so filthy that it was unlikely anyone could see in through the layers of dirt and grease. The Russians were likely wired to record their conversation, but that was to be expected.

"So, where do we stand at this point?"

"I can't tell you that we have a deal yet." The senior GRU man said as he dropped a handful of crushed ice into his glass. "But I believe our people are leaning in your direction."

"You must understand that something like this takes time," the junior man added. "Even if we were to get the go-ahead today, it might take some time for the details to be ironed out, for various aspects of the deal to be conducted to everyone's satisfaction."

"Of course," Panteros said, "but I confess I'm becoming impatient."

"I'm afraid there's not much we can do about that." The senior GRU rep caught the tone and rubbed his jaw as he stared at the Cuban spymaster sitting stiffly across the table. There was something unsaid here that made him uneasy. "The product on offer is still in good shape, I presume?"

"Yes, of course. We are taking good care in that regard. But I would like very much to get this deal done and get the product moved as quickly as possible."

"Why? What's the rush? You said we had all the time we needed."

"And you do, I assure you of that. But you must understand the longer things like this are allowed to run without satisfactory conclusion, the more chance there is that problems might arise. I want to avoid any potential problems and move this deal along. Please convey that to your sponsors."

"I will let them know."

"And let them know one other thing." Panteros leaned across the table and refilled glasses. "As a good will gesture to prompt a speedy decision, I am willing to lower the asking price a bit."

The two Russians exchanged a quick glance. "How much is a bit?"

"If we can get a deal completed within the next week," Panteros swirled the liquor in his glass and smiled. "I can offer a reduction of five million—total price would be twenty-five million—all other aspects of the deal remain the same. I am just attempting to speed the process here."

"We will communicate the new terms and get back to you."

Manuel Panteros nodded, picked up the tab from the table and walked out the door. He felt quite confident that the overall impression he'd left behind with the Russians was simply that of a greedy man trying to get richer quicker.

Carla Koehler watched the Cuban emerge into the sunlit street where he was immediately flanked by two security men. She couldn't identify the man, but he was obviously someone of importance. And even if he wasn't, he was meeting with the two Russians she'd been assigned to watch and that got the guy—whoever he was—plugged into her surveillance plot. She dug the phone out of her purse and shot a couple more photos as they crossed the street and walked away in the opposite direction. She had ordered a second coffee and chewed halfway through a sticky pastry before the Russians emerged. They took off on foot toward a side street where a black BMW was parked.

She finished her pastry, paid the bill, and walked across the street toward the same alley she'd entered an hour earlier when she followed the Russians from their embassy on Playa Miramar. The narrow little aisle between buildings was a dead-end and served mostly as a depository for kitchen trash from the restaurant. It was empty except for a row of overstuffed cans and a few stray cats. She ducked into it and moved to a crusty, grease-spattered window, the only one that illuminated the private room in the back of the restaurant. The bug was still where she'd planted it in the corner of the window frame held in place by a strip of plumber's putty. She peeled it off, dropped it into her purse, and then stooped to reach behind a reeking garbage can where she'd left the digital recorder. She put the recorder into a Styrofoam fast-food container and walked casually out of the alley.

The dead-drop arranged by the man who called himself Bayer was in a little park across from the Hotel Saratoga on *Esquina Dragones* in old Havana, an easy walk. On the way she sent the pre-arranged text from the phone to let him know she was making a pass and then stuffed the phone with its file of photos into the container with the recorder. The drop was a trash can near a crumbling, waterless fountain at the center of the park. She stopped by it, wiped her lips with a paper napkin as if she'd just finished eating and then, like a thoughtful tourist, she lifted the lid and dumped the container in the trash. Carla strolled casually out of the park, holding a sun hat onto her head against a gentle breeze and hoping whatever she'd collected would help Shake Davis in some form. Maybe she'd ask about a contact number. Even after all these years, she still had a thing for that man.

Inside the Russian Embassy on Playa Miramar, the two GRU field operators sat in a soundproof room with walls, floor and ceiling sewn with wires that constantly generated surveillance-defeating white noise. In the middle of the only table was a high-tech, ultra-secure phone that opened a direct line to a similar room and a similar phone at Moscow Central. It was time for their regular report and that phone should be buzzing shortly.

What they needed to decide before that happened was whether or not to take some initiative. Their Moscow principals were fretting over the huge asking price for Carlos Ruiz-Romero and had been for more than a week now. Officials weighed the risks of such a high level deal with the Cubans who were about to become larger, more independent, and more significant international players. Naturally, they would be happy with the discount offered by Manuel Panteros, but it was a relative pittance. Perhaps there was a way to squeeze the greedy little bastard for an even lower price. It seemed to be moving from a seller's market to a buyer's market. The way Panteros was sweating and gasping to get the deal done and get his hands on the money, it looked like the leverage was shifting in their direction. What if they recommended further delays or a counter-offer?

"You know if it was up to me," said the junior GRU man, "we would eliminate the middle man—just send some *Spetsnaz* operators into Fidel's mansion and snatch this man right out from under their noses."

"We're not even supposed to know where they're keeping him, so don't let that slip in conversation." The senior man crossed his arms and looked up at the padded ceiling. "Of course, Surkov knows. He's got agents running through Cuban intelligence like rats. If he wanted to take the guy, he would."

"Why doesn't he? It would save a lot of money and time."

"Director General Surkov plays the long game, my friend. He knows how quickly the Cubans will be corrupted when the Americans finally open the flood gates. He wants to be sure the emerging oligarchs continue playing for our side. That's worth the money to him."

"Well, maybe we can do something to make the long game less expensive."

When the phone rang, the junior GRU man leaned over the table to punch up the connection. There was no need for preamble when reporting to Director General Igor Surkov of the GRU, so the senior man leaned in toward the speaker. "We have some good news—and a recommendation."

The man who calls himself Bayer knew from experience and observation that Havana Municipal trash collection was an iffy, irregular proposition. Refuse receptacles, sited practically anywhere you looked in the Cuban capital, were habitually overflowing and besieged by squadrons of fat black flies. It was the reason he designated the can near the fountain in the park across from his hotel as a dead drop. Anything deposited there was likely to remain there.

When he got the text from his NOC indicating she was making a pass on the drop, he left his hotel room carrying his briefcase and wearing the Panama straw that he used to protect his scalp from the broiling sun. He was in shirt-sleeves as he usually was in the afternoon when he left the hotel to spend a little quiet time in the park. The obvious crowd of Cuban spooks that habitually hung around the lobby of the hotel where members of the American Normalization Task Force were staying barely glanced in his direction. His little excursions to the park were routine by now.

He sat on a rickety wrought-iron bench near the dried-up fountain and pretended to be studying something inside the briefcase propped on his knees. He sat there for about 15 minutes watching a few pedestrians rushing through the park in one direction or another. Cubans in Havana didn't do much loitering in parks, and there was no spray of water from the fountain to provide relief from the heat of the day. He waited five more minutes and then pulled a room-service sandwich in a Styrofoam container out of the case. He popped it open, removed a sandwich, and began to chew on it. It was spicy *chorizo* sausage stuffed between two slabs of thick bread that always tasted mildly gritty. He ate slowly for a few minutes, then dropped the remainder of his sandwich into the container and strolled toward the fly-infested trashcan.

Another Styrofoam container—an exact duplicate of the one he was holding—was resting on a pile of rotting fruit peels. He waved his hand to frustrate the swarm of flies that rose when he opened the lid and bent to trade his container for the one in the trash. Then he straightened up contemplating for a moment. He put the lid back on the trashcan and looking entirely like a man who suddenly decided he might want the rest of his meal later, walked back to the bench, tossed the container inside his briefcase and closed the lid. He sat for a few minutes more watching for watchers and then carried his briefcase back into the hotel lobby.

It took him less than half an hour to scan the photos on the NOC's phone and listen several times to the recorded conversation between the GRU Russians and Manuel Panteros, Director General of Cuba's *Dirrecion de Inteligencia.* It was a bad recording full of background noise and parts of it were completely unintelligible, but a little repetition and some guesswork allowed the man who calls himself Bayer to reconstruct most of it. What he knew for sure at the end of it all was that Cuban Intelligence had Carlos Ruiz-Romero and the director general of that outfit was putting him up for sale, discount price twenty-five million—not specified—but likely U.S. dollars or Euros.

He learned back in his desk chair and stared at the ceiling for a few long minutes, letting it all sink in and trying to decide on a course. In terms of actionable intelligence, he really had nothing. He could call a few conservative journalists he knew and leak the story, but they'd stir up a storm digging for corroboration and the heat might get Carlos killed. If he sent a series of rockets up the official government chain making accusations of kidnapping, international espionage, and a bunch of other wild claims involving Russians, anyone willing to listen would want to hear and see what he had—

and it wasn't much or very solid. It was all weasel-words. They talked about a "product on offer" and that could mean anything. Carlos Ruiz-Romero was never mentioned. If he tried to generate interest with what he had so far, he'd wind up locked in one of the rubber rooms reserved for conspiracy theorists.

What he needed was hard evidence, and that would require finding Carlos Ruiz-Romero before the Russians cut a deal and spirited the poor bastard out of Cuba and into some high-tech interrogation center in the bowels of GRU Central. He was standing at the window of his hotel room, contemplating the personal audience with the Normalization Task Force director he had in just under an hour. There was no telling what that was about, but it couldn't be good. He was distracted by an aircraft roaring over downtown Havana, descending toward a landing at Jose Marti International airport. Then he reached for his phone.

Scrolling through his contact list, he found the private number for Lieutenant General Gordon Fowler, who was still running the U.S. Southern Command near Miami. Gordo was a kindred spirit, an old compatriot from their operations in Belize and elsewhere in Central America. These days he was also under an official cloud for his outspoken opposition to the normalization process. Most pundits thought the general was due to be fired and retired shortly for his comments about the Cuban situation. Fowler was just the kind of loose cannon he needed.

An aide answered the call and promised that his general would get back to the man who calls himself Bayer in less than an hour.

Oceanside Marina, Key West

The *Junebug* was a 54-foot Chris Craft Roamer that slept four comfortably and powered through the water pushed by two big Detroit diesels. The boat was usually slick topside, rigged for cruising, leisure activities or deep-sea fishing, but Commander Ralph "Steamer" Bartlett USN (Ret.) had draped a huge 300-gallon fuel bladder across the foredeck to provide extra juice for extended cruising in the Caribbean where obtaining reliable diesel fuel was often problematic. High above the weather decks was a glassy and classy flying bridge with a spread of sophisticated gauges, LED screens, and instruments that Shake could just barely understand.

"Damn, Steamer." Shake looked around the control station that featured a plush Captain's chair situated in the middle of all the controls and monitors. "It looks like the bridge of the Enterprise up here."

Bartlett leaned an elbow on the chair and smiled. "June calls it my play station," he said. "We've got the boat rigged to take us nearly any place in the Carib, and she's been good as gold in fair weather and foul so far."

"How the hell does a retired squid afford something like this?"

"Navy shipmate of mine works for Chris Craft. He got me a deal we could afford. We sold the house and decided to just live on the boat. We make do."

"And you've been to Cuba before?"

"Twice so far, Shake, and no problem either time beyond the usual bureaucratic hassles. As long as we've got the right paperwork, no guns aboard, and a pile of twenties we're will-ing to part with regularly, it goes pretty smoothly. The Har-bor Master has got us on file by now. It's all a lot easier when you're a known boat."

"Are we gonna have to leave the pistols?"

"Maybe not." Steamer pointed to a line of plastic fenders rigged along the edge of the deck below them. "I've got an idea about that. I'll let you know before we leave."

Mike Stokey, wearing shorts and an outrageous Hawai-ian shirt covered with leaping game fish, climbed the ladder to the bridge carrying cold drinks. "We got all the provisions, Steamer. Everything on the list. The girls are stowing it all below. We burned the numbers clean off Shake's credit cards."

"Yeah…" Shake sipped his beer and shrugged. "Bayer assures me an electronic transfer of funds is imminent. Chan's not gonna be happy when the statement hits Lock-hart."

"No chicken, turkey, or any fowl with bones in it, right?"

"June checked it all personally, Steamer. What's that all about?"

"Beats me, but when the vet comes aboard at the marina, he has a shit-hissy if we've got any chicken parts containing bones. First time we went down there we had a couple of roasting birds in the freezer and you'd have thought we were bringing in the black plague." Bartlett walked across the bridge, pulled a padded envelope out of a compartment, and pawed through a stack of papers. "I think we've got all the passports and other paperwork in order. Did you guys pick up the mail?"

"June's got most of it down below," Stokey dug an en-velope out of his pocket and handed it over. "She said you'd want to see this right away."

Bartlett opened the envelope, shuffled through a few enclosed sheets, and then handed it to Shake. "We're all set. As of now the *Junebug* out of Key West is an official entrant in the Ernest Hemingway International Billfish Tournament which starts in two days."

"Great idea, Shake." Stokey slipped his beer into the cup holder, retrieved the papers from Shake and began to read. "How the hell did you come up with it?"

"Guy down at Gitmo told me about it. Apparently, the tournament has been going on down there for 60 years or so. There's all kind of big boats and big fishermen show up to try for Marlin every year. It's a big money-maker for the Cubans. I got Bayer to get us registered and pay the outrageous fee they demanded. We go motoring around all over their offshore waters with an official Cuban cruising permit and tournament sanction."

"Uh huh—except we aren't fishing for Marlin, are we?"

"I wouldn't mind if we hooked into one, Steamer. But we're mostly gonna be flying that drone that's down below. While you guys are fishing, Mike and I steer the Scout in to take a look at the place Bayer told us about."

Bartlett opened a locker at the rear of the flying bridge and spread a nautical chart on the map table. "I never heard of *Cayo Piedra* myself, but a guy who's been cruising down there for years says it's right here." Bartlett tapped a spot on the chart off the southwest coast of Cuba. "Chart doesn't show much, but I might be able to get an update from some Navy sources."

"Ain't gonna be easy, Shake." Stokey set a protractor to scale and placed it on the chart with one leg on the Cuban coastline and the other on a barely discernible dot that they suspected might be *Cayo Piedra*. If they were correct, their objective was located about 10 nautical miles south by southeast of the Bay of Pigs. "We talked to Steamer's buddy just after you called. He says any boat comes within sight gets warned off or shot at without warning. That's the Castro's private island, and they're serious about trespassers and gawkers."

"And that's why I think Bayer might be right about where they've stashed Carlos Ruiz- Romero. The drone's got a two-mile range, so we sit off out of sight and fly it in to snoop around for us."

A shrill buzz from the control console interrupted and Bartlett reached for a handset. "They've got chow laid on belowdecks," he said. "Let's eat, do some final checks, and then we'll get underway for Cuba."

Headquarters, U.S. Southern Command

Marine Lieutenant General Gordon Fowler was stuffing paper into his briefcase with one hand and holding his personal cell phone to his ear with the other. His aide sat at a nearby desk pouring over their trip itinerary. He made it a point not to listen too closely when the general was talking on his private line.

"You think this is for real, Bob? They snatched a DIA guy and they're gonna try and sell him to the Russians?"

"Everything I've got points that way, Gordo. I wouldn't be asking unless I was fairly sure. I can't shoot it up the chain for support because the White House has got the clamps on tight. I need an unofficial hand here."

"Yeah, I know all about that kind of shit. We got a blazer from the Pentagon last week reminding all hands we are expected to express full support for Administration policies— or else. I don't know if I can help you, but suppose I could rig a UAV over flight. What do I do with the data?"

"You just take a look. That's all I'm asking. You're the expert here. Anything looks suspicious to you, you let me know. It would be a onetime deal. I'm just trying to find this guy before they either kill him or sell him off. He's got a butt load of classified information that can't fall into the wrong hands."

"Let me see what I can do. I'm about to leave for an inspection tour down south."

"They still letting you travel, Gordo?"

"Yeah, but they've imposed a complete press black-out. After that interview I did with the Miami Herald about the

Cuba proposals, I am officially on the short-list for the shit-can."

"You think they'll fire you?"

"They'll retire me with a lot of bullshit about what a great guy I am. You know the drill. Whatever happens, I'll go out on my own terms. I don't wear three stars to be some kind of PC toady sucking up for one more."

"That's what I love about you Marines, Gordo. Have a good trip and call me back if you think there's something you can do."

The general dropped the phone into his briefcase and turned to his aide. "Doc Mills has still got the 96th Test Wing at Eglin, right?"

"Yes sir." The aide tapped a few computer keys to check. "General Mills is still in command. Should I get him on the line?"

Fowler took a look at the beautifully burnished Marine Corps emblem mounted on his wall and then let his gaze drift to the fringed American flag in a stand behind his desk. *Support and defend against all enemies foreign—and domestic.* "Yeah, get him on the phone for me." *Fuck the White House,* he thought with a smile. *They can kiss my about-to-retire ass.*

Ralph Bartlett kept the *Junebug* motoring westerly once they left Key West's southeast channel to take advantage of slack water until he was about 20 miles west of Sand Key. Now he was ready for a sweeping U-turn to port that would put them in position to pick up the Gulf Stream thus saving fuel and adding a few knots to their speed. He spun the wheel, immediately feeling the push from the current, and plugged a waypoint into the GPS. Their course was set for Cuban waters, and the next stop would be a few nautical miles from Hemingway Marina where they could clear immigrations and customs to obtain their cruising permit.

Below the flying bridge, his wife June fussed around the open weather decks sorting out deep-sea fishing rigs and showing Linda Stokey how the serious angling game is played. While her husband knew just about all there was to know about seamanship and navigation, June Bartlett was the duty expert on fishing including gear and techniques. Over a sumptuous dinner in the *Junebug*'s well-appointed cabin, the Steamer bragged about her bonefish and snapper catches that won a couple of tournaments staged in the Florida Keys. On this trip, June and Linda would spend most of the time in the chairs rigged aft trolling with rods and reels. Mike and Shake would keep an eye on the outriggers when they weren't actually flying the Scout drone which was the subject of their study belowdecks at the moment.

"Looks like some kind of weird little spider," Mike Stokey was twirling one of the drone's three propellers arranged around a circular body that housed the UAV's ultrahigh tech electronic heart including a high-resolution day/night camera system. "Or maybe something out of Star Wars—hard to believe this little deal can cruise at forty miles an hour up to a thousand-foot altitude."

"Manual says it can." Shake closed the operator's instructions he was reading and picked up the Scout drone. It weighed just less than four pounds including a rechargeable lithium polymer battery. "Range is listed at two miles, which means the *Junebug* can sit out over the horizon while we fly it."

"So how does a Neanderthal like you find out about a whiz-bang toy like this? You been reading Mechanics Illustrated?"

"It comes courtesy of a good buddy I knew in the Marine Corps when I was out in Hawaii with the Brigade. Jim Wiatt—he's a Canadian by birth and a damn fine cannon-cocker by trade. He was on the cutting edge of fire control systems when the Corps finally stopped counting on fingers and toes. He's high-tech savvy, so when he got out he went into UAV research and development. Now he runs Aerydon Labs. This is one of their best products, all kinds of military applications. He demonstrated it for me one time when he was at Quantico trying to sell it to the Marine Corps."

"Well, we better get in a little flight time." Stokey picked up a square console with a high-resolution screen in the center surrounded by buttons, switches, and joysticks. Shake carried the drone and the user's manual and followed him up onto the open decks.

They spent the next two hours switching off at the controls and test flying the little drone around the *Junebug*. When they began to get a feel for the surprisingly simple system, they sent the Scout further and further away, navigating by the images that appeared on the console screen and the GPS data that was constantly fed back to them by the UAV's onboard navigation system. On a last flight before dinner, they sent the Scout out to its longest rated range of two miles. There wasn't much to see except white caps and a school a bait fish being chased by a shark, but the system never faltered and the images were crystal clear.

Duke Field, Eglin AFB Complex

"So how do I log this?" The sensor operator perched next to the pilot in a darkened, soundproofed cinder-block building at Eglin's Auxiliary Field #3, his fingers poised over a keyboard. The pilot kept his eyes on the screen before him which was showing nothing but Caribbean white caps and a school of dolphins at the moment. "Systems check—open water—long range," the pilot mumbled into the microphone in front of his mouth, "authority: CG, 96th Test Wing."

"What's General Mills doing snooping around Cuba," the sensor operator sniggered, "looking for a new place to open a cereal factory?"

"Focus," said the pilot as he brought the RQ-4 Global Hawk onto a heading to overfly *Cayo Piedra* at 10,000 feet AGL on a southwest to northeast pass parallel to the Cuban coast. "We're coming up on the GPS intersect. Roll tape."

With a recorder rolling and the Tier II Global Hawk performing beautifully, the Mission Control Element watched their screens casually. They weren't really looking for anything in particular. There was no area or object specified in their mission brief. It was just a flight test plus a systems check coupled with a little clandestine aerial reconnaissance over an island off the Cuban coast. They certainly weren't seeing anything special as the Global Hawk Block 30 model flew straight and level over the objective area at 300 knots indicated with bright sunlight flashing off its 130-foot wing-span.

The pilot brought the bird around to a reciprocal heading as the sensor operator zoomed the cameras for a closer look. Courtesy of the drone's sensitive optics, they were seeing and recording images of what looked like some rich play-boy's island refuge. There was nothing much of interest be-yond an L-shaped concrete structure that was probably a residence, another smaller building with a swimming pool, and a huge yacht that was chugging slowly toward a long pier.

"That's some big bucks for you." The pilot put the Hawk into a slow left hand turn. "Wonder who owns that little is-land hideaway?" The sensor operator was rolling in some more magnification on his optical system whiz-wheel. "Drop it down for me. Let's do a low-fast pass in the other direction. I'm seeing what looks like bunkers or something around the biggest building and something under a camo-net at the far north point of the small island."

The pilot made the necessary flap and power adjustments to bring the Hawk into a dive and then leveled off at 2,500 feet AGL for another pass over the island. "Oh, shit!" The pilot saw a man in uniform step out of a bunker at the corner of the block structure. He was shouldering a long, dark tube. "What's he doing?" Before they could speculate, both men saw the tell-tale launch signature of a man-portable anti-air-craft missile. The Global Hawk's missile warning system be-gan to scream as the pilot jinked the drone hard left, poured on the power and clawed for altitude. The sensor operator hit a switch on his console to activate the onboard jamming sys-tem and chewed on a lip until the altitude indicator showed 5,000 feet.

"Looked like a Grail—SA-7—heat-seeker," he said. "They max out at around fifteen hundred." Both men sat qui-etly, eyes fixed on the altitude indicator. When it read 10,000 feet, the sensor operator sat back and scratched at the sweat pooled beneath his flightsuit. "We should be clear."

"Some sonofabitch took a missile shot at us!"

"Better bring it home." The sensor operator reached for the direct line to wing operations. "I'll call it in. They're gonna want to see the tape."

"Yeah, Doc, I understand you're pissed." Lieutenant General Gordo Fowler had been listening to the Air Force general's rant about the missile attack on the UAV off the coast of Cuba for the past five minutes. "Just report it up the chain according to SOP. If they want to know who steered you down toward Cuba on a test flight, just send 'em my way. They didn't hit the thing and you might have done some good for us. Don't worry about it. I'll keep your skirts clean." Fowler hung up and reached for his personal phone. He hit the speed dial and waited, listening to the beeps and static rush of a secure frequency, until the man in Havana answered.

"I think you're onto something," he said. "We overflew the island and they fired a missile at the drone. That's out of character even for the Cubans. I haven't seen the tapes, probably won't until I get back off the road if they'll even let me, but my gut says there's something on that shitty little island that they think is worth risking an international incident."

The man who calls himself Bayer explained that he had "certain assets" heading toward Cuba with the gear to take a closer look. "Have you got anything down this way that might serve as back-up for my people?"

"That depends on who your people are and what they've got in mind."

"It's Shake Davis and Mike Stokey."

"Damn, I should have known. Shake's just bound and determined to get himself killed or caught, isn't he?"

"They're aboard a private yacht in Cuban waters, Gordo, supposed to be competing in a fishing tournament, but they've got a small drone aboard. It was Shake's bright idea, but I'm worried it might get too heavy for them."

"Well, that's a valid concern at this point. Listen, I've got a team of MARSOC operators doing quals down on Andros Island. Give me Shake's contact information and make sure he's got mine. I'll see what I can do to help him out."

Ground Zero

Carlos Ruiz-Romero sat staring out the window of his little room wondering why he was not being taken out for his nightly exercise period. Likely it had to do with this afternoon's excitement. Shortly after his noon meal, there had been what he presumed to be a missile launch from one of the positions surrounding the courtyard. While he was eating, he'd heard shouts and a large bang followed by a whooshing sound. By the time he'd reached the window to take a look, all he could see were soldiers running in different directions. Some of them had launchers shouldered and all of them were staring at the sky.

He began to pace around the room, trying to figure it out based on what he'd seen and could speculate. The little shoulder-fired missile launchers were designed to engage aerial targets. He didn't know the technical details, but he'd seen enough battlefield coverage to understand how they were used against low-flying helicopters in places like Iraq and Afghanistan. So—some low-flying aircraft had likely intruded on Ground Zero's airspace. Maybe it was a surveillance aircraft, a drone or a helicopter? And where would something like that come from?

The only likely source was the United States. The Cubans wouldn't be shooting at commercial or private aircraft—at least they never had before. So maybe it was an American military aircraft from Florida, or maybe even Guantanamo Bay? He'd seen plenty of them during his stay there and he'd arrived aboard one of the Marines' tilt-rotors.

But they were extremely loud, and he hadn't heard any engine noises before the uproar started. About 10 minutes after the missile shot, a senior soldier had barged into his room and looked around in a panic. The only response to his questions about what was happening outside was a terse command to shut up. Shortly after the senior man left, two more soldiers arrived and completely tossed his room, obviously searching for something. They found nothing because he had nothing to hide. When they finally left, they took his radio with them.

And now it was well past the usual time for his nightly exercise session. Tomorrow would tell the tale, but it seemed likely that he might not be allowed outside at night any longer. Carlos continued to mull over the possibilities with a small glimmer of hope forming as he did his regular exercise routine on the floor of his room. The S and the O were complete but he couldn't be sure about the final S. To make it clear, he needed a couple more days of trampling saw grass.

General Enrique Constanza studied the photo in his hand for a few long moments and then tossed it on his desk amid a pile of other photos showing the known inventory of U.S. drones. "This is everything?"

"This is everything listed in the threat aviation order of battle, sir." His pawed the pile of photographs—some clear and detailed; recently copied from internet sites and some indistinct and grainy from clandestine sources—and attempted to put them in some sort of order on his general's cluttered desktop. "There may be a few very new RPVs for which we don't have imagery, but these are the ones most often used by the American Air Force and Navy."

"RPV?" The general stared at his aide and swept his hand over the pile. "I asked for photos of all the current American UAVs."

"For some reason the American Air Force now refers to their drones as Remotely Piloted Vehicles or Aircraft rather than drones or Unmanned Aerial Vehicles. It's the same thing, General." He plucked one of the photos out of the pile, "This is the one that the officer in charge says flew over *Punto Cero*."

General Constanza took the photo and examined it with a magnifying glass. It was a strange looking thing with a bulbous nose, v-tail, and jet engine mounted atop the fuselage. The wings were thin and barely looked sturdy enough to keep it airborne. "RQ-4 Global Hawk," he said reading the caption.

"Full specifications are on the back of the photo, sir. The drone in the picture shows U.S. Air Force markings but the guard force at *Punto Cero* all swear that the one they saw had no markings. It was painted a sort of haze-grey or light blue."

"Typical," Constanza said. "They aren't going to advertise on a mission that involves flying through restricted airspace, are they? The range is listed at twelve-thousand nautical miles or more—normal operating altitude from twenty- to thirty-thousand feet."

"Yes, sir. I would have said it was just a random over flight. The Americans have been known to fly through our airspace on reconnaissance missions before. But this one made several passes, the last one at lower level."

"So, they were looking for something on the island."

"Obviously, General—but there was nothing for them to see. The over flight occurred at 1345 and there was no one outside the building except for the security guards."

"One of which launched a Strela at this Global Hawk drone."

"Correct, sir. The officer in charge said the SA-7 indicated a lock, but the drone was just out of range when the gunner fired. The SAM site at the north end of the island did not engage due to malfunctioning fire control radar."

General Constanza slumped in his desk chair and waved for his aide to dispose of the file photos. "Thankfully, the MANPADS gunner missed. If we had managed shoot the damn thing down, we'd never hear the end of it. Something like that is not what we need with the American normalization team in Havana."

"The *Aquarama II* was just pulling back into the jetty from some engine tests. They know its Fidel's pride and joy.

Maybe they thought he was aboard; maybe they were interested in that."

"Maybe," the general mused aloud. "They might be cozy with Raul these days, but the Americans are still afraid of Fidel. Just look at the news reports: one week Fidel is alive, the next he's dead." General Constanza walked over to a window and stared at a gathering of Military Intelligence cadets gathered in a lecture circle outside his headquarters building. "Who else knows about this incident?"

"No one as far as I know, sir." The aide closed the file folder and stood waiting for orders. "The security force is our men, our responsibility. They made only the initial report to this headquarters and have been instructed to say nothing further to anyone as you ordered."

"We'll keep it that way for now. When I have more information, I'll make the formal incident report."

"Was there anything else, sir?"

"Nothing for right now, but I may want to visit *Punto Cero* on short notice. See that there is a helicopter standing by."

When his aide was gone, General Enrique Constanza returned to his desk and distracted himself with pending paperwork. He had no intention of making any formal incident report, especially one that would inevitably come to the attention of Director General Manuel Panteros. If that nefarious bastard found out *Punto Cero* had been over flown by an American drone, he would likely panic and destroy any evidence of the scheme to cut a private deal with the Russians. That would be the end of Carlos Ruiz-Romero and the end of the expected windfall that would set Enrique Constanza up as a very powerful man in the new Cuba.

North of the Cuban Coastline

Ralph Bartlett was wrapping red tape around one of the white plastic fenders that the *Junebug* carried to put over the side when the boat was docked or moored alongside another vessel. A line of these 24-inch plastic tubes, secured to cleats by line and hung over the side, kept the hull and deck edges from being damaged as a moored boat ground against a dock or jetty in a swell. Every smart skipper used fenders, and they were among the most common pieces of boating equipment seen in harbors everywhere around the world. Which is why the Steamer decided they would be the perfect hiding place for the .45 caliber pistols Shake and Mike brought aboard and unlikely to draw any kind of scrutiny from the Cuban *Guarda Fronteras* officials when they inspected the *Junebug*.

"I cut a section out of this one," he said, "and put the pistols inside wrapped in plastic. Then I used a soldering iron to reseal the cut. Your ammo's inside there too." Steamer held the finished product up for all to see. Even on close inspection, it looked like nothing more than a well-used and slightly dinged boating fender. "Just be sure when we tie up that the one with the red tape goes over the side next to the dock. They ain't gonna dick around checking fenders for contraband."

"Got it." Shake helped place the modified fender in a deck locker and then checked his watch. "What's next?"

"Now I call the Harbor Master at Hemingway Marina and the fun begins." He stood with one foot on the ladder leading up to the flying bridge. "You guys decided what we're gonna tell them when they find that drone?"

"It's a fish-finder, right?" Mike Stokey had recorded a few aerial shots of schooling fish during their practice flights on the trip down. "If they want to see how it works, we just roll some video and they'll get the idea."

"They probably won't be interested past the first couple of twenties that they pocket," Bartlett said as he climbed toward the VHF radio console on the bridge. "Just smile a lot and don't talk much unless they ask you a direct question. And Shake—try not to look like an old heathen on a trip down here to kill commies."

Bartlett plucked the VHF handset from his overhead console and checked to see the radio was set to Channel 16. "Havana Harbor Master...Havana Harbor Master...this is private vessel *Junebug*. We are about eight kilometers due north of you. We're requesting permission to approach for inspection and docking instructions."

There was some static-filled delay and then a voice responded through the cockpit speakers. The person on the other radio was speaking accented English. "*Junebug* this is Harbor Master. State your vessel details."

"Harbor Master, this is vessel *Junebug*, fifty-four-foot Chris Craft, American flag, registered in Key West, Florida. Our last port was Key West. We are headed for Hemingway Marina to participate in the billfish tournament and should arrive..." Bartlett checked his instruments and then his watch. "...in approximately one hour. We have five persons aboard."

There was some more delay but Bartlett just smiled and nodded. "They're probably looking us up in the known vessel logs."

"*Bienvenidos, Junebug.* You may proceed toward Hemingway Marina but do not enter. When you are within sight of the Marina, contact us for docking instructions."

"Copy all, Harbor Master. We will be in touch shortly."

Bartlett swung the wheel and goosed the throttles to send the *Junebug* churning toward the Cuban mainland. "You guys get below and tell June to lay out the paperwork. Have Linda stand by with cold beer and sodas. They probably won't take one but it never hurts to offer. Then get back on deck—one of you forward and the other aft—to handle lines and fenders. Don't forget about the one with the red tape."

Hemingway Marina was really a series of canals cut into the coastline. There were boats flying a number of international flags moored throughout the area, either waiting or partying in anticipation of the starting gun for the International Billfish Tournament. Bartlett maneuvered to point the bow toward the harbor entrance, fiddled with the engine and steering controls to hold position and reached for his radio handset.

"Harbor Master, vessel *Junebug* holding at the mouth of the harbor for docking instructions." He studied the marina complex through his binoculars and saw what looked like a hell of party going on in the third canal to his left. "We'd like to tie up in canal number three near *Cerca de Piscina* if you've got room for us."

"Vessel *Junebug*…Harbor Master…proceed with caution to canal number three. Your mooring will be at number eight. Do not attempt to come ashore. Secure your vessel and then stand by for inspections."

"Here we go," Bartlett shouted down to Mike and Shake on deck. "Stand by with lines and fenders."

As the *Junebug* maneuvered into a mooring point in canal three, they could hear raucous music from a Cuban *bolero* band that was entertaining celebrants near a huge swimming pool. It looked like a good number of the tournament fishermen were getting a head start on the festivities. A couple of hands in sweat-stained OD uniforms took the lines Mike and Shake passed and wrapped them loosely around pier-side bollards. Shake hustled all along the port side of the boat facing the sea wall and put the fenders over the side. The one with the red tape was amidships where it would be most difficult to retrieve.

With the engines and electronics shut down, Bartlett descended from the bridge and stretched. "Won't be long before the bureaucrat parade starts," he said. "Remember, nod, smile and act like dumb-shit gringos delighted to be visiting the Cuban workers' paradise. Let's go below and get a beer."

Three *Guarda Fronteras* officials scrambled aboard about 15 minutes later. They were all in faded uniforms that had been sun-bleached to an off-white khaki color. One man who appeared to be senior, took a seat on a couch, looked around and then turned his attention to Linda and June who were smiling at their visitors, wearing halter tops and shorts that showed off the tans they'd acquired during the trip from Key West. The second official seemed to be the admin guy. He perched a pair of crooked reading glasses on his nose and began to scrutinize passports and papers at the little dinette table. As he examined each passport, he looked up over his readers to match the smiling gringo faces in the cabin with the photos in the documents. Shake noted that Steamer had put a crisply folded twenty-dollar bill in each passport which the official pocketed when he was done with his reading. When he got to the tournament registration letter, he turned and handed it to the senior man who had yet to say a word.

"This requires a one hundred dollar additional fee for our fish and game department," he said in good English. When no one responded immediately, he locked eyes with each of the three men gathered in the main cabin and then cleared his throat. "This fee is due and payable before any fishing can begin."

"Can we take care of it now?" Bartlett got up from his seat and dug in a pocket.

The senior man merely nodded and held out his hand. When Steamer handed over a folded sheaf of bills, he stuffed it in his shirt pocket without counting. "Payment will be noted on your cruising permit." He went back to staring at the women. Linda offered him a cold soda from the little fridge in the cabin and he accepted with the barest hint of a smile.

While the paperwork and payola was being handled in the main cabin, the third *Guarda Fronteras* official, presumably the junior man and worker bee in the party was busily searching the forward cabins, heads, cupboards and lockers all over the boat. When he passed through to begin his inspection of the weather decks and bridge areas, Shake followed to see if he could get a feel for how they were doing. The underling didn't seem very surprised to hear the visiting gringo speaking fairly fluent Spanish.

"Looks like you get all the hard jobs, my friend."

"I haven't been here very long." The official opened a row of lockers and compartments but didn't seem overly curious about what he was seeing. "I just got posted from Cienfuegos."

"I'll bet you're gonna be very busy in a little while, when the travel restrictions are lifted."

The official snapped off the little flashlight he was using to examine the *Junebug*'s chart locker and turned to glare at Shake.

"Sorry, my friend," Shake shrugged and smiled. "I was just trying to make conversation." He pulled a cold beer out of Bartlett's stand-by cooler, wrapped a twenty around it and offered it to the inspector. The man softened his stance a bit, waved off the drink, and pocketed the bill.

"Got any tips on where we can find the big fish?"

"There are big fish everywhere in these waters. It's just a matter of using the right bait."

"You gonna be much longer?" Shake pointed through the windscreen at the party by the swimming pool. There was a bevy of scantily-clad dancers jumping around the bandstand at that point. "We'd like to get ashore and join the party."

"I'm through here," he said heading for the ladder leading below. "You can go ashore when customs and the medics are finished with you."

The Customs inspection was fairly perfunctory, involving mainly questions about firearms and liquor plus another stem to stern search of the boat. One of the customs agents expressed some interest in the Scout drone rig but he lost enthusiasm when Mike showed him some recorded sequences of blue water and bait-fish. Apparently, this was not the first high-tech gringo fish-finder he'd seen in his time. The aged veterinarian who came aboard last satisfied himself that they had no pet dogs or cats aboard and then went through June's freezer, carefully looking for provisions that might contain bird bones. He left after he consumed two beers and pocketed forty U.S. dollars. Two hours later, just as they were sitting down to a quick lunch, a *Guarda Fronteras* courier arrived with their cruising permit.

After their meal, Bartlett maneuvered the Junebug to the other side of the marina where they paid outrageous prices for low-grade diesel fuel to replenish their main tanks. When they were back at the assigned slip, they erected an awning on the after weather deck and sat around watching the party at the swimming pool which showed no signs of slowing or diminishing. Crowds from the moored boats were coming and going from the festivities in various levels of intoxication. Apparently Cuban communists were willing to overlook capitalist excess on certain occasions such as a big fishing tournament about to launch out of Marina Hemingway just nine miles west of their capital city.

Shake squinted through the afternoon glare at the line of moored yachts off their starboard side. The boats were richly appointed and well-equipped, flying national standards from all over the world. These were the kind of expensive vessels owned by sportsmen with enough money and leisure time to chase the giant marlin that cruised the underwater canyons off the Cuban coast. Most of the skippers seemed to know one another and those that were not at the swimming pool were partying in a more sedate manner aboard their boats.

"I can spot at least three other American boats," he said. "At least we won't stick out like a PFC in the Pentagon."

"We probably won't even see too many other boats once the tournament starts." June Bartlett looked up from the reel she was oiling. "Every fisherman has got his favorite spot and they like to stay spread out. They're all afraid some other skipper is gonna poach their big fish honey-hole."

"How's it work?" Linda Stokey asked as she mixed a jug of lemonade and spiked it with tequila. "I mean, it's a tournament, right? So they've gotta have judges and records and things like that."

"Boats can work anywhere they want, but they need to be back here by a designated time to register their catch with the Tournament Committee. A team of officials measure and weigh the billfish from each boat. There are a number of different prizes awarded at the end of it all, but it's mostly about bragging rights. The people who can afford to compete don't need prize money."

"So if we come in skunked we won't raise any eyebrows?" Shake saw a few Cuban police and coast guard people strolling along the jetty, but they seemed more interested in the parties on the boats than anything else.

"Won't be a problem," June said. "Lots of boats come in with nothing to show for a day's fishing. Some skippers stay out all night if they've had a bad day. Anyway…" She opened a locker near the stern transom and shook out a dark blue pennant with a leaping billfish in the center. "I don't intend to get skunked."

"We get underway tomorrow morning at dawn," Steamer said. "Or maybe we'll leave a little before that. This place is gonna be a zoo with a bunch of hung-over skippers trying to maneuver out of the harbor."

Mike Stokey jumped as his cell phone buzzed in a pocket and then pulled it out to check an incoming message. "Text from you know who." He handed the phone to Shake. "He wants you to call him ASAP on that number."

"Why didn't he just call me direct? That's what he usually does." Shake carried Mike's phone up to the bridge of the *Junebug* and got comfortable in the Captain's chair. The man who calls himself Bayer answered after the first ring.

"What's the deal? You lose your phone?"

"No—lost my job. I'm at the airport booked on a flight that leaves in about twenty minutes."

"What do you mean lost your job?"

"I shot my mouth off one too many times, I guess. Yesterday afternoon the Task Force director called me in to inform me that my services were no longer needed in Havana. They're bringing in some toe-the-line yes-man from Homeland Security who will keep his mouth shut and do as he's told. I don't know what they know or suspect, so I switched phones to my back-up number. We'll use it from now on."

"Are they likely to sic the dogs on us?"

"Hard to say, Shake. I didn't get any indication of what's on their minds. They obviously know about what happened down at Gitmo by now. Somebody might connect the two of us from past activities. State Department and the White House are obsessed with the goddamn normalization thing. Who knows what they might do—to me or to you. If you want to pull out, I'll understand."

"And that would be the end of Carlos and a huge hit for national security. You're not gonna let that happen, and neither am I."

"I was hoping you'd say that. You aboard the boat?"

"Yeah, we're at a Marina west of Havana. Tournament starts tomorrow and you know where we'll be heading."

"That's the spot, Shake. I'm almost sure it is. General Fowler had a drone fly over it yesterday. I asked him to do it and that might be another reason for my abrupt departure. Anyway, they overflew the island and somebody shot a missile at the damn thing. "

"They see anything interesting?"

"Not that Gordo knows about. He's on the road and hasn't seen the video but you've gotta believe they're in protective mode big time out there. Be very careful."

"Sounds like you've got General Fowler read into this deal. That might be helpful."

"Hopefully, but he's on the Administration shit-list. I asked him for some back-up in case you need it. He's got your contacts. Have you got his?"

"Yeah, he gave me his personals after the deal down in Belize."

"Good. You two need to talk soonest. I'll be in touch as soon as I get my feet on the ground back in Washington. If you've got anything for me, use this number."

Mike and Ralph climbed onto the bridge to find Shake deep in thought, staring through the windscreen at the parties on nearby boats. "You don't look happy," Mike retrieved his phone and stuffed it in a pocket. "Anything we need to know?"

"They shit-canned Bayer from the Normalization Task Force. He's headed home."

"Ouch! What's that do to the mission?"

"Depends on what we decide to do, I guess. Could be we're compromised. You guys get a vote. What do you think?"

"I say we go fishing." Bartlett reached into a cooler and wiped the sweat off a beer can.

"It might be better if we don't come back here once we leave in the morning. We got the gear to do that, Steamer?"

"Depends on how much milling around we do at sea. If we conserve, we'll be OK. The tanks are topped off and we've got that bladder up forward."

"Riddle me this, Shake." Mike Stokey closed the lid on the beer cooler and sat on it. "Suppose we find out our guy is on that island. What are we gonna do about it? You thinking the three of us just go in there ninja-style and kidnap him back?"

"My original plan was to use the drone to locate him for sure. Then we call Bayer with the evidence and he gets the SEALs or somebody like that to do a rescue."

"We might want to re-think that."

"Yeah, I need to call Gordo Fowler. Hopefully, he'll have some ideas."

Andros Island

The six-man team of Marine Critical Skills Operators had been on the southernmost Andros Island for nearly two weeks. Their original mission in this remote part of the Bahamas was learning to survive and operate effectively in the bug-infested mangrove estuaries and tidal swamps. Their parent command, the newly and officially titled Marine Raider Regiment, was big on training in the most adverse conditions available. Andros Island qualified as adverse and then some anywhere south of the only real settlement of Andros Town. The training had been mostly about navigating through the muck and mire, day and night, until it became repetitive and boring.

At that point, they took to doing clandestine reconnaissance on a little refugee camp that housed Cuban escapees who holed up on Andros until they were eventually plucked off the islands by paid refugee runners and taken to the U.S. or to one of the nearby Caribbean nations. The reconnaissance eventually turned into an unofficial Humanitarian Assistance mission when the Marines discovered how poorly the refugees fared. They began to help find and purify water, build shelters and distribute what food they could spare from their own meager supplies. That was sufficient distraction until an Osprey arrived carrying a representative from Special Operations Command in Miami.

Now they sat around a small, smoky camp fire in the middle of a muggy mangrove swamp, trying to ignore the swarms of mosquitoes buzzing around their heads and pay attention to the briefing. The SOCOM Major doing the talking had arrived just an hour before to cancel their training exercise and pitch a new mission, a real-world mission that would be very dark, very risky, and quite probably illegal as hell.

"So it's a four-man tasking, right, sir?" The solidly-built Marine Gunnery Sergeant who was in charge of the team training on Andros looked around at his junior men. If they decided to go, he'd be hard-pressed picking two to stay behind. These guys were Marine Raiders because they wanted to be in on any available action.

"That's the deal, Gunny Simmons." The major squeezed insect repellant out of a little OD bottle one of the operators provided shortly after he came ashore and slathered it on his neck and face. "And that's a hard number—General Fowler wants the smallest possible footprint on this thing."

"Just so I'm tracking here, sir." One of the corporals on the team rapped a can of Copenhagen against his knuckles, extracted a sizeable pinch and tucked into his lower lip. "The mission is to join up with civilians on a yacht and then stage a rescue of some American dude that the Cubans are holding on an island off their coast?"

"That's the short of it. The hostage is a very valuable DIA civilian that we think the Cubans are trying to sell off for his Intel value. He disappears into the ozone where he can be interrogated and it's very bad news for our country. If it helps, the civilians involved are a couple of Marines and the boat is owned by a retired Navy three-striper. One of the Marines, a retired Gunner by the name of Shake Davis, is a bit of a legend in our community. Some of you may have heard his name mentioned in connection with Vietnam, Beirut, and some other deals."

"Shake Davis?" Gunnery Sergeant Henry Simmons Junior laughed and stood to stretch the kinks out of his leg muscles. "That dude was in Vietnam with my Dad. I grew up hearing Shake Davis stories. The guy's got a rack of decorations that would make the Commandant blush. You talk about your Recon rock-and-roller, you're talking about Gunner Shake Davis. If he's in, I'm in, Major. How's it gonna work?"

"How about the rest of you?" The Major barely had the question asked when he saw six hands sticking in the air and all of them showed a thumbs-up.

"OK, the Gunny makes the selection. Two men remain here to clean up, secure the gear, and stand by for return to Lejeune. The other four put together a raid package and we move the people and gear to the Cayman Islands. If the raid is a go, the civilian boat picks you up and takes you to the objective. The detailed briefing comes from Gunner Davis, but Gunny Simmons is mission commander." The major stood, checked his watch and scanned the sky over Andros Island.

"The Osprey that brought me in is due back in about an hour. They've got some extra gear, an IBS, and live ammo aboard. Once you've done the prep and put the package in best shape possible, we'll fly the team to Little Brac in the Caymans where you stand by for launch." He handed the Gunny a small notebook. "This is burn before reading stuff, Gunny. It's got all we know about the situation right now plus the Opsec procedures and the Gunner's cell phone number. When you're set up on Little Brac, you give him a call. He's expecting to hear from you."

The major and Gunny Simmons walked away for a private word while the rest of the team began to police the harbor site and pack personal gear. "Just how dark is this thing, sir?" Gunny Simmons asked.

"It's so dark its damn near invisible, Gunny. You tell your selected people whatever you think is best, but the truth is that we've got to be deniable on this thing. Even if we pull it off, no one is ever gonna know who did it. From a political standpoint, it will likely blow this whole Cuba normalization thing right out of the water. And that is not gonna please our civilian leaders in Washington."

"Well, as I've been known to say in the past, sir: Fuck our political leaders in Washington and the horse they rode in on. Going dark and staying that way ain't what bothers me or any of my Raiders. That's SOP. What worries me is what if somebody gets dinged bad or even killed. Something like that happens on one of these clandestine deals and people start preferring charges and denying benefits and like that, right?"

"You know I asked General Fowler about that very thing when he sent me out here to brief you guys."

"What did he say?"

"He told me to promise you that he will never, ever, under any circumstances let something like that happen."

"Damn, Major. That's pretty bold."

"That's right, Gunny—so is General Fowler—and so is Gunner Davis. Whatever happens on this deal, they've got your six."

Aboard *Junebug* in the *Golfo de Batabano*

It had been a long, high-speed run from Marina Hemingway, west along the northern coast of Cuba before Steamer Bartlett sighted *Cayo San Antonio* and made a turn south to round the island's far western point. They reduced speed and put a couple of unbaited lines over the transom once they made the turn back east heading into the *Golfo de Batabano*. With Linda and June Bartlett in the fishing chairs aft, they steered for the mouth of the Bay of Pigs where Bartlett planned to turn south once again and bring the boat past *Cayo Piedra* at a distance of two nautical miles or better.

They'd seen a few other tournament boats during the trip, most of them working off the north end of the island. As they motored past *Cayo Corrientes*, they passed a *Guarda Fronteras* vessel, a Russian-built Stenka-class patrol boat with twin 30mm guns mounted fore and aft. The Cubans studied them closely through binoculars and did not return friendly waves from the ladies on *Junebug*. "No sweat," Bartlett told Shake and Mike as they watched the vessel pass headed in the opposite direction. "They've got the name and description of all the tournament boats. They won't bother us." After that they were mostly alone on the water with the exception of one Canadian boat that was fishing the waters around *Isla de Juventud*. The Canadians did return their waves.

It was late afternoon when they made the turn south. June Bartlett plugged her deep-sea rod into the chair socket and climbed up to the flying bridge where her husband was study-ing the GPS. "I don't see why we can't actually fish while we're out here spying."

"Have a glass of wine and relax, June." Bartlett swept a hand at the horizon. "We're less than an hour away from the island. Soon as we get set up out there, I'll troll and you can put some real lures in the water."

Shake's phone buzzed while he and Mike were program-ming the Scout drone for the first pass over *Cayo Piedra*. This one was planned for after dark, so there was some tweaking to do on the camera settings. Shake looked at the screen, but all he saw was a message that told him caller ID was blocked. He connected and answered cautiously.

"Hello?"

"Is this Mr. Davis?" He didn't recognize the voice but the gravel tone and clipped tenor were familiar. The caller was likely military and had spent more than a little time shouting commands.

"It could be. Who's this?"

"My name is Puller—Chesty Puller. I was told you'd be expecting my call."

Shake grinned and showed a thumbs-up to Mike. They'd been waiting for this. General Fowler said they'd be getting a call from the NCOiC of a Marine Raider team who would identify himself as the legendary Marine officer; a name every Marine worldwide would instantly recognize.

"Chesty, I'm very happy to hear from you. Can I assume you're in place at the designated spot?"

"We're there, Mr. Davis. If you approach the little place from the north you'll see a sign on the beach. Do you think you can find it?"

"Is it standard sign or neon?"

"It's a neon sign, sir. I'll send you some GPS information. Can I use this number?"

"That will be fine, Chesty. We have a few things to do and then we'll be heading in your direction."

"We'll be waiting, Mr. Davis. Hope to see you soon. My Dad sends his best regards."

The connection broke down, leaving Shake wondering about the caller's last comment. There was nothing about fathers or family in General Fowler's Opsec briefing. If he was missing something, he hoped it wasn't important.

"That was the call from our Marines." He pocketed the phone and moved across the cabin to look over Mike's shoulder. The night camera settings were almost complete and they were ready to make a test run as soon as it got a little darker.

"They all set?"

"According to Chesty Puller, they are standing by for word from us. They've got an IR beacon set up on the northern beach at Little Brac. He's sending us GPS data. You take the Scout topside for the test flight. I'm gonna check with Steamer and make sure we've got some kind of optics aboard that can see IR."

"I think we have a deal, Manuel. Can you come by the office?" General Enrique Constanza's aide looked up from the transcript of the phone call MI monitored from the Russian embassy. "Those were the exact words used."

"So the meeting will be at the embassy. Any indication of when?"

"No, sir, but we've got men watching. We'll know immediately when he leaves his headquarters."

"Probably just as soon as he finishes doing handsprings." General Constanza stood and pointed at the pre-packed bags in the corner of his office. "Get our gear out to the helicopter, round up the security detail—just the two men we designated—and then let's get out to *Punto Cero.* The Russians will want to see what they are buying before they pay for it. I want to be there in case Manuel Panteros decides to change the terms of our agreement."

A uniformed guard met Manuel Panteros' car at the Russian Embassy compound on Playa Miramar, cleared him through the gate and then turned him over to a gruff-looking civilian who greeted him in Spanish. "If you'll follow me, sir—the meeting is up on the third floor."

They rode a clanking, jerking elevator upward and then exited in a long sterile corridor. There were two locked doors opposite each other mid-way along, but their destination was the third door at the far end of the hallway. His escort punched numbers into a keypad and when the lock clicked, he pushed the door open and motioned for Cuba's Director General of Intelligence to enter. Manuel Panteros stepped inside and stood looking around a small, nearly airless cubicle as the heavy security door shut behind him with a resounding thud. He'd never been in this part of the Russian Embassy before and the security arrangements were something he coveted for his own offices across town. He stared at the dark, unblinking eye of a surveillance camera mounted high above a second door and waited.

The junior of the two GRU men opened the door to the inner sanctum and Panteros followed him into what looked like either a soundproof site for enhanced interrogations or a very secure communications center. He glanced at the sophisticated console in the middle of the table and decided it was the latter, likely the place where the GRU men talked over a secure circuit to their bosses in Moscow.

The senior GRU man was seated at the head of the table next to a silver serving tray that held glasses and a bottle of vodka stuffed into an ice bucket. "Please come in and sit down, Manuel." He smiled and pointed at the vodka. "We're all set to drink a toast."

"And so—we have a deal?" Panteros slid into a chair and folded his hands on the table. Both GRU intermediaries were wearing big grins and he thought that was encouraging. Maybe they could finally get this thing done and dusted.

"We have a deal, my friend…" The senior GRU man leaned forward and tapped the table with a thick finger. "…for ten million U.S. dollars."

Panteros tried to hide his anger at the squeeze, tried to ignore the smug looks on the GRU men's faces as they waited for his response. "That is unacceptable. You know the asking price and that has not changed."

"What has changed," said the junior GRU agent, "is Moscow's position on your proposal. It seems Carlos Ruiz-Romero is not as valuable to us as you thought." He pointed at the console in the middle of the table. "If you wish to talk directly to Moscow Central, it can be arranged."

Manuel Panteros had absolutely no desire to speak with Moscow Central. He'd had some previous dealings with them and nothing ever went well. His counterpart in Moscow, the man ultimately behind this proposed deal with the Russian Federation, was General Igor Surkov, who considered all Cubans flunkies or lackeys. His often expressed opinion of Cuban intelligence was less than complimentary. If he got on the phone with that man, the price might plummet even more—or the deal might collapse entirely. For lack of anything better to do at the moment, he simply crossed his arms and glared at the smiling men across the table from him.

The senior GRU man used both hands to rotate the vodka bottle in its ice bucket. "As I think you once told us in your office, Manuel: The price is not negotiable."

"You know there are other countries that would gladly pay what's being asked."

"Yes, I'm sure Venezuela might bite," the Senior GRU man popped the cork on the vodka bottle to let the liquor breathe. "Or maybe even some little shit-hole like Guatemala, but could you trust them? Could you be sure they wouldn't fold under pressure? Could you be sure they wouldn't betray you?"

Manuel Panteros felt the sweat pooling in his armpits. He needed to do something before it showed through his shirt. There really was no Plan B. He'd been so sure of the Russians that he hadn't made one. Perhaps if he accepted this deal, if he allowed himself to be short-changed, it might buy

him some favors from the Russians down the road after normalization. It was a much smaller cake, but he might be able
to bump Constanza and eat it all. He needed a little time.

"You understand," he said to the senior GRU man, "if I
accept this deal, I will demand cash—no negotiable instruments or anything of that sort—cash only, in U.S. dollars."

The senior man began to pour vodka into glasses. He'd
been expecting something like that, and Director General
Surkov indicated he would send a diplomatic courier with
the money if they made a deal. "We can have it for you by
the end of the week. Do we have a deal?"

"We have a deal."

The senior man slid a glass across the table top. "Then
let's drink to our deal with good Russian vodka."

June Bartlett had hooked a sizeable snapper shortly after she was allowed to put a lure in the water and she was below preparing chunks of it for their dinner. It was nearly dark and her husband had the boat throttled back, barely making way as they drilled a long oblong pattern in the Caribbean just under two nautical miles to the seaward side of *Cayo Piedra*. Not that it really made much difference, but their position put them right on the edge of Cuban territorial waters at the 12-mile limit. They were cruising with minimal light showing besides the port and starboard running lights on the cross-tree above the flying bridge.

Shake was busy rigging the after awning so they could fly the drone without showing too much light from the LED screen. Linda Stokey was holding a hooded flashlight for her husband who was putting final GPS settings into the Scout drone. There was very little wind beyond a slight breeze, and even that was blowing in the right direction. They planned to launch the first reconnaissance flight as soon as Mike, who had proved to be the better remote pilot, declared the system ready.

"It's amazing how little noise this thing makes," he said when Shake came to check on his progress. "It's got to be really close for you to hear it and even then it just sounds like a little bird or a big bug."

"It's designed for clandestine surveillance, brother. Awning's rigged. We can launch whenever you say."

Mike hit a button to activate the night camera and wiggled a joystick to maneuver the lens around the deck. The screen showed the familiar green and yellow images they had both seen hundreds of times looking through the dark on all sorts of military devices. He aimed it at Linda and laughed. "Damn, girl, you even look good on a night vision device."

"Let's launch this thing," she said. "I'm ready for dinner."

Ground Zero

General Enrique Constanza and his aide were taking the night air on the northern part of the island complex, walking back south after checking with the soldiers manning an SA-8 Surface to Air Missile launcher located at the far northern end of the island. It was not an encouraging visit. The three missiles in the Transporter-Erector-Launcher were showing signs of rust and corrosion from the sea air, and the senior NCO reported that their targeting radar was out of commission and had been for the past month.

"You'd think they'd send someone out to fix it," the aide commented as they strolled past the pool and guest house where the Castro's housed the few select VIPs they allowed to visit the island. "If Fidel or Raul were here, they would."

"Yes," said the General as they approached the 700-foot bridge that connected the northern and southern islets, "and if that SAM site was operational when the Americans sent the drone, we might all be standing in front of a firing squad." The general returned the salute from the sentry at the bridge and continued to walk. "What do we hear from Havana?"

"I checked right after dinner, sir. Director General Panteros left the embassy less than an hour after he arrived. He went directly back to his office. We are monitoring the phones. So far, it's been nothing but routine business."

"Have them keep a very close eye on him," the General said as they crossed the bridge. "My guess is the deal is done. We should have some visitors shortly."

"Yes, sir—and what do we do about our guest's request?"

"Is he still complaining about his nightly exercise?"

"He is, General. He's being reasonable but he wants to run. Apparently, he's used to that kind of thing. He says it keeps his mind off his situation."

"I don't think it would hurt to let him out to take a little night air. Let's go talk to him."

They were just passing the long jetty where Fidel Castro's private yacht was moored. The skeleton crew was mostly belowdecks and the big boat showed only a few standing lights. They were nearly at the door to Fidel's mansion when the aide suddenly stopped. General Constanza followed the man's gaze up toward the night sky over *Punto Cero*. "What is it?"

"I thought I saw something—more like I felt something, General—passing overhead."

General Constanza scanned the sky but he could detect nothing beyond a quarter-moon, and a field of bright stars. "Probably a bat," he said continuing toward the mansion door. "The damn things nest in the trees around here."

"You're recording all this, right?" Shake peered over Mike Stokey's shoulder trying not to jostle him as he flew the Scout on a second pass over *Cayo Piedra*, in the opposite direction. So far the little UAV was performing beautifully, and Mike was proving to be a skilled hand at the controls.

Stokey pointed at a blinking green light at the bottom corner of the LED screen. "It's all going onto the disc. Even if we lost the Scout, we'd still have the images." He brought the drone around into a sweeping turn and set up for the north to south run. "Did you see the two guys walking on the bridge?"

"Yep, couple of officers—or at least one of them was. I saw the sentry salute."

"I'm ready for the next pass, Get the sketch and I'll call what I'm seeing here."

Shake reached for a sketch-pad on which they'd drawn two big circles representing the north and south islets of the *Cayo Piedra* complex. The plan for this run was to rough-in the location of various things on the island. They would re-fine the sketch and turn it into an operational diagram after they recovered the Scout and studied the imagery. "OK, I'm ready," Shake said. "Start at the north tip and call what you see. If we need a closer look at anything, you can put it into a hover." He checked the timer on his watch that he'd started when they launched the drone. "I figure we've got about thirty minutes remaining."

Stokey glanced at the elapsed time indicator on his screen and nodded. "That checks with the instruments. Here we go." He brought the drone to an altitude of 150 feet AGL and adjusted the camera lens. "Far tip of the northern islet—there's what looks like a SAM site under canopy. Unknown type but its mounted on a wheeled vehicle. Two troopers in hammocks between a couple of palm trees." Stokey flew the drone southward where two Cuban soldiers were sweeping flashlights over the road surface. "Two sentries, looks like a roving patrol—both armed with AKs. Coming up on the smaller house; two more sentries also armed with AKs and not very alert. Swimming pool on the north side of the house—small truck parked near the pool house. Trees, more trees—lots of sand."

"Got it." Shake scribbled on the pad and looked over at the LED screen. "Let's go south across that bridge we spotted."

"OK. One sentry at the bridge, weapon on shoulder—unknown type. That's a long damn span—gotta be over five hundred feet. There's another sentry at the south end, looks like he's talking on a small radio. Road forks here..." Stokey brought the drone to a higher altitude and recorded the Y intersection. "Fork to the right is the jetty that leads out to a big yacht, left leads to the bigger house—which way?"

"Let's look at the big house. We can come back and take a closer look at the yacht if there's time."

"Copy." Stokey sent the Scout off to the left and overflew one more armed sentry on the road before he put the UAV into a broad circle over the L-shaped structure. "Looks like three small security bunkers or OPs at each end of the L, set up for defense. I'm seeing something that looks like a LAW or an AT-4—or maybe a Stinger?"

"Probably some kind of MANPAD, I'd guess. Fowler said they took a shot at his drone with what the pilot thought was an SA-7. They all manned?"

"Yep. One man in each position it looks like. Every damn one of them is smoking a cigarette—wait—look at this."

Stokey made another altitude adjustment and they could see two men walking out of the back of the building toward a field between the two legs of the L. They separated and the one with a rifle on his shoulder walked back toward the building. The other man began doing jumping jacks. "What the hell is that—some kind of nighttime PT session?"

"Beats me. Let's come back to it. Go ahead south."

OK. Not much to see. Three GP tents—one, two, three—looks like five troopers gathered around a cooking fire. I'm betting that's the island garrison—where the guards live."

Shake watched for a while, trying to compute the number of Cuban soldiers they'd seen. It looked to be a few more than 20, but they could review the imagery and fill in the blanks later. "How much time have we got?"

"Bingo in ten minutes." At the bingo point the drone would have just enough juice remaining to make the return trip. "You want to take a quick look at the boat?"

"I'm curious about that dude doing PT in the courtyard. Let's take another look at that, but stay up high so we don't get the Scout silhouetted against the structure or the trees."

Stokey added altitude and swung the Scout around toward the big house. The man they'd seen exercising was now running around in irregular patterns in the grassy expanse at the rear of the building. "What the hell is he up to?" Stokey zoomed out for a wider view. "It looks like he's doing some kind of agility drills or something."

Shake saw it immediately. "Mike, pull up and hover over that field!"

At altitude, Stokey saw it too in the dim pools of yellow from standing lights on the roof of the big house. "Looks like letters or shapes in the grass. "S...O..." They stared at the running man below the cameras. He was making looping tracks on the other side of the O. "S O S..." Shake jabbed a finger at the LED screen. "I think we're watching Carlos Ruiz-Romero sending a distress signal! Can you get any better definition on him?"

Mike Stokey fiddled with the camera controls, but what they mostly saw was an unruly shock of dark hair. The running man kept his head down, concentrating on the pattern he was making. "We could get a hell of a lot more detail in daylight. I can't get anything better without bringing the damn thing down and flying around his head."

"Bring it home, Mike. I think we've found our guy."

Arlington, Virginia

The man who calls himself Bayer really, really wanted to break something. He looked around his Spartan townhouse idly wondering which little memento, statue, or keepsake collected over more than 30 years of overt and covert service he'd miss least after he smashed it on the fieldstone fireplace. He tried pacing off some of the heat by storming from room to room, but nothing seemed to bank the fire of resentment he was feeling.

In all of those years, working for or with the CIA, DIA, FBI, NSC, ICE, U.S. Special Operations, Homeland Security, even directly for three sitting Presidents, he'd never been called on a carpet and dressed down like an errant amateur. Apparently his years of service, his admirable record and demonstrable successes, counted for nothing with the current Secretary of Homeland Security. He was barely off the plane from Havana when one of the department's noxious ass-kissers stuffed him in a town car and delivered him to the Nebraska Avenue Complex for a one-way, personal conversation with the Secretary himself. He was subjected to a full half-hour of cliché-ridden tirade about being a team-player, getting with the program, skating on thin ice, and so much more bullshit that it was hard to remember more than the bottom line. And that was that the man who calls himself Bayer would likely be looking for another job soon and that job would not be with the Federal Government.

"Regardless of how we may feel personally," the Secretary of Homeland Security said as the man who calls himself Bayer did a sharp about-face and headed for the door, "we are expected to support the Administration's positions fully and enthusiastically on matters of national security!"

Seeking distraction, he found the remote and buzzed his flat-screen to life. Naturally, the TV was tuned to Fox News where he caught a few clips from the President's announcement that an American embassy was about to be opened in Havana and a Cuban embassy would be operating in Washington in the very near future. That drove him to the wet bar where he was nursing a tumbler of scotch when one of the three phones on the bar top began to dance. It was his scrambled back-up line, and the only one who would be using it right then was Shake Davis. He snatched it up and connected, hoping for something that would lift him out of his dark mood.

"Fortunately, you caught me working on my first glass of scotch," he barked.

"In a bit of a foul mood, are we?"

"Shake, it has been a hell of a day. And it ended with the Homeland Secretary personally calling me a bitter, antiquated subversive still fighting the Cold War."

"I've got some news that might cheer you up. We found our guy. He was right where you thought he'd be."

"The cloud is lifting." The man who calls himself Bayer tossed off the remaining liquor in his glass and poured another generous shot. "Can you get him?"

"We're damn sure gonna try. We're headed over to pickup the Marines now. We got good surveillance of the island layout and I'm putting together a scratch plan. It'll be better once I see what the Marine Raiders have to say. I think we can make it work."

"If anyone can do it, it's you and Mike."

"Maybe—but we're gonna need some help on the ass end. You still got your job?"

"They're threatening but they haven't served the papers yet."

"Listen, if we get this guy the Cubans are gonna go ape-shit. We need to get him off our boat and onto something that they won't challenge—say, something like a Coast Guard cutter that would meet us out beyond their twelve-mile and take Carlos off our hands."

"And the Coasties belong to Homeland Security. I see where you're going with this."

"Can you do it?"

"I'll make it happen, Shake—one way or another. Give me the details."

"**G**ot the info you wanted." Steamer Bartlett looked up from the GPS screen as Shake and Mike climbed up into the flying bridge. "I called my buddy at ONI. The *Aquarama II* is Fidel's private yacht. She's an eighty-eight-footer with a top end of around forty knots. The boat's got all the bells and whistles, very plush, made to impress VIP visitors and like that. My guy says it's all tricked out in exotic woods and lots of chrome. Fucking thing was apparently a gift from Leonid Brezhnev, personal from him to *El Supremo*."

"Any idea how many crew it carries?" Shake took a quick look at the GPS and punched up a wider scan. They were still about three hours north of the Cayman Islands.

"My guy didn't know for sure. He said the boat likely carries a crew of a dozen or more but that's toadies and flunkies when one or both of the Castro's are aboard. I'd guess that she only has a skeleton crew other times. Call it four men—maybe six."

"Yeah, I'd go with that, Shake." Mike Stokey made a note in the enemy order of battle they were compiling. "And they're gonna be civilian sailors on payroll, not soldiers."

"I don't want to make assumptions about something like that, Mike. We'll stay away from the boat unless it becomes a factor."

Bartlett opened a cabinet in the bulkhead and pulled out a set of U.S. Navy 7x50 binoculars. He rooted around in the case, came up with a pair of dark-red filters and snapped them on the objective lenses. "These will let you spot the IR beacon once we get to Little Brac." He handed the glasses to Shake. "I've got their position plugged into the GPS. We'll cruise the coast until we spot it. And they've got a small boat, right? I don't know how close to the beach I can get."

"Our man Chesty Puller reports they've got an Inflatable Boat, Small and a muffled outboard with them, Steamer. Just get us as close as you can to the spot and they'll come to us."

"You guys better get with the girls and figure out where we're gonna put 'em. This bucket sleeps four—six at a stretch if you don't mind getting cozy—but we're gonna have a lot of extra gear and nine souls aboard for the run back to the objective."

Shake flicked open the Kershaw pocket-knife he always carried and handed it to Mike Stokey. "I'll do that, brother. You take this and carve open that fender. We need to clean a couple of pistols and do function checks."

Little Brac, Cayman Islands

Dawn was breaking on the eastern horizon as the *Junebug* cruised just outside the reef surrounding the smaller of the two Cayman Island land masses. There wasn't much to see through the gloom except a stretch of white sand backed by a line of wind-warped ironwood trees. The GPS on the cockpit console showed a blinking arrow pointing toward a spot on the beach just behind a shallow tidal pool. Shake swept the binoculars across that area slowly until he saw the blinking infra-red strobe tied to a tree.

"There it is." He handed the binoculars to Steamer Bartlett and pointed. "Line us up with the strobe while I make a call."

"Good morning, sir." The voice on the phone was familiar and cheerful. "We've got you in sight."

"Good morning, Chesty. We're gonna anchor outside the reef and then bring you aboard."

"Copy, sir. I've got a total of four Marines plus gear." Shake looked toward the beach where he saw a black Marine in a bush hat waving at him. At his back three other Marines in digital-camouflage were pulling a small boat piled high with gear onto the beach. "Soon as you've got an anchor dropped, we'll motor out to you with the IBS."

Shake watched the Marines shove their small craft into the tidal pool and felt the stern of the *Junebug* lift as Bartlett engaged the bow thrusters and dropped an anchor onto the coral bottom that was just becoming visible in the first full light of dawn. He saw a small plume of smoke as the Marines piled into their boat and started the engine. He could hear a low-pitched hum and a few resonant burbles, but otherwise the little outboard was surprisingly quiet. June Bartlett and Linda Stokey arrived on deck with a carafe of fresh coffee and a heaping plate of pastries. "Good idea," he said. "Most likely those guys have been on MREs for a week or so."

Steamer shut down the engines to save fuel and gathered on the after deck with everyone else, watching the Marines approach. "Just like the old days," he said with a big grin. "Here I sit taking Jarheads aboard and hauling 'em to the action. Been there; done that." He poured coffee and sipped. "We could let 'em take a Navy shower—or we could just hose 'em down on deck. Your call, Shake. You're in command of the landing force."

"Once we launch, I won't be." Shake moved to take the bowline of the boat that was maneuvering alongside. "No way I'm gonna challenge Chesty Puller for command."

The Marines clambered aboard and grabbed at the offered coffee and pastries. Shake introduced everyone in his party and stuck out a hand toward the black Marine who was obviously in charge.

"Welcome aboard, Chesty Puller. If you tell me your names will you have to kill me?"

There was some laughter from the Marines but they were mainly interested in wolfing down donuts and slurping the coffee June and Linda were pouring for them. The senior Marine grinned and mumbled around a mouthful of bear-claw. "We're all from 2nd Marine Raider Battalion out of MARSOC at Lejeune, Gunner—and we've heard about you." He nodded at Mike Stokey and Ralph Bartlett. "Glad to be working with members of the family." Then he turned and pointed at his men to begin introductions.

"That one is Sergeant Mark Ebenhoch. He's second in command." The handshakes began as he continued in a voice that had a distinct southern lilt. "Then there's Corporal Gus Hasford, demo man, and Corporal Earnie Grafton, communicator. We had to leave two guys behind on Andros. They're gonna be pissed."

"That's everybody but you," Mike said extending his hand. "Do we just call you Chesty or Gunny or what?"

"Sorry, sir. I'm Gunnery Sergeant Henry Simmons."

"Oh, my God..." Shake grabbed the NCO by a shoulder and turned his face to the morning sun. "Henry Simmons? As in Henry Simmons Junior, son of Henry Simmons Senior, U.S. Marine Corps?"

"That's my Dad, sir. He called me before we left Lejeune and told me he'd met up with you in Tupelo. I've heard him talk about you for what seems like most of my life. I don't know why or how we wound up meeting like this, but it's an honor."

"I assure you that most of what your Dad said about me is likely nonsense, Gunny. He's one of the best Marines I ever met or served with and I'm betting you're cut from the same cloth."

"Maybe we should give him and my Mom a call when we've got time. He'd sure get a kick out of that."

"We'll do it for damn sure. Can you guys get your gear aboard while I try to recover from the shock? We've got some serious planning to do."

As the Marines and everyone else available brought the combat gear aboard *Junebug*, Gunny Simmons outlined what they had in the raid package. "We're fairly light. We've got personal weapons, M-4s and pistols all with suppressors and there's a pair of MP-5SDs plus a pot-full of ammo for everything. We've got NVGs and spare batteries. There's Inter-Squad Radios so we can talk to each other on the mission plus a sat-comm radio in case we need to talk to highers.

There's a standard breeching and demo package plus some odds and ends I thought might come in handy. We'll know what to leave and what to carry once we've got a plan hammered out."

"We've got a sketch of the objective and some video for you to see," Shake said as he watched the gear being passed up from the IBS. "Plus we've put together what we think is the strength and armament of the security forces. We know basically what needs to be done," Shake led the Marines below decks. "Once you've had a look and a chance to think it over, we'll refine that. You guys are the experts, and I'm open to any and all suggestions on how we do this."

The Marines took turns in the *Junebug*'s small shower and caught cat-naps in the bunks so they'd be fresh for the operational planning session. Steamer Bartlett weighed anchor and set them on a course for their objective at *Cayo Piedra* with the IBS tied on aft and bobbing along in their wake.

Back on the *Junebug*'s weather decks, Shake stood beside Gunny Simmons who had a satellite phone pressed to his ear. "Dad? Yeah, it's me. How you doing?" Simmons held the phone a little distance from his ear so Shake could hear the familiar voice on the other end. "No, no—I'm fine. Still on that training mission I told you about last time. You and Mom OK?"

Apparently Master Sergeant Henry Simmons USMC (Ret.) and Mara Simmons in Tupelo, Mississippi were fine and they'd just that morning talked to their daughter-in-law and grandson at Camp Lejeune who were also fine. So what else is new?

"Well, I'm out here with somebody you know, and I thought you'd want to say hello." Gunny Simmons could barely control his voice as he handed Shake the phone.

"Henry?" Shake grinned and tried to get the younger Simmons to be quiet. "I met your boy. He's not nearly as ugly as you are."

"What the hell is going on here, Shake? How'd you two get hooked up?"

"It's a long story, Henry. I'll tell you all about it—or he will—next time we meet. Can't really get into it now, but we're involved in a little project. He's gonna babysit me through this thing and then we'll all get together—either in Tupelo or you all can come see us in Texas."

There was a long pause before Henry Simmons responded. He didn't have the details but he knew enough about this kind of thing to understand such meetings were not happenstance. "I don't know what you two are up to, but it likely ain't a tropical vacation. Shake, you know I never asked for nothing much, but I'd like to be sure you're gonna watch his back—same way you watched mine in Nam."

"You can count on it, Henry. I'll take care of him. Put Mara on so she can talk for a minute. See you soon." He handed the phone back to Gunny Simmons and stood looking out at the ocean until the big Marine was finished talking to his mother and disconnected the call.

"Funny thing." Simmons stuffed the phone into a pocket and walked toward the main cabin, "I heard my Dad asking you to take care of me, right?"

"Yeah—Dads are like that."

"Well, the last thing he said to me was to be sure I take care of you."

Havana

The GRU contingent arrived right on time. They didn't bother with preliminaries, merely nodded and strolled into the office struggling with the weight of two large canvas satchels. They eased the weight off their shoulders and plopped the satchels on a coffee table. The Director General of Cuban Intelligence rose from behind his desk to get a first look at his prize. The junior man unzipped each bag and pointed at the bundles of U.S. currency bound in plastic sheeting. "Five million," he said, "in U.S. currency."

"Five million?" There was a squeak in Panteros' voice as he contemplated being ripped off or short-changed again. He'd already made arrangements for a large payment to a banker colleague who would secretly store the cash until time to start spreading it around in the right places. "What's going on here? The agreed upon price was ten million!"

"Relax, Manuel." The senior GRU man walked to the desk and helped himself to a cigar from Panteros' humidor. "You didn't think we'd buy a pig in a poke, did you? This is your down payment. The remainder is at the embassy. It will be turned over to you once we have Ruiz-Romero safely on his way out of Cuba."

"I want to see that money."

"Certainly, at your convenience. In the meantime, we should discuss how to move our man."

"He will be taken from his present location to an airfield where I have arranged for air transportation to Guatemala.

Once he's there, you can pick him up or I will have him delivered to any destination you require. Arrangements have been made."

"I don't think that's the best course of action, Manuel." The senior GRU man said as he lit the cigar and waved at a cloud of aromatic smoke. "Too much unsecured travel, too many air miles—who knows what might happen enroute?"

"And you have a better idea?"

"Actually, Director General Surkov came up with the best idea. As you know we have the Viktor Leonov, an intelligence collection ship, in Havana harbor right now. When we are satisfied with the conditions, the Leonov will be dispatched to *Cayo Piedra* to pick up our man Very safe and very secure for passage back to the homeland."

Manuel Panteros tried to hide the shock he was feeling as he nodded and began to pace around his office. He'd underestimated Surkov and his spies. They knew where he'd been keeping Ruiz-Romero all along. So why hadn't they just sent in commandos to steal the man? Likely Igor Surkov was being his usual cagey self, establishing a debt he could call in the future. And who knew what that might involve? Of course, there could yet be a *Spetsnaz* team waiting somewhere nearby—perhaps aboard the spy ship—to kill him, to avoid complications, to keep from paying the rest of the money. He took a deep breath and tried to chase away the doubts.

"You must know that I've got trusted people on the island. If anything happens to me, if anyone tries to violate the terms of our deal…" He stared at the GRU men with what he hoped was the look of a serious, dangerous and capable man. "I can have Carlos Ruiz-Romero killed immediately."

"And why would we do something like that, Manuel? We have a deal. Director General Surkov has approved that deal." He pointed at the satchels still lying open on the coffee table. "He sent the money as promised."

"He sent half the money—as far as I know."

"You can see the rest of it anytime at the embassy, even count it if you wish. You are reading too much into this thing, Manuel. When you are ready, my associate will accompany you to the island to inspect the product. When he's satisfied, he calls me and I hand over the remainder of the money when and where you specify. It's really that simple."

"Very well. I will inspect the money tomorrow morning at your embassy. If all is in order, we will fly to *Cayo Piedra*. After that, what you do is your business."

When the GRU contingent departed, Manuel Panteros sat for long moments examining the money they'd delivered. There were no blank sheets hiding under the one-hundred dollar bills on the top of the bundles, no markers, tracers or any other devices he could detect. It seemed to be what it looked like: Five million U.S. dollars in bundles of large bills. Apparently, Director General of the GRU Igor Surkov was playing it straight, at least so far. What he's doing, Manuel Panteros realized as he fingered the plastic-wrapped bundles of cash, is doubling down. He gets a very valuable intelligence asset on one hand and buys power over Cuban Intelligence on the other. It made him feel a little more secure, so he returned to his desk and picked up the phone.

"I need you in here," he said to his trusted personal assistant, the only other man beside General Constanza and his aide that was privy to the deal. "Bring a calculator."

"Count it," he said when his assistant walked through the office door cradling a laptop computer. "Then take it to the bank. Tell Senor Aguinaldo to lock it in the vault. Give him his fee and tell him there will be more to deposit tomorrow or the day after."

The plan was really very simple as Shake and Mike outlined it for the Marine Raiders. That's when it started to get complicated.

"So you guys go dark and loiter out over the horizon about two miles from the objective." Sergeant Mark Ebenhoch pointed at a spot on the chart they were examining. "The raid force goes in with the IBS—motor for about a mile and then paddle the rest of the way to this point." He shifted to the sketch Shake and Mike had made of the island complex indicating a stretch of beach about 200 meters southeast of the main house where they expected to find Carlos Ruiz-Romero. "That means we've got to infiltrate right past this garrison area. That's risky. Video showed four or five of them sitting around a campfire, right? It might be a nightly ritual with them. We need to find a better landing spot."

"Maybe not." Gunny Simmons spun the diagram and pointed at the long jetty where the *Aquarama II* was moored. "Maybe what we do is create a diversion and wait for everyone to respond before we move on the main house and start the search."

"I like the idea of a diversion," Shake said. "That's good raid tactics."

"How about something like this?" Simmons sat back and stared at a bulkhead, letting his imagination run. "We put a man—maybe two—in the water. It's an easy swim from the landing site to the jetty." He glanced at Corporal Hasford on a nearby couch. "Gus, have we got some Willy Pete?"

"Four M-83s in my demo pack. If you're thinking about starting a fire, a couple of those will damn sure do it."

"Check." Simmons went back to the sketch. "So the swimmers heave a couple of White Phosphorous grenades up on the deck of this yacht. That starts a fire on Fidel's baby and everybody rushes to land a hand. That's when we make our move on the big house."

"That's gonna bring a lot of bodies milling around the area." Mike Stokey pointed at the northern islet. "We don't know how many people they've got up around that SAM site."

"Yeah, but they can't come south across a bridge that ain't there anymore. Suppose we cut the grenade toss to one man—say, Earnie Grafton handles that. Meanwhile, Gus hauls his demo gear to the south end of that long bridge and drops it. Now we got the north island cut off from the south island. That leaves me and Mark Ebenhoch to get in there, start kicking doors and find our man."

"You've got at least three men in the security positions around the big house and who knows how many more inside, Gunny. It's too much for two men." Shake went to pour a fresh cup of coffee from the jug on the sideboard. "You'd have to shoot a bunch of them to give you any kind of chance and I'd really like to limit the number of dead bodies on this deal."

"Is that a statement about Rules of Engagement, Gunner?"

"No, it's not, Gunny—not by a long shot. I know how things like this get messy. I would expect your people to defend themselves at all times—lethal force and whatever else it takes to accomplish the mission—I get that. I was just hoping we wouldn't have to blow away every swinging dick on that island."

"We shouldn't have to, if we do it right. But you know we're likely to have to cap a few of the bastards."

"I know that Gunny. I just wish we had more hands on this thing."

"No question I'd like to have the two guys we left back on Andros."

"You're ignoring the elephants in the room." Mike Stokey pointed at Shake and Steamer Bartlett. "We may be old but we ain't feeble. And this wouldn't be the first rodeo for any of us."

"Mike's right." Shake returned with his coffee and set to measuring the distance between their selected landing beach and the jetty where the *Aquarama II* was moored. "I could easily make the swim from here to there and light up that yacht."

"Yeah, and that's a chance you shouldn't take." Mike Stokey flicked at one of Shake's ears. "Remember you had to quit diving because of a blown-out eardrum. You damn near drowned hanging onto that doper mini-sub down in Belize." He swept a hand over the assembled Marine Raiders. "If we go with something like that, we'll get one of these amphibious monsters to do it."

"You guys are all combat swimmers, right?" Ralph Bartlett walked over and stood staring down at the objective sketch. "Did you bring masks and fins?"

"Never go anywhere without that gear, Mr. Bartlett." Sgt. Mark Ebenhoch pointed at a pile of equipment in the corner of the cabin. Strapped to each Marine's rucksack was a pair of Navy issue black swim fins.

"Back in my younger and stupider days, I went through a UDT course at Coronado. How about I do the Willy Pete thing for you? I'd know where to heave it for the best effect anyway. Once I get the party started, I'll just swim back to where we left the boat and meet you there."

"Can June handle the boat while you're away?"

"I can handle this thing as well as he can," June Bartlett said. "And Linda's a good hand on the deck. She's on the controls right now. We'll have the boat right where you want it when you come off the island."

"That leaves two men to handle the demo at the bridge," Shake agreed, "and four of us to hit the big house. The demo team can join up and pull security for us on the outside while we go in and find our man."

"OK, basically sound," Gunny Simmons went back to the chart. "Let's talk about exfil after we get him."

"Yeah, let's talk about that." Corporal Earnie Grafton said. "Gonna be a tight squeeze aboard that IBS with seven of us plus the hostage. We better cut it down tight and only take what we're really sure we're gonna need."

"Biggest bulk is the demo package and your radios, Earnie."

"Yeah, but Gus won't have the demo package on the way out. Let's leave the radios except for the ISR gear and we'll be wearing that. I've got two extra sets so the Gunner and Mr. Stokey will have one, but that's all we'll need. I mean who you gonna call? Ghostbusters?"

"Good idea," Bartlett agreed. "I've got a little Motorola portable that we can waterproof. If we need to talk to June on the boat, we can use that."

"Commander Bartlett, how much time before we're at the departure point?"

"At current course and speed, we'll be in position two miles off the island no later than 2100 tonight."

"Check…" Gunny Simmons began to page through his notebook. "I want to go around midnight when everyone on that island is hopefully asleep except for the dudes on watch. Let's call it 2300 for launch time. That gives us some transit time and a little room to adjust if Mr. Murphy decides to throw anything at us on the way." He glanced at Sergeant Ebenhoch. "Mark, let me know if I miss anything. Situation: We know what we're facing per the Gunner's brief on opposition forces. Mission: Simple, find that guy and get him out of there. Execution: We got that covered for the most part but stand by for any changes or adjustments. Admin/Logistics: We'll go over that again in prep to make sure we've got what we need. That starts right after this briefing. I want everybody as light as possible, so ditch the SAPI plates. Command and Signal…"

"A word about that, if I may, Gunny." Shake looked around at the assembled party and then pointed at Simmons. "This is the mission commander. All decisions are his and we all do what he says the way he says to do it. In his absence, we take our orders from any of the other Raiders. Steamer, Mike and me are herewith reduced to privates last class. I want to make that clear."

There were nods from the civilians and huge grins from the Marines as the assembly broke up to begin readying gear for the rescue at Ground Zero.

Ground Zero

The helicopter carrying Director General Manuel Panteros and the junior GRU agent from Havana settled with a thump on the helipad southeast of the main mansion at mid-afternoon. For Panteros it had been a frustrating morning. Right after breakfast he'd gone to the Russian Embassy where he sat in an airless little room like some overworked and underpaid accountant verifying the remainder of his money was there. Then his banker wanted more than they'd agreed upon and he'd been forced to pay it after listening to some not-so-veiled threats. Panteros had plenty of power within the Cuban government, but these damn bankers were another story entirely. And now, the pilots informed him that General Enrique Constanza was on the island and waiting for him at the big house.

"Don't go anywhere," he told the pilots. "We won't be long. I will be returning to Havana inside the hour." He led the GRU man along the walkway at a fast clip, intending to get this day over with as quickly as possible.

Constanza was waiting for him inside the parlor, sitting comfortably beside his aide on one of Fidel's over-stuffed couches. "Welcome, Manuel." He pointed at a sweating pitcher in a silver salver on the coffee table. "Can we offer you and your guest something cold to drink?"

"What are you doing here?" He didn't bother to introduce the GRU man who simply stood to one side looking around at the ornately appointed room.

"We came out yesterday. Some trouble with the SAM site on the north end of the island. I'm trying to be sure it's fixed or replaced before Fidel returns."

"And this is the kind of trouble that requires a general's personal attention?"

"All problems within my organization get my personal attention, Manuel. Are you going to introduce your associate?"

"You know who he is—and you know why we're here. We need to see the guest."

"Of course," General Constanza rose and gestured to the door. "If you'll follow me, we'll go see Senor Carlos Ruiz-Romero."

They rode the elevator down one level and walked up the hallway where General Constanza's aide punched in the lock code. Then he held open the door and gestured for them to enter. Carlos was naked from the waist up, lying on his bed with his hands behind his head. He was shaggy and unshaven with some ribs showing from a reduced caloric intake, but otherwise the American looked in good shape as he rose from the bed. He'd long ago learned it was useless to ask questions, so he simply stood silently looking at his visitors.

The Russian walked over and looked at Carlos as if he were examining a piece of meat in a butcher's shop. "You are Carlos Ruiz-Romero?"

"I am. Who are you?"

"I am your new best friend. You will be moving soon. Don't bother to pack. Everything you need will be provided." The Russian nodded to his Cuban hosts and started for the door.

"I'm not going anywhere until you people tell me what's going on!"

The Russian spun and stormed over to stand very close and poke a finger into Ruiz-Romero's chest. His tone was an evil whisper. "That is not the kind of attitude that we expect from our guests, Senor Ruiz-Romero. Let me assure you that play time is over for you. You will do exactly as you're told from this point on—no questions and no complaints. Do you understand me?"

When Carlos simply locked his jaw muscles and returned the man's glare he was rewarded with a resounding back-hand that split his lip. "What's your American expression?" The GRU man hissed into his ear. "We play hard-ball now? Get used to it." Carlos slumped back onto his cot. The GRU man nodded to his escorts and walked out the door reaching into his pocket for a phone.

"I need to make a call," he said. "Is the cellular service OK out here?"

"It's better outside," General Constanza's aide responded. "I can show you. If you have trouble, you can use my phone."

Back in Fidel's sitting room, Director General Manuel Panteros tried to defuse the tension. He accepted a glass of lemonade and stood by the windows watching the Russian make his call. "I'll be very glad when this is all over, Enrique."

"I'm assuming the deal is done—the money has been paid?"

"About that…" Panteros placed his sweating glass on a side table and turned to look at his co-conspirator. "The Russians reneged on our deal."

"They did what? Then what's that GRU goon doing here?"

"The price was cut. They will only pay ten million. Your share will be three million—one third as agreed."

Enrique Constanza moved closer and tried to spot the deceit in the man's eyes. It was there, he was sure of it. This was some kind of trick, some excuse to short him on his share which was supposed to be ten million dollars. He tapped the pistol holstered at his hip. "You know, I suppose, that I will kill you if you are pulling some kind of stunt."

"I assure you, Enrique…" Panteros held up his hands and smiled. "It's the truth. They had me over a barrel. It was a final offer—ten million or nothing. Igor Surkov is behind it. I had to accept the offer or we would have wound up with nothing for our trouble."

"They would never know what happened to you, Manuel. They'd never find the body."

"There's no need for threats. Working together we can turn this ten million into twenty and then thirty. We will be the power in Havana after normalization."

"So now we're friends and business partners? You know I've been in this business a long time, Manuel. I can smell lies."

"No one is lying here! You can return to Havana with me. You can talk to the Russians. You can count the money."

"I will do precisely that—all of it—but not before I see this thing played out. What are their plans for moving the American?"

"They are sending that spy ship that's parked in Havana Harbor to pick him up, probably tomorrow sometime. They didn't give me all the details."

"Very well." Constanza kept one hand resting on his holster and pointed with the other. "You go back to Havana. I will remain here to see that there is no more nonsense. When the Russians have our bird in their hands, I will return by helicopter. Plan to meet me immediately. I want to talk to the

Russians—Surkov himself—and I want to see the money. This whole thing stinks!"

"Let me know when you'll be arriving." Manuel Panteros shoved past the angry man and headed for the door. "I'll see you get everything you want." *And I'll see that the fucking helicopter carrying your ass never arrives in Havana.*

Aboard USCGC Mohawk (WMEC-963)

"**M**aintain present course and speed," Lieutenant Commander Priscilla Walker USCG said to the Junior Officer of the Deck as she collected her phone and a roll of charts. "You have the Deck and the Conn."

"Captain is leaving the bridge!" The Boatswain's Mate of the Watch announced for the benefit of the cutter's bridge crew. Walker nodded at him and headed for the ladder leading down to the wardroom where her command team was waiting for a little more information on their unexpected mission. Yesterday at mid-morning, the Mohawk, a 270-foot Medium Endurance Cutter, was ordered to cut short some badly needed maintenance work in Key West and head south into the Caribbean. Only the captain was briefed on the short-fuse mission, but everyone aboard knew it was something important. Now that they were at sea and headed in the right direction, the Captain intended to bring everyone up to speed as much as she could.

She stepped into the wardroom, nodded for everyone to be seated and then counted noses. Except for the watchstanders on the bridge, she had all her commissioned and senior enlisted leadership waiting for word. "As you've all probably surmised from our abrupt departure, this is a hot-ticket mission. It's also highly classified so Opsec applies. You can brief your people as required to get the job done but the details we keep inside this room." She looked around to be sure all hands got the message and then spread a nautical chart on the wardroom table.

"This little flyspeck off the southwest Cuban coast is where we're headed. It's called *Cayo Piedra* and its Fidel Castro's private island getaway. The Cubans are very touchy about approaching vessels or aircraft so we will stand off outside their 12-mile. The bridge already has the GPS data and I want to be in position right about here…" She sketched a circle on the chart with a fingernail. "…no later than 2300 tonight. That's the navigation piece. The operational piece goes like this: Sometime in the early morning tomorrow, we will rendezvous with a civilian vessel. She's called the *Junebug*, a 54-foot Chris Craft out of Key West. Aboard that vessel will be four Marine special operators and one DIA agent. We take them aboard and make turns for Key West at best speed."

Lieutenant Commander Walker looked around the wardroom table. Some of her critical people were taking notes but most of them were just staring at her, waiting for the other shoe to drop. "I didn't get a complete briefing, some of the background is need-to-know only, but here's what I could put together. Apparently, the Cubans kidnapped the DIA agent from Gitmo and stashed him on this little island. There has been no official U.S. response. I'm guessing it's because of the delicate normalization talks. On the other hand, this DIA guy has a lot of classified info and the Administration wants him back in the worst way. SOCOM and Homeland Security got the tasking for an unofficial, low-key solution. That's where the private boat and the Marine Raiders came into the picture. Sometime tonight they're gonna snatch this guy back from the Cubans."

The Mohawk's navigator raised a hand and got the nod from his Captain. "I'm assuming we won't want to be hanging around outside Cuban waters very long, Ma'am. Can we contact the *Junebug* and get an idea of where she'll be?"

"I don't want to be too chatty on VHF, Gator." She ripped a page out of her notebook and slid it across the table. "The skipper of the *Junebug* is a retired Navy Commander, a salty old destroyer man with plenty of operational experience. His name is Ralph Bartlett and that's his cell number." She nodded at an enlisted man on the other side of the table. "Get with Senior Chief Larimore and work out some kind of recognition signal and then call Commander Bartlett."

"We'll have him set his radar to pulse mode, Captain." The Chief made a note and pocketed it. "Any old tin-can swabbie can do that. He'll stand out like a lighthouse beacon. We'll ID the pulse and keep tracking it. Once he's ready, we can motor right up to him."

"How are we gonna know when he's ready?" The Mohawk's First Lieutenant wanted to know. "I mean, how will we know he's got the guy aboard and he's ready to make the transfer?"

"Work it out with Commander Bartlett," the Captain responded. "You people can come up with something—but no pyrotechnics or fireworks. Remember we want to be low-profile and out in international waters at all times. Anything else?"

"Rules of Engagement, Captain?" The Chief Gunner's Mate asked as everyone else began to rise for dismissal.

"I'm hoping that won't be an issue, Chief. We won't be advertising that we've got this guy aboard. If we are challenged or threatened in international waters, we will respond according to SOP. Best bet is to have the weapons manned at all times after we go to General Quarters. I expect to do that at around 2200 so make sure the crew gets proper rest. It's probably gonna be a long night."

"Commander Bartlett? This is Lieutenant Scott Redding, sir. I'm the navigator aboard the Mohawk, a cutter out of Coast Guard Station Key West."

"It's nice to talk to you, Lieutenant. What can I do for the Puddle Pirates?"

"I was told by my CO that you'd be expecting a call from us, sir."

"Roger that. We got the word a couple of hours ago that some Shallow Water Sailors were coming on station."

"Yes, sir. Well, you know how it goes. Us Shallow Water Sailors are always standing by to help the U.S. Navy when they get dazed or confused."

"Yeah. So how is this thing gonna work?"

"I've got my Chief right here, sir. He suggests you set your radar to pulse-mode so there won't be any confusion with emissions from other vessels in the area. We'll see that and know it's you. How's that sound?"

"It sounds like your Chief is a good man. I'll set it up with my gear. Depending on range, you should start seeing something around 2300 tonight."

"We've also been asked to arrange a recognition signal, Commander—something that will let us know when you're ready to meet up with us?"

"Let us not over-complicate the issue, Lieutenant. How about I just call you? I've got this number in my phone now."

The navigator looked inquiringly at the Senior Chief listening on speaker. He just smiled and shrugged. "Easy way is usually best, sir."

"OK, Commander Bartlett. That will work for us. I'll have this phone charged and standing by. If that fails, VHF is the default. I'll send you a text with the frequency and call sign, but our CO doesn't want to use it unless necessary."

"Copy all. We'll be seeing you out in deep water before dawn tomorrow."

Ground Zero

General Enrique Constanza pulled off his boots and massaged his aching feet. He was looking forward to a soak in the Jacuzzi tub located just off the plush guest bedroom at the back of Fidel's mansion. When he got himself paid and set up in the new Cuba, he was determined to install a Jacuzzi in his own home on the outskirts of Havana. There might not be enough money for the other improvements he planned now that Panteros had caved to the Russians, but the Jacuzzi was a definite priority.

His aide knocked and entered carrying a fruit plate and a bottle of rum. One of the other things he'd enjoyed during their stay on the island was the nightly drink and conversations they had on the guest room's breezy veranda overlooking the ocean. No wonder Fidel claimed this place and poured millions of the people's money into creating a private resort with all the capitalist amenities, he mused. They had come a long way from starving revolutionary scarecrows up in the mountains. And clearly communism was dead, a failed experiment. In the new Cuba he would spend his last years in peace and comfort—if all went well in the next 24 hours.

"I've been thinking about this thing with the Russians," he said as they took their drinks to the veranda. "I trust them about as much as I do Manuel Panteros—which is not at all."

"It's seems odd that they'd send one of their spy ships into Havana Harbor during the normalization negotiations, doesn't it?" His aide lit a cigarette and propped his feet up on a wrought-iron rail.

"Yes, it does. It's like thumbing their noses at the Americans, unless they've got something else in mind."

"Do you think it has something to do with our guest, General, something beyond just picking him up tomorrow? Director General Panteros made it sound like a fortunate coincidence that the ship was available."

"With the Russians, my friend, there are no coincidences." General Constanza stared out into the dark. There was nothing much to see except a few yellow lights showing through the portholes of the *Aquarama II* and a sentry or two strolling through pools of standing light. "Suppose that ship has a squad of commandos aboard? Suppose the GRU has plans to save a little money and just steal Carlos Ruiz-Romero out from under our noses?"

"It's a possibility, I suppose. Would you like me to call our man on watch at the harbor? We can determine if the ship is still docked or if they have moved it. That may be helpful."

"Yes, do that. And tell the guard commander I want to double the watch around the building tonight. If he has to eliminate some of the walking posts, do that. I want this building guarded well and properly until we deliver Senor Carlos Ruiz-Romero to his new hosts."

"Yes, sir." The aide gulped his drink and stood. "And how about our guest's exercise period tonight?"

General Constanza checked his watch. It was just coming up on 9 p.m. "Give him one half-hour. It may be the last exercise he gets for a long while. Have him back inside and locked up by ten."

Aboard *Junebug*

"**Y**ou need to lose some weight." June Bartlett was struggling with the zipper at the back of her husband's black wetsuit. "A little less beer would help."

"Don't worry," he gave her a kiss and headed for the main cabin. "I've got a feeling I'll burn a few calories tonight. The radar is set to pulse mode. Power it up as soon as we're over the side. The phone is on the chart table. If you go anywhere, keep it with you."

He entered the main cabin and looked around at the landing team in final preparations. The Marine Raiders were in full stealth mode with all exposed skin mottled and blotched in camouflage cream. They looked like the real deal with fighting gear tightly strapped around their torsos and night vision devices hooked into the brackets on their FAST helmets.

Shake and Mike Stokey, on the other hand, looked like something between knock-off ninjas and railroad tramps in jeans and old dark-colored sweatshirts. Stokey had the ISR comm rig strapped to his bare head while Shake had pulled one of Bartlett's old Navy watch caps over his white hair. The war paint on their exposed skin only increased the hobo look as if they'd spent the night sleeping in a coal car. "Well, you guys look ready to go—some of you anyway." Steamer Bartlett strapped a web belt bearing the plastic-wrapped Motorola radio around his waist and checked his diver's watch. "We're over the side in fifteen. Who's got the Willy Pete?"

Corporal Gus Hasford looked up from screwing a suppressor onto his M-4 carbine, reached into his demo kit and
tossed him two M-83 incendiary grenades. "You know what
to do with those, Commander?"

Bartlett hefted one and studied it. "Pull pin and heave—
after the pin is pulled, Mr. Grenade is not our friend." He
clipped the grenades on his belt and secured them with tape.
"You guys gonna trust me with a weapon? It's gonna be
lonely out on that beach waiting for you to show up."

Gunny Simmons glanced at Shake for inspiration. "Give
him this," shake handed over one of the MP-5SD sub-guns
with a dual-point sling. "I'll take the shotgun." Simmons
nodded and dug a Remington 870 Modular Combat Shotgun
out of a satchel. He opened the action and handed it over
with a handful of 12-gauge rounds. "All we've got is breeching rounds for that thing, Gunner. I didn't figure on using it
for anything else."

"No problem." Shake patted the MARSOC custom
M1911 he had tied to a lanyard around his neck and stuffed
into the waistband of his jeans. "I've got old slab-sides as a
back-up."

"Showtime, gents." Simmons stood up and bounced to
check his gear. "We are good to go. The IBS is fueled, paddles aboard, and we know the scheme of maneuver. My compass is pre-set so I'll navigate from the bow. Earnie, watch
for my hand signals. You've all been through the brief-back,
any questions, concerns, comments?"

The silence was disturbed only by the sound of bolts
ramming live rounds into weapon chambers. "Final comm
checks on the ISR up on deck. Let's do this."

On deck, the raiding party slipped over the side and into
the IBS. The Marines were on the gunwales with Gunny
Simmons up front as navigator and Corporal Earnie Grafton

aft to handle the muffled outboard. Mike and Steamer Bartlett were tucked uncomfortably in the middle of the crew. Shake was the last to board. He untied the mooring lines and turned to Linda Stokey.

"Listen, I don't want this to get all dramatic, but if anything happens to me tonight…"

"I'll talk to Chan. Don't worry about it." She gave him a peck on his grease-smeared cheek. "And also don't make me have to make any condolence calls. You guys just get this done and get back here safe and sound."

June Bartlett and Linda Stokey stood in the dark watching the IBS putter away from the Junebug. In three minutes it was out of sight and two minutes later they could no longer hear the outboard. "They never really retire do they?" There was a hint of sadness in June's tone as she climbed up to the bridge.

"Yeah, they do." Linda followed her on the ladder. "They retire all the time. Trouble is they never *stay* retired."

Ground Zero

It didn't take long after Corporal Earnie Grafton shut down the outboard for the Raiders to catch a rhythm with the paddles. The boat was heavy with so many people aboard, but it was deathly silent on the final approach to the objective. They reached the splash point for Steamer Bartlett a little after midnight. "Go get 'em, Steamer," Shake whispered as the big sailor slid silently over the side, adjusted his face-mask, and began an energy-saving breast stroke toward the *Aquarama II* which they could see as a big dark silhouette off to their left. Gunny Simmons gave the signal and the Marines along the sides of the IBS began to stroke toward the beach.

They maneuvered through gentle surf lapping against the island's white sand and backstroked to stop just short of touchdown on the beach. When the little boat was snug up against the shore, they slithered over the side, careful not to splash. When everyone found their footing, Simmons gave another silent signal and they hoisted the boat out of the water and onto their shoulders. Dragging a rubber boat across firm, fine sand made a lot of noise, so they carried the IBS up across the beach and into a stand of low scrub about 20 meters from the high-water mark. Simmons sent Corporals Gus Hasford and Earnie Grafton, carrying the demo-kit, on the hustle toward the bridge and then the remaining raiders returned to the sand to obscure their footprints. When that was accomplished, they took a knee and stared into the inky darkness waiting for the planned diversion to stir up a hornet's nest.

Steamer Bartlett swam with his head low in the water as he approached the big yacht trying to keep any glare from a couple of lighted portholes from reflecting off his face mask. The *Aquarama II* was moored port side to the jetty with her bow pointed seaward. It was a big, beautiful boat and he was about to damage it badly, maybe even sinking the thing right there at her mooring. It was both a damn shame and an absolute requirement, he thought as he rounded the seaward end of the jetty. He'd seen no sentries on the long pier nor any crewmen on the decks during the approach swim, so he added a little power to his stroke and quickly brought himself up on the starboard side of the boat.

As he hugged the side and pulled himself toward the stern, he put an ear to the hull and listened for sounds that might indicate crew activity. All he heard were waves gently lapping against fiberglass and the hum of life-support machinery. The yacht was dead in the water, all hands turned into their racks. He maneuvered himself down the side, but not for long. His plan was to heave one of the WP grenades up onto the weather decks aft where it would likely roll down into the hatch that led belowdecks. At that point he'd work himself toward the bow and toss the second grenade in through an open port he'd spotted.

Bartlett steadied himself with his back to the yacht's hull, tugged at the tape, and pulled the first grenade off his belt. When he got the pin worked out of its recess, he rolled over and heaved it up onto the deck as close to the superstructure as he could manage. He heard the spoon release and the primer snap and a dull thud when the grenade hit the wood decking. Trusting he'd made a good toss, he immediately started kicking his way seaward while he pulled the second WP grenade off his belt. He was treading water off the yacht's beam when he was nearly blinded by a flash. A hollow boom rolled out over the water as the first grenade detonated sending a shower of sparks and glowing chemical spears skyward over the boat's fantail.

Bartlett ignored it and concentrated on the free-throw he needed to make with the remaining incendiary. He kicked away from the hull a bit to give himself a better angle and studied the target. He needed to hit the two-foot open porthole perfectly or the grenade would bounce off the superstructure into the water. Treading water gently to keep his body as steady as possible, he pulled the pin and set himself for the toss. "Nothing but net," he whispered with a grin as the second grenade disappeared into the interior of Fidel Castro's yacht.

He was stroking for the end of the jetty when that one detonated. Bartlett rolled over into a backstroke and saw flames licking at the dark from the interior of the yacht. He could hear the shouts and screams of the crewmembers and saw a few of them rushing outside in their skivvies to escape the fire. By the time he reached the beach rendezvous point, he'd seen at least five Cuban soldiers rushing down the jetty toward the burning yacht. *And that*, he thought as he crawled up out of the water and headed for the scrub brush where the IBS was hidden, *is what you call a diversion.*

In the light of the growing conflagration aboard the *Aquarama II*, the raid party saw soldiers from the tent-city garrison scrambling to respond. First to move were four or five who had been sitting around a campfire. They rushed toward the jetty yelling for their comrades to follow. A flood of sleepy soldiers spilled out of the tents pulling on shirts and trousers as they rushed to follow. Simmons let the crowd thin and then led the team on a diagonal cut, past the back of the garrison compound, heading for the Y intersection of the main road.

Mike Stokey was bringing up the rear as the raiders hustled past the third GP tent. He was squinting, trying to keep Simmons and Sgt. Ebenhoch in sight with no NVGs to improve his view, when he ran headlong into a Cuban trooper. They both staggered around in the dark, but there was enough ambient light at this point for the Cuban to realize whoever he'd bumped into was not one of his buddies. He shouted something in Spanish and whipped the AK off his shoulder. Mike dropped to a knee and brought the MP-5SD to bear on the man's torso. At a range of just two feet, there wasn't much point in aiming, so he simply squeezed the trigger and sent a burst of sub-sonic nine-millimeter slugs into the man's ribcage. There were maybe five rounds in the burst, but it didn't make much noise. The suppressor reduced the muzzle blast to what sounded to Mike like someone running a thumb across bubble-wrap. *So much for quick and dirty*, Stokey thought as he stepped over the body and ran to catch up with the raid team.

At the Y intersection, they were in a tight perimeter, tucked into a stand of palm trees, waiting for the next distraction. They saw at least six more security guards hustling toward the big blaze on the yacht, but none of them bothered to look along the sides of the road as they ran to lend a hand with the firefighting efforts. The big house was in sight off to their right where they could see a few lights coming on in darkened windows. Stokey caught up and whispered a report about his confrontation at the tent camp. Simmons just shrugged and keyed his ISR to get a report from the demo detail.

Corporals Hasford and Grafton were in no position to
verbally respond to the query coming through their headsets.
Hasford merely tapped the transmit button on his ISR three
times to send the stand-by signal. They were hunkered down
in a patch of low scrub at the southern end of the bridge connecting the two *Cayo Piedra* islets. About 20 meters away
from them a sentry was milling around the end of the bridge,
staring at the blaze in the distance and jabbering into a radio.
He had his AK off shoulder, cradling it in the crook of his
free arm. This guy needed to either move or be eliminated
before they could slide under the bridge and rig the demo.
The sentry might stand his ground or he might head off toward the jetty to help with the firefighting. Hasford tapped
his wrist and showed three fingers. If the guy didn't hustle
off or otherwise disappear out of their way in 90 seconds, he
was going down.

The sentry finished his conversation and clipped the radio to his belt but he made no move to leave his post. Hasford
finished counting seconds and then raised his suppressed M-
4. He caught the image he needed in the ACOG sight, took
a deep breath and squeezed the trigger. The two rounds he
fired were barely audible in the rising bedlam on the island
but they were on the intended target. The sentry staggered
backward as the 5.56mm slugs tore into his chest. Then he
collapsed, hitting the bridge planking like a wet sandbag.

Hasford and Grafton dug the pre-rigged demo charges
out of a satchel and headed for the foot of the bridge. They
snatched up the dead sentry and shoved him into the water
where the weight of his equipment rapidly pulled him under
and out of sight. The water this close to the shore was likely
not deep but there was no way they could gauge the drop-
off, so Hasford led the way, stepping slowly to measure
depth and find any potholes. He was standing waist deep on

firm footing near one of the big wooden pilings when he signaled for Grafton to come ahead.

Back on the *Junebug* Hasford had rigged the kind of demo they needed to drop a section of the long bridge after studying the reconnaissance video from the drone. He had cutting charges rigged in a daisy-chain. There were three charges, each one composed of two slabs of C-4 wrapped in det-cord that connected all three for simultaneous detonation. They had a remote-control blasting kit that would set it all off after they got it rigged and then cleared themselves out of the blast zone.

Hasford moved to a second piling opposite the one Grafton was tending and went to work. They were using long strips of waterproof adhesive to glue the charges to the wood barely above the waterline. The tamping effect of the water would direct some energy of the blast upward and that would be enough to cut the pilings according to Hasford's estimate. When the cutting charges were in place, Hasford stepped into Grafton's cupped hands and got a boost that allowed him to reach the underside of the bridge planking. The third charge was attached there with a hard plastic shield covering it as a tamping device. They had it all in place within the allotted six minutes.

Hasford poked a wireless blasting cap into the charge and then they both waded to shore, avoiding the glow reflected off the water by the growing blaze down by the jetty. Hasford hit the transmit button on his ISR as they were hustling away from the bridge toward the big house. "Demo going in five…four…" He flipped the power switch on the remote initiator and watched the red light turn green indicating the device was reading the signal from the blasting cap. "Three…two…shot." He mashed the fire button and the south end of the 700-foot bridge connecting the north islet with the south islet erupted with a blinding flash and a thunderous bang. Hasford took a quick look through his NVGs. When the ocean breeze cleared some of the smoke, he could see that at least 30 feet of bridge was missing. There was still dust, debris, and wood chunks raining down on them as they rushed toward the primary objective.

His aide came rushing into his room holding a portable radio to his ear as General Enrique Constanza was lacing his boots. The last reports he'd gotten indicated pumps were being rigged to fight the fire on the yacht, but it didn't look promising. The officer in charge said there was too much wood, too much flammable material. Saving the boat was likely out of the question, but they were struggling to keep the flames away from the fuel tanks. Two of the crewmen were dead from smoke inhalation and none of the survivors had any idea about what caused the fire to erupt so suddenly in the middle of the night. And now there had been another explosion down by the bridge. That was too much. Whatever was happening at Ground Zero, General Constanza knew it was no accident.

"None of the sentries reports seeing anything around the bridge, General." The aide moved to the veranda and stared out at the huge fire lighting up the night sky. "There is a big section missing so the people on the north end can't get across to investigate."

"You tell those bastards to swim across if necessary—or find a boat! I want to know what caused that explosion. We are under attack! Am I the only one here who understands that?" The general took a look through the veranda doors and chewed on his lip. This was likely what he'd feared. Somewhere out there was that damned Russian spy ship. And somewhere on this island was very likely a *Spetsnaz* commando team that would very soon come bursting through the mansion doors.

He turned and strapped on his pistol belt. "Find a rifle for yourself and check on the building sentries," he shouted reaching for his cap and heading for the door. "It's the Russians. I'm sure of that—and they're after the American."

"Where will you be, General?" The aide followed him out of the bedroom door.

"I'm going to get a quick look around. When you've got a weapon meet me in the room where we're holding the American."

Gunny Simmons, Shake, Mike, and Sgt. Ebenhoch were gathered in a drainage ditch about 50 meters from the entrance to the mansion. They had been studying the situation for five long minutes when Hasford and Grafton showed up to slide into ditch. "There's four of 'em jinking around right there by the entrance. We didn't see that on the video." Simmons spoke to his demo team and pointed. They could see four soldiers with AKs cutting impatient little circles on the terrace and steps of the building. "Nervous in the service," said Grafton. "They know something serious is going down, but they don't know what."

"I want you two to move left. This ditch curves toward the house down there. You'll be about thirty meters from the entry. Set up on those sentries. When I pass the word on the ISR, you take 'em out. Then move up on the veranda and stand by. Nobody gets in or out." He turned to Shake, Mike, and Ebenhoch. "We're looking for that door that leads out to the courtyard where you spotted the signal. We'll go around the flanks. Me and Mark to the right, Shake and Mike to the

left. There's no way around the posts at the ends of the buildings, so we gotta drop the sentries. Everybody check in with
me on the ISR when you're in position. Gunner, we'll meet
in the center at the apex of the L after the sentries are down.
There's gotta be a door there. We saw our guy come out of
it on the video. And don't worry about noise at this point. Do
what you gotta do. Quick in, find our guy, quick out and back
to the beach."

Simmons was set up about 30 meters from the bunker on the
right side of the mansion. He'd been expecting one sentry in
the position but there were two, both of them peering intently
into the dark. Ebenhoch was lining up on the position with
his M-4 propped on the branch of a gnarled old pine tree. "I
got the guy on the left," he said. "Ready when you are."

"Ready out front…" Grafton and Hasford radioed. They
had the front entrance guards in their sights with the targets
designated as two apiece. The Marines were aiming in from
deep in the shadows provided by the drainage ditch. Once
they dropped the Cuban soldiers, it would be a quick sprint
to covered positions where they could control access and
egress to the mansion.

"Ready on the left..." Shake and Mike were a bit closer
to their targets. They'd made a slow crawl through the saw
grass and found a hole that kept them out of sight. Their shots
would be from just 20 meters—maybe a little less. "There's
two of 'em," Shake whispered. "You take the one closest to
the building." He slipped his .45 out of his waistband and
thumbed the safety off. "When we get the word, pop up and
shoot."

The word came over the radio five seconds later.
"Ready…ready…ready…fire!" The loudest report was from

Shake's pistol, but nobody in the guard force on the perimeter of the mansion was alive to hear it. Mike's rounds spun the first man around and left him hanging dead over a pile of sandbags. The big .45 caliber slugs from Shake's pistol took his target in mid-torso and blew him backward over the low wall of the guard post.

The general's aide stormed down the stairs looking for one of the extra sentries they'd posted near the front of the mansion. There was no one on the interior. They must have gone outside when the shooting started, he thought, as he scrambled for the front door. He swung it open and saw two dark shadows running toward the house carrying weapons. The next thing he saw were the four sentries, all sprawled on the portico and steps. None of them were moving and all of them were bleeding. He could smell the fresh blood as he grabbed for the nearest man's rifle. Two shots blew wood off the archway near his head as he ducked back inside to slam the big main doors. There were huge internal locks on those doors that would keep intruders at bay for a while, but determined men could always gain entry.

The general was right. They were under attack. The Russians had come to claim their prize. The aide checked to be sure the rifle had ammunition in the magazine and then ran for the elevators. He decided not to wait after he'd impatiently pressed the call button several times and ran for the stairwell that led to the lower floor. Surely an old campaigner like General Enrique Constanza would know how to handle a situation like this. His aide most certainly did not.

Carlos Ruiz-Romero heard the gunfire and rushed to his window. There were muzzle flashes in the inky night but he couldn't see who was doing the shooting. He thought for a moment that he'd seen someone in blackface with wide white eyes, peering into the window of his darkened room but wrote that off as his imagination running wild. There was no way for him to tell what was going on outside the building. Clearly the Cubans were fighting with someone out there in the dark. Maybe it was a rescue attempt. Maybe someone had seen his signal. He might just get out of this thing alive. He was pacing and thinking of what he might do to help when the door burst open and he found himself staring at the muzzle of an AK-47.

The senior officer and his aide rushed into the room and slammed the door behind them. He was grabbed and jammed hard down into the desk chair. The man with the rifle pulled a knife out of his pocket and began to slash at the bed sheets, tearing them into long strips. The senior man stood with his ear pressed to the door.

The search teams ran down sloping ground and met at the apex of the structure. They glanced quickly in a few windows but saw nothing in the dark. The door they wanted was the only access to the building from the rear. It was securely locked when Simmons tried the handle. From the looks of it, that door probably led to a basement or some space below the main level. "We'll take what we've got," Simmons said stepping aside and pointing at Shake and his shotgun. "Blow the lock off this thing and we'll search from bottom to top."

Shake jacked a breeching round into the shotgun and stepped up to the door holding the muzzle about six inches from the place where the lock fixture met the door jamb. The disintegrating slug blew a big hole in the wood and the door swung inward easily when Shake gave it a hard kick. As they piled inside a long corridor, a man carrying an AK came skidding around the corner near what looked like an elevator station. Simmons dropped him on the move. The dead man slid across the polished tile and his AK clattered against a wall. They looked around quickly to get their bearings. There were just three doors leading off the corridor. All of them featured key pads requiring security code numbers for access. Simmons nodded at the nearest one and the search team stacked up ready for kinetic entry. Shake moved forward with his shotgun.

"They're inside the building!" General Enrique Constanza shouted. "I can hear them out in the hallway!" His aide was just finishing the task of strapping Carlos to the desk chair. He reached for the AK and pointed it at the terrified hostage. "Do you want me to take care of it, sir?"

Constanza heard another loud report echoing through the corridor outside the door. The Russians were shooting their way into another room. They would find this one soon, he understood, and at that point the best he could hope for was to escape alive. "No, no. Not yet. We need to delay them— find a way out of here." His initial thought had been to just come down here and shoot the American and rob the damned Russians of their prize, but that seemed to be giving away what little leverage they might have. General Constanza decided to wait. Perhaps they could bargain and get out of this thing with their lives. He needed to make some kind of overture to the assault force. He needed to let them know there was no need to kill everyone just to get what they wanted.

He looked at his aide and decided there was no other way. The man was loyal and smart. He'd been with Constanza from the day he was promoted to general but there was just no other way. "They're searching the other rooms. See if you can make contact. Tell them we are willing to bargain! They want the American, not us."

The aide hesitated at the order. He was not a combat soldier and he certainly didn't harbor any delusions about surviving if there was a shoot-out with Russian commandos. On
the other hand, he would most certainly die in this little room
if he didn't do something. Maybe the General was right.
Maybe the Russians would be willing to let then live if they
just surrendered the American. He could feel sweat running
from his forehead and blinked his eyes against the sting.
From what he knew of the subject, Russian *Spetsnaz* were
notoriously ruthless, the kind of men who would instantly
gauge the situation in the little room where the American sat
trussed up and shoot them both dead. Perhaps, he could just
find the commandos and surrender. He considered leaving
the AK behind and walking out into the hallway with his
hands in the air. He looked at his general and decided that
seemed cowardly, unbecoming of a Cuban officer. Holding
the AK-47 loosely in his hands, ready to drop it at the first
sight of a commando, he moved to the door.

The general turned the knob and then put his arm around
his aide for a reassuring squeeze. "Just let them know we
have the American and we will bargain—we will turn him
over without a fight. You'll be fine." He hauled open the
door, shoved his aide into the hallway and slammed the door
shut behind him. Then he rushed over to the American, drew
his pistol and waited.

The General's aide saw two men crouched by a door on
the opposite side of the hall. One of them was looking toward
the elevators. The other was staring directly at him and raising his weapon to a shoulder. They didn't look like any Russian *Spetsnaz* he'd seen in photos. In fact, he realized
standing there frozen in abject fear, they looked like Americans. He raised his weapon in both hands, extending it out at

arm's length, offering it to the crouching soldier aiming at him. It was the last thing he ever did.

Sergeant Ebenhoch pulled his smoking M-4 out of his shoulder and stuck his head around the door frame to shout at the team that was searching inside. "One down out here—he came out of the last room on the right."

Shake and Gunny Simmons came bolting out of the empty room they'd been searching, leaped over the bleeding body in the hallway and headed for the indicated door. "Same drill," he said. Mike Stokey and Sgt. Ebenhoch stacked up on either side of the door as security. Simmons nodded at Shake who jacked a round into the chamber of the shotgun and pointed it at the door jamb. Wood chips flew and he snap kicked at the door, heading inside with Simmons hot on his heels.

"There's no need for this!" The general was shouting as the two commandos charged into the room with their weapons shouldered. "You can have him!" He watched as the two men split apart, the black one was clearly aiming a vicious little carbine at his head. There was no doubt in General Constanza's mind that a bullet would be heading in his direction in just seconds. He pressed the muzzle of his pistol tight behind the hostage's ear. "One more step and I kill him!"

Shake understood the Spanish clearly. Simmons got the picture without understanding the command. They halted abruptly to assess the situation. Over their gunsights, they saw Carlos Ruiz-Romero tied to a chair with a terrified look on his face and a Cuban general standing right behind him holding a Makarov pistol. The general officer was flushed and breathing in little gasps of the smoky air inside the room. He glared at the two men pointing weapons at him.

"You're not Russians."

"No," Shake replied in Spanish. "We're Americans and we've come to reclaim our countryman. Drop your weapon and step back."

"You will drop your weapons—right now." The general said sounding a bit more confident. "If you comply, I will walk away from here. You can have him. If you do not, he dies!"

"And so do you, General. You know that."

"It's your choice. I will not wait much longer."

Shake turned to Simmons and spoke in English. "He wants us to drop the weapons, Gunny. Or else he kills the guy. I think we better go along with it."

"I can probably drop him." Simmons redirected his muzzle. Shake looked at the General's eyes and saw that the man understood what was being said.

"No, that's too dangerous. This is a determined man." Shake saw the hint of a smile on the general's face. "Let's just do as he says." He lowered his shotgun, keeping his eyes on the general, calculating range and trajectory. He heard Gunny Simmons at his side unsnap the sling from his M-4 and let the carbine clatter to the floor.

"OK, General, you win." He switched back to Spanish. "I'm gonna toss my weapon over on the bed." With a flick of his wrist, Shake sent the shotgun swirling toward the bed. As he calculated, the Cuban officer turned slightly to watch it land and in that action, he brought the muzzle of his pistol clear of Ruiz-Romero's head.

Shake immediately snatched the .45 out of his waistband, gripped it firmly with the weak hand, and dropped into a crouch. He found the front sight blade instantly and squeezed on the trigger. The single 230-grain hydra-shock round hit General Enrique Constanza a quarter-inch above the right eyebrow. The man's head snapped back violently enough to break his neck but that didn't matter. The general was dead before he hit the floor.

"Nice work Gunner!" Simmons retrieved his carbine, snapped it back into his sling and moved to cut Carlos Ruiz-Romero free. The man was slipping into shock and began to babble questions. "Save it, sir." Simmons hauled the man toward the door. "We'll give you the complete 4-1-1 once we get you off this island." He hit the radio transmit switch. "We got our man. Muster at the door where we came in."

When they got Carlos Ruiz-Romero outside, they heard what sounded like a hot firefight on the other side of the building. "We got a little thing going on here, Gunny." Hasford's voice was steady but everyone could sense the pressure. "Bunch of guys showed up a few minutes ago headed for the house. Looks like ten or so from what I can see. We stopped 'em but now they're in that ditch and busting caps all over our ass. We're about to go black."

"Running out of ammo," Simmons said to Mike and Shake. "We're gonna have to help 'em break contact. "I'll take Ebenhoch around to the ditch and hit 'em in the flank. You two take our guy down to the beach and meet up with Commander Bartlett and stand by. We'll be right behind you."

Simmons and Ebenhoch rushed off in one direction while Shake and Mike headed off in the other with Carlos Ruiz-Romero sagging between them on shaky legs. It was 0100, just short of one hour since they first set foot on *Cayo Piedra*.

Aboard USCGC Mohawk (WMEC-963)

Lieutenant Commander Priscilla Walker was pacing the bridge trying to look confident and unruffled for her first-team that had been standing watch with her ever since they reached the loiter point for the expected rendezvous with the civilian boat. She glanced at the cell phone on the chart table, willing it to ring, but it was silent. They were running at darkened ship, just drilling holes in the Caribbean about a mile outside Cuban territorial waters. She'd checked their position so many times it was becoming an irritation for the bridge watch. She decided to think about something else for a while.

"Range and bearing to the contact?"

The Navigator looked up from the radar screen. "Which one, Captain?"

"Both."

"The *Junebug* is still showing pulse emissions. She bears zero-niner-five relative at two-five-double zero. The other contact bears zero-two-four relative at eight thousand. The *Junebug* is barely making turns, just cruising back and forth in a kind of racetrack pattern. Contact Two is also moving dead slow but heading in our direction." The Captain walked over to the chart table and stood staring at it for lack of anything better to do. "And we're sure about the ID on Contact Two?"

"She lights up like a Christmas tree, Captain." Chief Larimore responded from his corner of the bridge. "It's the Russian. *Viktor Leonov*, three hundred eight feet. Vishnya class Intel ship. Top speed is only about sixteen knots and they aren't making anything like that. It'll take her a while to see us."

"It's a spy ship, Chief." The Navigator left the radar repeater and walked to the chart table. "They saw us a long time ago. Maybe we should light up a little, Captain. You know look all innocent and like that."

"We *are* innocent, Gator—at least so far. And we're in international waters. I'm not gonna be intimidated. We'll continue to steam around out here in the current pattern. When we get the call, we'll light up and slide ourselves between the *Junebug* and the Russian. I'll get with the Boatswain and set it up so the meet looks like the Coast Guard rendering assistance at sea or something. And for God's sake—when the call comes, keep it neutral. If that chatty retired commander starts running off at the mouth, you cut him off in a hurry. That Russian is rigged to monitor everything up to and including a fish-fart."

Ground Zero

Gunny Simmons and Sgt. Ebenhoch could see the fire-fight clearly as they dashed around one leg of the mansion and maneuvered for the drainage ditch. The Cubans had set up a firing line with shooters in the ditch and in two little clusters of potted plants closer to the mansion entrance. Grafton and Hasford were conserving ammo and snap-shooting from behind a pair of concrete columns on the mansion's porch. Simmons elbowed Ebenhoch and pointed at the nearest Cuban position. It looked to be two shooters blazing away with AKs between them and the ditch. He hit the radio transmit switch to let Hasford and Grafton know what he planned to do. "We're gonna take out the two on your left and then go for the ditch. Soon as we start busting caps, you two break contact and move left. Try to get to the Y intersection. We'll rally there."

They had the drop on the Cubans who were focused and concentrating their fire on the Marines on the mansion's porch. That made them easy prey when Simmons and Ebenhoch charged directly at them. The Cubans died in a shower of pottery shards as the Marines pumped rounds into their position. Their move brought a fusillade of fire from the Cubans in the ditch as they quickly swung their weapons to address the threat from their flank. Simmons and Ebenhoch changed magazines huddled behind what was left of the shattered pottery and glanced through their NVGs to see Grafton and Hasford rushing out of the fight. They were nearly clear of the porch when Simmons saw one of them go down hard.

"Hasford's hit!" The call came from Grafton who had hold of the evac strap on his buddy's gear and was hauling him across the tile and into the shadows.

"Can you handle it?" Simmons asked over the radio. The Cubans in the ditch were now moving in his direction.

"He's bad, Gunny! I need to get some of the bleeding stopped before I try to move him."

"Find some cover and do what you gotta do!" He turned to Ebenhoch and pulled a grenade from his modular vest. "Frag goes and we go right after it into that ditch." Simmons got the nod of understanding and then pulled the pin.

The Cubans on *Cayo Piedra* were getting organized and aggressive. Groups of them that had been helping to fight the fire on Castro's yacht had returned to their quarters, found their weapons and equipment, and rushed off into the dark hunting for whoever it was assaulting their island stronghold. Shake and Mike could hear a bunch of them shouting and thrashing their way through the low scrub leading to the beach. "They've got it figured that we must have come from the sea," Shake said to Mike and Ralph Bartlett. "They're gonna be sweeping the beach."

"Where the hell are the Gunny and his guys?" Mike Stokey was peering into the dark, guarding Carlos Ruiz-Romero who sat dazed with his back against a palm tree. "Sounds like they're in a hot fight," Steamer Bartlett said listening to rounds being exchanged to the north of the beach position. "Think we should go ahead and get the boat in the water?"

"Better wait on that, Steamer." Shake was about to radio for a situation report when he heard shouting and saw the first Cubans stomping through the bush. "They're organizing a sweep. We don't want them to spot the boat."

He looked at Carlos Ruiz-Romero and decided the man was not likely to panic or pass out. "Carlos," he said as he crawled over to the man, "we're gonna get you out of this but it's not gonna be quick or pretty. Are you gonna be OK?" Carlos nodded. He was finally beginning to understand the situation. "I'm OK. I'll do whatever you need me to do."

"Steamer, I'm gonna leave him with you. We need to pull these guys away from the beach." He pointed at the MP-5 hanging around the big sailor's neck. "Don't pick a fight, but if they come at you, open up and we'll come running back to help out."

Shake led Mike Stokey off into the dark, sound ranging on the approaching Cuban search parties. When they hit a well-used trail to the rear of the guard garrison, he called a halt. "They'll come this way rather than tromp through the boonies." He motioned at a stand of palms on either side of the trail. We'll set up in there and take 'em as they come. You OK for ammo?"

"Two mags plus what's left in the gun." Mike glanced at Shake's empty hands. "Where's the shotgun?"

"I left the damn thing back in the big house. Give me your spare .45 mags."

They set up in the palms with 70 rounds of 9mm and 20 rounds of .45 ACP, hoping it was enough to slow up an unknown number of Cubans approaching from their right.

Steamer Bartlett touched Carlos Ruiz-Romero on the shoulder and whispered. "Listen, shipmate—you just sit here and guard the boat. Don't panic and don't do anything stupid." When he was fairly sure his message was received and understood, Bartlett checked the chamber of his MP-5SD for a ready round and slid off to the left toward the blaze on the jetty. With that conflagration as illumination he'd spotted two Cuban soldiers strolling down the beach in their direction. They were gabbling loudly in Spanish and sharing a cigarette, so he was fairly sure it was just a routine search party. Probably the only two bodies they could spare, he thought, as he set up in the scrub brush for a shot on both men as they passed to his left or seaward side. There were a lot of armed Cubans running all over the island but these two were the only ones he'd seen actually on the beach. That made them threats and threats had to be eliminated.

Bartlett snuggled into the soft sand behind a sprawling bush and tried to remember his Navy small arms training. There hadn't been much and as he advanced in rank what there was mostly involved pistols. Gunny Simmons and the Raiders had run him through a familiarization exercise with the MP-5SD back on the *Junebug*, but now he couldn't remember which way he was supposed to move the selector switch for semi-automatic, burst, or full-automatic fire. All he could remember as he watched the Cuban soldiers approach jabbering at each other in loud voices was that there was a bunch of little red projectiles painted on the left side of the gun: One for single-shot, two or three for burst fire, and a whole bunch of those little red things for full-auto. Steamer decided the middle was safe enough, so he thumbed the switch and stared at the front sight.

The Cubans were back-lit perfectly by the blaze that was illuminating the sky to their backs. When they were directly opposite him, he squeezed the trigger and felt the weapon jump in burst-fire mode. Got it right, he thought and fired three more controlled bursts into the Cubans. They collapsed cooperatively in a pile on the sand and Bartlett rushed to check his shooting. It looked like he'd been on target but both men were still alive. He solved that by pumping a couple more bursts into each body before he hauled them into the surf and rushed back to check on the American they'd been sent to rescue.

"Here they come," Shake whispered to Mike Stokey as a column of Cuban soldiers came into view moving along the trail leading to the beach. They were bunched up and not very disciplined, he noticed. The guy in front with the flashlight looked like a leader, so he put the luminous dot of his front sight blade on the man's torso and squeezed the trigger. The man went down immediately and Shake switched targets as Mike opened up at his side with the suppressed MP-5. The fight was short and sharp. Shake figured they'd probably killed or wounded two or three in the ambush but the rest of the Cubans were pulling back, just pumping desultory rounds in their direction to cover the withdrawal.

"Let's work our way back to the beach," Shake turned to Mike and pointed in the direction they needed to go. "We need to get off this island before this thing turns into World War Three."

Gunny Simmons and Sgt. Ebenhoch followed their grenade into the drainage ditch, maneuvering shoulder-to-shoulder and shooting at anything that moved. The frag had disposed of about four of the tightly-clustered shooters but there looked to be about four more scrambling up out of the ditch to put as much distance as possible between themselves and the sharpshooting attackers. The two Raiders stomped their way over the dead and wounded taking snap shots at the escaping Cubans. They got two more before the remaining pair disappeared into the dark.

"Worth chasing them?" Ebenhoch dropped his empty magazine into a dump-pouch and snapped a full one into his M-4. "Let 'em run," Simmons said and hit the transmit switch on his radio. There seemed to be little firefights going on all over the island and he was starting to lose his situational awareness. "Earnie, say your position."

"I'm about fifty meters south of the big house, Gunny. Couldn't go any further with Hasford. He's in really bad shape."

"Stay where you are. We're coming to find you. We'll be approaching from the direction of the ditch. When you hear us, sound off on the ISR."

Simmons led Ebenhoch on a run to their right where he could see a huge clump of palms disrupting the flat horizon. That's likely where Grafton and Hasford were. It was the only concealment between the house and the road intersection. Ebenhoch caught the Gunny's elbow just before they crashed into the trees. He was pointing off the left where Simmons could see a squad of Cuban soldiers piling out of a small boat. Reinforcements were arriving from the northern islet and fanning out into an assault line. He hit the transmit switch and sent a warning. "All hands this net, be advised we've got company coming our way from the north island. Scrub the rally at the intersection. Everybody head for the boat!"

"I hear you, Gunny!" Grafton transmitted. "We're about twenty meters to your right near a big palm. Look for a glow-worm." Grafton snapped a little chem-light into action and then stuck it under the band around the base of his helmet. When he heard Simmons and Ebenhoch thrashing toward him, he turned back to Hasford. The man was still breathing, but that was about all. Earnie had done everything he could with his combat medical kit, but it was superficial stuff and Gus was torn up badly inside. A round had entered near his right armpit and ripped directly across the chest. God only knew what kind of damage the bullet had done to Hasford's internal organs, but it was most definitely serious.

Simmons and Ebenhoch spotted the light and changed direction to find Grafton on his knees pumping at Hasford's chest in an attempt to keep the wounded man's heart pumping. The Gunny dropped to a knee and took a quick look at his wounded Raider. He'd seen a lot of shot-up men in his time and this one was not likely to survive the damage inside his torso. Hasford was struggling to breathe and his skin felt cold and clammy. If there was any off-chance of saving Hasford, they would have to get him to expert medical attention in a hurry and that meant getting him off the island. The immediate priority for Gunny Simmons was now the survival of his men.

"Help me get him up on my shoulders," he said grasping Hasford's modular load-bearing vest. "We go directly for the beach. Mark, call the Gunner and tell them to get the boat in the water."

Ebenhoch made the call on the fly as he led off in the direction of the beach. Simmons, struggling under Hasford's nearly dead weight, followed with Corporal Grafton bringing up the rear. It was slow going on a direct line for the shore. Carrying Hasford they couldn't afford to make much speed, and they needed to avoid any trails where they might run into Cuban patrols. They were just passing the road intersection when they bumped the right flank of the Cuban sweep line.

There were loud shouts in Spanish and an immediate fusillade of AK fire. Grafton and Ebenhoch jumped for cover, spun, and started pumping rounds back at their pursuers. Gunny Simmons staggered on, trying to gain some distance and get closer to the beach. He'd made about ten meters when a Cuban soldier stepped out from behind a palm tree and drilled a burst into his left side. Simmons went down hard under the impact of the rounds. Hasford's weight drove him into the sandy scrub. He was struggling out from under the wounded man and trying to get to his weapon when Ebenhoch arrived. Grafton had killed the shooter who got the Gunny but there were plenty more on the way now that they had the Raiders located and stopped.

Simmons struggled to take stock against the pain. His left leg was useless but he managed to scoot around and take a look at the situation. He could see nothing but a slow-moving wall of muzzle flashes that stretched about 50 meters end-to-end. The Cubans intended to roll them up, but they were taking their time about it. They'd been hurt sufficiently in earlier engagements and that was enough to make them cautious. Simmons and his surviving Raiders had a little time. What they didn't have was good options.

"We'll hold here, Mark." Simmons gritted his teeth so hard against the pain in his left hip and leg that he tasted blood. "Contact the Gunner—we're gonna need some help."

They had the IBS bobbing in the surf line, waiting for the Raiders to arrive, when the call came over the radio. "Gunner, if you're receiving this…" Shake recognized Sgt. Mark Ebenhoch's voice. "We've got a situation here. We're gonna need a hand."

"Where are you?" Shake jumped out of the boat and signaled for Mike Stokey to follow across the beach and back into the scrub.

"We're about fifty meters south of the Y intersection. Bad guys closing on us—maybe fifteen or twenty of 'em."

"We're headed in your direction. Move toward the beach as fast as you can."

"Can't move, Gunner—we've got two down. "

Shake spun toward the boat bobbing in the surf. "Steamer, you stay here with Carlos. Give us twenty minutes. If we don't show up, you take him out to the *June-bug*."

Shake didn't wait for argument or discussion. He led Mike at a run toward the sound of gunfire they heard ripping through the night air. Two down, he thought as they tore through the trees and scrub brush, and the number two man transmitting. That likely meant that Henry Simmons was one of the wounded men. Shake increased his speed, praying that down meant wounded and not dead.

As they approached the intersection, Shake spotted two Cuban soldiers with AKs dashing through the dark on their left. Likely a scouting element, he realized, pointing them out to Mike Stokey. "Get those two," he said. "I'm gonna find the Marines." Stokey set up between two large rocks and waited for the Cubans to break cover. When they did, he put short, accurate bursts into both of them and then charged off after Shake.

Shake spotted the chem-light still glowing in Ernie Grafton's helmet band and shouted to let Stokey know where they were. Stokey came charging up a moment later indicating the flank threat was eliminated. "They'll try it again shortly," Shake said eyeing the advancing assault line. He moved quickly to where Simmons was propped up against the bole of a palm and tried to determine how badly the man was hit. Simmons had been struck by two rounds, one high on the left hip and the other slightly below it in the meat of the left thigh. Between firing at the bad guys, Grafton had found time to apply quick-clot and wrap the entry wounds. Simmons had lost significant blood and was slipping in and out of consciousness, chased by and then stimulated by excruciating pain. Hasford, Ebenhoch reported, had died shortly after Gunny Simmons got hit.

"Not too bad, Henry." Shake moved close and got set to haul the wounded man up onto his shoulders. "We're gonna get you out of here. Just lay back and enjoy the ride."

He stood staggering under the load and got his balance. "This has got to be quick," he said to the others. "Mark, Earnie, you guys just drag Hasford by his gear straps. No need to be gentle with him now. Mike, you cover our rear, but don't stop to gunfight with those guys. Just keep 'em from running up our ass. And tell the Steamer to get the engine started."

With rounds from the Cubans cutting through the brush around them, Shake led the damaged assault element as fast as they could maneuver back toward the beach.

Shake's sweatshirt was soaked with blood when he staggered onto the beach followed by Grafton and Ebenhoch dragging Hasford's body. Mike Stokey arrived moments later, still snapping shots at the Cubans who were chasing them. Shake didn't stop to rest. He hustled directly into the surf and gently laid Gunny Simmons on the bottom of the idling boat. Grafton and Ebenhoch lifted Hasford's body in next and then piled into the IBS. Mike Stokey came splashing through the water and got aboard, trying to help arrange the casualties and leave room for Shake.

But Shake wasn't coming. "Steamer, toss me your subgun." When he had the weapon in hand, he stooped to give the IBS a shove away from the shore. "You guys head out to sea. I'm gonna buy you some time."

He was nearly set up in a good firing position when he heard someone splashing through the surf in his direction. It was Sgt. Ebenhoch and he was holding his Beretta pistol in his right hand. "I'm black on five-five-six," he said flopping down on the sand next to Shake. "But this will help a little."

"Mark, put that damn thing away and get the boat launched!"

Ebenhoch didn't move, he was just staring into the dark watching the muzzle flashes like a solid professional, barely bothered by high rounds that buzzed overhead, showering them both with pieces of bark and palm frond. After a moment, he turned to look at Shake. His voice was calm and firm.

"Gunner—private last class—remember? You go and I'll do this."

"Negative on that, Sergeant Ebenhoch. I just promoted myself—and I'm the old fart with experience at this kind of thing. What those people need right now," he nodded in the direction of the IBS that was bobbing in the surf at their rear, "is leadership—and that's you. Your mission is to get that hostage out to the *Junebug* and get some help for Gunny Simmons."

Ebenhoch turned to look at the boat. He could see the hands waving for them to come aboard. "Gunner, listen…"

"No, you listen, Sergeant Ebenhoch. I'm gonna buy you guys some time and that's the way it is. You can sit here and argue with me, but it's not gonna change anything. Now carry on and get the mission accomplished."

Ebenhoch rose to a knee and watched the Cubans advancing on the beach. If they waited much longer to go, the pursuit would be close enough to blow them all out of the boat before they could get out of range. "I'm probably gonna regret this." he said.

"Don't. Don't even think about it." Shake caught his elbow. "You got any frags?"

Sergeant Ebenhoch tapped his modular vest. "Yeah. Why?"

"Frags will drive 'em to ground. If I can get 'em stopped, I'll swim for it."

Ebenhoch dumped three M-67 fragmentation hand grenades in the sand and squeezed Shake's shoulder. "I'll tell Mr. Bartlett to steer on a diagonal so we won't be too far out." Then he raised his pistol and fired the magazine clean before he turned to run for the boat.

Shake was up and moving parallel to the beach, probing for a firing position on the Cuban assault line when he heard the burble of the muffled engine pushing the overloaded IBS out into the deep, dark waters of the Caribbean. He was alone on the island with a bunch of well-armed, pissed off Cubans but the mission was good—at least one mission was good. He'd failed miserably in the other mission—the one about taking care of Henry Simmons' kid.

When he heard a Cuban NCO shouting at the search detail to get a move on, he had a sound bearing. Shake shouldered the MP-5 and walked rounds in a wide arc until he heard one of the Cubans yelling that he was hit. Then he dug for the grenades. He had two more in the air when the first one exploded with a loud crack. He didn't wait to hear the others detonate. He spun for the beach and stormed into the water splashing and thrashing. The IBS was barely visible on the dark horizon. The boat was well out beyond the surf line, moving from his right to left. He had a long swim ahead of him, so he dropped the sub-gun and began to stroke in a long, powerful crawl.

As he turned his head to breathe, Shake could hear the rattle of gunfire from the beach. He'd bought a little time, enough to get the boat launched, but it might not be enough. He realized he was still in range when close rounds began to sizzle in the water around him. Suddenly, the horizon to his front lit up like a blowtorch. He heard the rumble of the outboard as it approached and he could see Mike Stokey and one of the Marines kneeling up in the bow exchanging rounds with the Cubans on the beach. They were coming back for him, deliberately moving back into range of the incoming fire. He didn't feel very worthy of their effort, but there was not much Shake could do but keep swimming.

"Heads up, Shake!" He heard Stokey's shout and then saw a long manila line arcing through the night sky in his direction. Shake grabbed at it and looped it under his arms. "I'm good," he yelled and immediately felt the tug as the IBS engine wound up to speed. Steamer Bartlett brought the boat about smartly and dialed up all the revs the little outboard could deliver. In seconds Shake was ripping through the dark water like a game fish on a taut line. After gagging and choking on huge gulps of salt water, he finally quit fighting the ride and rolled onto his back. It was easier that way and Shake could see what was happening behind them on the island. Bartlett was steering the IBS seaward at an acute angle from the shore to avoid the glow from the fire still burning on Castro's yacht. That illumination on the water was allowing the Cubans on the beach to continue sniping at them as the rescue party drove hard away from the island with everyone now hugging the gunwales and staying as low as possible.

Shake rode it out bobbing and churning behind the speeding IBS, watching the tumult on the island they'd just left. He could see running figures, silhouetted by the blaze on Fidel's yacht. He could see soldiers on the beach and in other places closer to the center of the island still pumping rounds at something. *Probably at each other,* he thought. Those guys never knew what hit them. And all they'll know

when the sun comes up is that they lost a very valuable human commodity. Someone was going to pay for that. Those
that survived the chaos on *Cayo Piedra* would probably
wind up in front of a firing squad or inside some dark, dank
gulag. Shake let that thought distract him as he was towed
away from the island, hoping he wouldn't get hit by a hungry
shark and dreading what he would have to say to his old
friend Henry Simmons Senior.

Caribbean Sea, 12.5 nautical miles off the Cuban coast

June Bartlett was studying the radar repeater while Linda Stokey stood out on a bridge wing staring into the dark. They could see a glow on the horizon to the south. Both of them knew that likely came from *Cayo Piedra,* but neither knew if it was a good sign or bad. There had been no word, no communication of any kind. Nothing from Ralph on the portable radio and nothing via the cell phone she'd been squeezing in her hand for the past hour.

"There's another boat out here." She pointed at the repeater when Linda came in to check for progress or information. Every time the *Junebug*'s radar pulsed to send emissions out into the dark, the screen showed two big, solid returns. "This one is the Coast Guard," she said when the screen illuminated next. "I don't know what this other one is, but it's big and headed in our direction."

"Where is that?" Linda watched as June pointed in the general direction and then she swept the horizon with binoculars. There was nothing to see but black sky and blacker water. "I don't see anything." Linda dropped the glasses into a rack on the dashboard and tried to sound confident. "They should be getting back soon. I'm gonna go down and see that the coffee hasn't burned." She was nearly at the ladder leading below when the little portable radio squawked.

"*Junebug, Junebug*...we're inbound. Can you flash some lights?"

June and Linda slapped a resounding high five and rushed to the starboard side of the flying bridge to stare into the dark. There was nothing to see but at least they knew the rescue party had made it off the island. June couldn't tell anything from Ralph's voice but he didn't sound desperate or hurt. She reached for the lighting panel, hit the switch for all running lights and turned them up to full intensity. Then she grabbed the radio.

"We are showing all the lights we've got. Can you see us?"

"We have a visual. We're slightly south and west of you. Hold your position. We should be coming alongside in fifteen or twenty."

"Is everybody OK? Do you want me to call the Coast Guard?"

"Hold off on that until we're back aboard, June."

She dropped the radio, pocketed the cell phone and cut the engine propulsion to dead slow, trying to hold position against the current. "Better go down and stand by to help," she said to Linda who was already scrambling down the ladder leading to the deck.

Steamer Bartlett let the others recover Shake and haul him into the boat. He was scanning the horizon and motoring slowly toward the *Junebug*'s running lights. As Shake flopped aboard trembling with cold and crippled with muscle cramps, Bartlett heard the outboard begin to cough and sputter. They just might have enough fuel left in the outboard to make it he estimated. If not, the *Junebug* could maneuver to pick them up. Either way, they were home free—except for the dead Marine. And it wasn't looking good for Gunny Simmons who was slumped, dosed with a morphine Syrette, and rolling like a corpse against the swells that smacked into the IBS as they chugged across the current.

Sergeant Mark Ebenhoch also sat staring at the lights on the horizon, struggling to think clearly now that he was in command of the mission. He was fighting the adrenaline surge as well as a flood of depression that hit him every time he glanced down at Hasford's dead body. It wasn't the first dead man he'd seen in his time, but this was Gus Hasford, the guy who helped haul them both through the most difficult times in training, his hard-charging running-mate. He couldn't imagine that life in the Raiders would ever be the same. At least Gus died in a fight, on a mission, doing what they all signed up to do. *He wouldn't have wanted to go any other way,* Ebenhoch thought. Gus was a player, always had been, and he knew the stakes in the Marine Corps game. He tried to hold on to that thought and focus on the remainder of the mission. There was still a lot to be done.

The outboard quit, starved for fuel just 30 meters from the *Junebug* and they had to paddle to come alongside. Linda Stokey, standing on the deck, tossed them a line and hauled them in close where the Marines could secure the rubber boat firmly against a growing Caribbean chop. Those that were able immediately jumped onto the deck and began to offload. The first thing handed up out of the IBS was a shivering Carlos Ruiz-Romero. Mike and Linda Stokey hustled him down to the warmth of the cabin where they could get something hot into him and fend off shock. The guy was in a zombie state but that wouldn't last long now that he was safe. Next up was Gunny Simmons who was thankfully unconscious and didn't react as they struggled to get him up onto the *Junebug*'s deck. The last thing handed up was Corporal Gus Hasford's body. Sgt. Ebenhoch retrieved a poncho-liner from his rucksack and wrapped the dead man neatly before they carried him below.

With Simmons groaning and gasping on one of the bunks, Shake sent June Bartlett for the onboard medical kit and considered the situation. "This is a combat lifesaver drill," he said. "No more morphine. We'll look for bleeders and treat those with quick-clot. Break out the inflatable splint and let's get that leg immobilized." There was no question about command or responsibility as they rushed to carry out the orders. Shake had both at this point and he was not about to hear any arguments.

"Steamer," he shouted as Bartlett scrambled up the ladder to the flying bridge, "get us underway—best speed. Find that Coast Guard vessel and tell 'em we're gonna need emergency medical care!"

On the bridge of the Mohawk, the Captain and the Navigator nearly collided jumping to answer the cell phone that was sitting on the chart table ringing stridently. Captain Priscilla Walker snatched the phone, checked the caller ID, and tossed it to her officer. "It's him. Find out what he wants to do." Then she turned back toward the helm and hopped into her chair. "All hands stand by for maneuvering. Tell the Boatswain to muster his crew and get the accommodation ladder ready for rigging out."

"Lt. Redding, sir—can I help you?"

"I believe you might, Lieutenant. We need to meet ASAP."

"Yessir. We are standing by here. Do you have us on radar?"

"Yeah, I can see you. I can also see another vessel not far off. What's that about?"

"We can discuss that at another time, sir. I think we should really concentrate on the rendezvous, don't you?"

The Navigator hoped the man on the other end of the conversation caught his tone. He didn't want to have to explain that a Russian spy ship was closing on their position. There was some hesitation, but the response was guarded as if the old sailor got the message.

"Yeah, I understand what you're getting at here, Lieutenant. I'm gonna steer due north from my current position. That should put me close to you in about a half hour or so. You'll see my running lights. Be advised we have casualties aboard. We're gonna need a doctor or a senior medical corpsman right away. Can you provide?"

"We've got an independent duty corpsman aboard, sir. He'll be standing by. Can you say the nature of the injuries?"

"Call it penetrating wounds to the hip and a leg. Your guy should get the drift. We're doing what we can here, but he's gonna need a professional soonest."

The Navigator looked over at his Captain and saw her signal. "The Captain has asked me to find out if you picked up the package you were after, Commander."

"Affirmative, Lieutenant. The package is in good shape. Call on this number when you've got us in sight."

"They've got the guy, Captain." The Mohawk's navigator dropped the phone on the chart table and went to look at the radar repeater. "He's heading toward us now. I've got him on the scope. They've got wounded aboard, Ma'am. Apparently one is serious."

Captain Priscilla Walker nodded and then leaned over to take a look at the screen. "The Russian is holding course and speed. Let's get ourselves to a point about right here." She tapped the screen for the navigator and the helmsman. "Then we'll come about and go dead slow. I want the Russian on our port side, and we'll take them aboard on the starboard side. Let the boatswain know and tell him I want it done in a hurry. Alert the Doc and tell him what we know. Soon as we've got the hostage and the Marines aboard, hustle them all below with no delays."

Aboard the *Viktor Leonov* (SSV-175) the Russian Captain was reading a dispatch he'd just been handed by one of his communicators. "Come left to course two-seven-zero," he said to the conning crew on the bridge. "Make turns for ten knots."

"The American Coast Guard vessel is maneuvering," his Executive Officer said pointing at the radar repeater. "And the smaller vessel has turned onto a parallel course."

The captain shrugged and waved the message form in his hand. "We are directed to proceed directly to the island. No change in orders or priorities."

"Still leaves me wondering," the XO said as he stared at the running lights receding into the darkness. "What the hell are the Americans doing out here—this close to Cuba?"

"No concern of ours anymore, XO." The Captain hefted himself into his bridge chair and picked up the sandwich he'd been eating before the Russian Embassy answered his query for orders regarding the American vessels. "Apparently, we have bigger concerns tonight."

They could see the Mohawk dead ahead as the Junebug maneuvered through the chop heading directly for the starboard side of the Coast Guard vessel. In the glow of her running lights, they could just see a crew working feverishly on the deck to get a boarding ladder rigged. The Raiders' gear was packed and they were all kneeling on deck surrounding Corporal Gus Hasford's body, waiting for the transfer and the trip home. The IBS had been punctured and sunk at sea. It was deemed too difficult to deal with and expendable as a combat loss. Gunny Simmons was nearby with his wounded legs isolated by an inflatable cast. Shake was kneeling next to him whispering at the wounded man and fairly certain what he was saying was not being heard. Still, he needed to say it and he did.

"This is gonna sound like bullshit, Henry, but I know exactly what you're gonna be feeling when you wake up in sick-bay." He nodded toward the poncho-wrapped corpse. "You'll be wishing the dead man was you—and God knows, I wish it was me. When the hurting inside gets bad, try to understand that what we did—what Hasford died doing—was important. It's hard to care very much when you're grieving, but our country is safer and more secure for what we did out here. When it's time and you've got your own head straight, you be sure your Marines know that."

Simmons made no response and Shake didn't expect he would. This was about cleansing, not communicating, and he'd been down that road a time or two. "I'm gonna have to call your folks before long, Henry. Don't know what the hell I'm gonna say, but one of the things I want them to know is that when they talk about the right stuff, they're talking about guys like you."

When the two vessels slid into position side-by-side in the deep, dark Caribbean, Shake and Mike stood waiting below the Mohawk's accommodation ladder while the Raiders and several Coast Guard crewmen carried Simmons up onto the deck of the cutter. The next thing up the ladder was Corporal Gus Hasford's corpse. The Raiders insisted on carrying him without assistance and they did it with great dignity despite the pitch and roll of the vessels. Watching the transfer, Carlos Ruiz-Romero stood waiting his turn, sad and silent. It was the first time he'd shut up since they boarded the *June-bug* an hour earlier.

The rescued man chattered ceaselessly when he came aboard, spending his time between mourning the casualties and excitedly thanking everyone involved with his rescue. Now at the last moments of his ordeal, he'd turned morose and thoughtful. He had a lot of explaining to do and very likely a tough task ahead answering for transgressions and finding a new job outside the intelligence community. He had no idea what might have happened to his sister and her family. Even if she was still alive, he might never see her or meet what was left of his family. There was a lot on his plate and none of it seemed very appetizing.

"OK, buddy." Mike Stokey pointed up at the deck of the Coast Guard cutter where a crewman was signaling for the next boarder. "They're ready for you. Let's go." Carlos Ruiz-Romero turned to Shake and offered his hand. "Thank you again for all you did, Mr. Davis. I'm truly sorry one of your men was killed."

"He's not my man, Carlos. He's America's man and he died doing what our country asked him to do—no questions and no regrets. You'd do well to remember that."

When all of the new passengers were aboard and the deck crew was hauling in the accommodation ladder, Shake and Mike saw a female officer on the bridge wing waving at them. Shake waved back and watched as she smartly saluted and then disappeared back inside the ship.

The Mohawk flashed running lights and they heard the engines spool up as she gathered speed and turned away from them.

"Where to?" Commander Ralph Bartlett USN (Ret.) shouted from the flying bridge above them. "Now that the party's over."

"Key West at best speed, Steamer—and tell June she can do all the fishing she wants on the way."

Shake went below to find the satellite phone he'd pilfered from Gunny Simmon's gear. The first name on the contact list was Mom & Dad. He glanced at a bottle of tequila sitting on the counter and decided that would have to wait. He had a condolence call to make—and a lot of explaining to do.

Director General Manuel Panteros' trusted aide met the GRU man at the back door of the headquarters building and led him to a small room off the deserted passageway that was mainly used by the housekeeping staff. The Russian was dressed in drab coveralls with a tool belt wrapped around his waist. He looked like the phone repairman the aide had called earlier in the day, speaking loudly enough for the receptionist and one or two others who milled around the Director's private anteroom to hear.

"He's in his office. Most of the staff is at lunch. We will go up the stairs to his private entrance. The door is unlocked. I'll leave you there."

The GRU man nodded. "And the stairs lead back down the parking garage?" The aide tugged at his uniform collar. "The door leading to the street is at the back to the left of the elevators as you face them."

"He has no scheduled appointments?"

"None. I told the receptionist that he left orders that he was not to be disturbed." The aide held out his hand and snapped his fingers.

The GRU man dug in his coveralls and handed over a thick envelope. Ten thousand was a small bite out of the five million on hand at the embassy. It would barely be missed.

The aide pocketed the envelope without bothering to count his fee. It would all be there as agreed in his meeting with the Russians after the debacle at *Punto Cero*. The Russians were paying for his cooperation and they wouldn't dare scrimp or cheat. The recriminations and turmoil had already

started. Raul was said to be rushing home from his trip to
begin damage control. There had even been a report from the
hospital that Fidel was apoplectic over the ruin of his prized
yacht and was threatening to run a bloody broom through the
entire government. Ten thousand U.S. dollars and a Ukrain-
ian passport would get him out of Cuba and a long way from
any fall-out.

"You have the passport?"

"Almost forgot." The GRU man reached back inside his
coveralls. When his hand reappeared it was holding a suppressed Makarov pistol. Pressing the startled man backward
against a rack of cleaning supplies, GRU man jammed the
muzzle under the aide's chin and pulled the trigger. The sub-
sonic round tore upward into the man's brain and he collapsed on the floor. The GRU man stuffed the pistol back
inside his coveralls and walked out of the maintenance
closet. He left the cash in place with the corpse. It would
make a nice piece of incriminating evidence.

He was an experienced and detail oriented man, so the
Russian paused outside the private entrance to Manuel Panteros' office and pressed his ear to the door. He could smell
cigar smoke and hear the squeak of the springs on the man's
desk chair. Assured that his victim was where he was supposed to be, the GRU man pulled his pistol and checked for
a ready round in the chamber. He took just a minute more to
review the office lay-out in his mind and then shoved
through the door.

Director General Manuel Panteros looked up from his
desk in confusion. Then he recognized the intruder and saw
the pistol swinging up in his direction. He was just beginning
to duck under his desk when the first round caught him in
the neck. He tumbled sideways behind his massive desk and
lay staring up at the ceiling. The last thing he saw was the

muzzle of the pistol pointing directly at the bridge of his nose.

Camp Lejeune, North Carolina

So much had changed aboard the sprawling Marine base that Shake had to ask an MP for directions to the Naval Hospital. Hopefully, they'd have somewhere to get coffee. He needed to take a few minutes after the hectic drive from Texas to assemble his thoughts before he was forced to try and put them into words. Chan had been a big help on the trip, mostly listening and letting her husband talk about some of the mental pain and anguish he was so obviously feeling. She knew him to be fairly quick in recovering from the post-operation analysis and recrimination, but this was different. She came to understand all that as Shake told her about Simmons and his special connection with the family they were about to meet.

"I've been thinking about it constantly since we left Lockhart," he said as they parked in the hospital's lot. "And beyond sorry, I don't know what the hell I'm gonna say to Henry and Mara."

"Deal with the wife first," Chan said as she followed him into the red brick hospital building. "It's his son, but Henry Senior has been through this kind of thing before. Henry Junior's wife is the one that will need your immediate focus. She'll probably have a million questions."

"And I don't have any good answers," Shake said as they approached the reception desk. A civilian hospital worker checked their IDs and signed them in as patient visitors. They were informed that the Simmons family was in the top-side waiting room. The elevators would carry them up when they were ready. She couldn't provide any updates on Gunnery Sergeant Simmons' condition, the post-op staff would do that. If they wanted coffee, they would find the snack bar just down the passageway.

They sat at a little aluminum mushroom that passed for a table in the snack bar, inhaling coffee aromas mixed with the pervasive smell of disinfectant. "I guess every hospital in the world smells like this," Shake said as he toyed with his coffee cup. "Always makes me feel like I fell into a vat of Lysol—brings back too many bad memories."

"Consider a few of those memories, Shake." Chan reached across the table to touch her husband's hand. "You've been hit before—at least once or twice fairly seriously—and you got good care in places like this. You survived and thrived. Henry Simmons will too. That's the message you need to send."

"Yeah, I guess so. I mean the round that hit him in the leg broke the femur, but that's not a big problem—couple of pins, some rehab time—he'll be fine. It's the one that hit him in the hip that's got me worried. A thing like that can get a guy retired on disability in a hurry."

"Don't buy trouble." Chan gave his hand a squeeze. "Drink that coffee and let's go meet the Simmons family."

Mara Simmons sat on an upholstered couch with her arm around her daughter-in-law. Both women looked fairly stoic and in control when Shake and Chan emerged from the elevator and walked into the post-op waiting room. Henry Simmons Senior was nowhere in sight. Shake walked over and introduced his wife. Mara gave him a warm hug and Shake could feel some of the tension drain from her body. Reiko Simmons just shook his hand and listened while her mother-in-law explained the relationship between the tall craggy man and their family.

"Henry went down for coffee," Mara said when they were seated. "You probably passed him on the way up. He'll be back shortly."

"How's he doing?" Shake asked and reached for her hand.

"He's OK. Just worried like the rest of us. The doctors are saying the hip replacement surgery is going fine. They send somebody out every once in a while to keep us updated."

"Reiko, listen…" Shake turned toward the Asian woman and took a deep breath. "I'm truly sorry for what happened."

She nodded and chewed on her lower lip for a while. "Can you tell me about it?"

Shake scooted closer and told the women what he thought was pertinent about their mission and Gunny Simmons' role in it. He didn't skimp too badly on the details. They deserved to know about the kind of jeopardy everyone faced on that island and the magnificent performance of the Marine Raiders. "What's important for you to know," he said when the story wound down, "is that Henry was calm, cool, collected and utterly professional through it all. I've seen a lot of good men, a bunch of really good Marines in combat, but I can honestly tell you both that I've never seen anyone better than Henry." Shake looked up to see Henry Senior walking down the corridor carrying a box of steaming coffee cups. "And that includes his Dad."

They left the women alone and walked toward an isolated corner of the waiting room. Chan had stepped up to take charge, distributing coffee and then sitting down to talk about things from the female perspective. It's at times like these, Shake thought as he gave the senior Simmons a hug, when Chan shows her emotional strength. Now he needed to do the same.

"Henry…" Shake sat opposite his old friend in a little conversation-cluster of heavily-padded chairs. "I need to say this and you need to believe I'm serious. I'm so very, very sorry for what happened to your son. If there was any way I could trade places with him, I'd do it in a heartbeat. I told you I'd take care of him and I screwed that up. Sorry don't quite cut it, but it's all I can offer."

"I talked to him just before they took him into surgery." Henry Simmons blew some heat off his coffee and shook his head. "When he found out you and your lady was coming, first thing he said is that you'd be apologizing. Next thing he said was to tell you that's bullshit. That's exactly what Henry Junior said, Shake. He said it was bullshit. I know that's true and so do you."

"Maybe, Henry—maybe so—but you know I've gotta say it. My heart is damn near broken. I can't tell you…"

"You don't need to tell me anything, Shake. I heard what went down when I met with the other Raiders yesterday. They all say it was you got them off that island with the hostage in hand. They said you were willing to stay behind and buy them time to escape."

"Stuff like that doesn't mean much…"

"It ought to mean a bunch, Shake. They also told me what happened to Henry Junior was just fortunes of war—the kind of thing guys like me and you know all about, don't we?" Henry Simmons sat back in his chair and watched his old friend and mentor struggling with his emotions. "They also told me it was you carried my boy out of the fight and down to the beach. How about I accept your sentiments and you accept my gratitude for saving his life?"

Shake nodded and tried to blink away the tears pooling in his eyes. "He's a motivated man and the Corps needs guys like him more than ever these days. I just hope the docs can put him back together in shape to continue the march."

"He's motivated all right. He's also harder than woodpecker lips, Shake. I've seen that boy go up and down so many times, I've lost count. The docs say the hip replacement deal is fairly routine these days—no big deal—and there wasn't too much other internal damage. Guy I talked to down in the Wounded Warriors Regiment said he's seen guys hurt a lot worse come back and remain on active duty. If that's what Henry Junior wants, it's what he'll make happen."

"It's a lot different than it was for us back in Nam, ain't it?"

"Different times, different medicines and surgeries, different attitudes about keeping good men on active service. What ain't different is that old warrior grit. Most Marines got it and Henry Junior certain does. He'll be fine, Shake. You'd do me just one more great service if you'd quit blaming yourself for what happened."

The chief surgeon that did the hip replacement met them in scrubs wearing a big grin. His operation went well. Gunnery Sergeant Simmons had a brand new titanium hip joint and while he wouldn't be doing PT for a while, the doctor felt he'd make a full recovery. He was recommending a period of rehabilitation training and continued active service.

"Can we see him?" Reiko Simmons was smiling for the first time since Shake had met her. "He's gonna be out for some time," the surgeon said checking his watch. "But if you want to peek into the ICU, I think that would be OK. Just a peek, mind you, he needs rest. We'll call you when he's awake and aware enough for visitors."

They all stood gathered around Gunnery Sergeant Simmons in the ICU. He looked clean and rested, very different from the last time Shake had been him off the Cuban coastline. There were a lot of beeping and humming machines monitoring his condition, but it was fairly obvious that Gunnery Sergeant Henry Simmons Junior was resting comfortably. Shake reached into the pocket of his jacket and felt for the little blue box he'd brought along on the trip. Inside was one of the four Purple Heart medals he'd been awarded for combat wounds over the course of his career. Gunny Simmons would get his own medal in the near future, pinned on by some general who would make him swear not to reveal how his wounds were suffered, but that was largely impersonal and officious. The Purple Heart is a thing that fairly drips with emotion for those that wear it.

It was likely a weak gesture on his part, but Shake wanted Gunny Simmons to have a little piece of him, something that he could contemplate when the time was right or the going got tougher than usual. Nothing connects people more strongly than blood spilled in combat. And the Purple Heart is awarded for wounds suffered on those seminal occasions. He plucked the medal out of its box and pinned it to the pillow where Henry Simmons would be sure to see it when he awoke.

"You're a good man, a good Marine," he whispered. "I was proud to serve beside you."

"**Y**ou're gonna miss having them around." Chan Dwyer Davis stood in the doorway of her husband's new workshop and watched him hanging hand tools on the wall. "Who's gonna help you keep all that grass mowed?"

Shake walked outside and looked at the low ground of his property. It was neat and pristine after the week-long riding mower assault he and Mike Stokey had staged on their return from the Caribbean. The fertile soil and Texas heat would produce a new crop of weeds shortly. "Well, the plan always was to get you a couple of those little Mexican goats. Let's do that. We'll just turn the little buggers out down there and let 'em eat."

"Probably best," Chan said heading for the house to make lunch, "You damn sure won't be spending much time on lawn care since you and Mike got this workshop built."

"Production on Bushcraft by Davis begins tomorrow morning."

"Yeah, Linda says the first thing you need to do is build yourself a little stall so you can hawk that stuff on the sidewalk. We're gonna need the extra money to get those credit cards settled."

Shake followed her into the kitchen and washed his hands at the sink. "Don't let it bother you, Chan. The money's inbound. He promised me."

The cell phone sitting on the kitchen counter began to vibrate. Chan glanced at the caller ID, picked it up and handed it to her husband. "Speak of the devil…"

It was the man who calls himself Bayer. Shake carried the phone onto the screened porch and slumped in a wicker chair.

"I'm feeling the heat down here. You better get that check in the mail."

"Wire transfer was made yesterday, Shake. I saw to it personally—and there's a little kicker in there to reward your excellent service. Check your bank balance and let me know if you need anything more."

"What's the latest on your end? Should I be watching for a nuclear news flash?"

There was a long silence until the man who calls himself Bayer finally responded. "They slammed a lid on it, Shake. They've got him sequestered, quarantined, and he's probably been told they'll shoot him at sunrise if he says a word."

"They can't keep something like that under wraps—not in America, they can't! It'll leak somewhere, sometime."

"Maybe—and maybe there'll be a little furor and tub-thumping, but in the end the Administration will get what it wants. The Cuba thing is a go and there's nothing I can do to derail the train. I'm officially ordered to retire next month. We tried, my friend—and we failed."

"You know a good man died in the effort to save that guy. The Cubans should be held responsible for that."

"Frustrating as it is, it won't work out that way, Shake. We'll get the guy decorated and the family compensated— General Fowler has got that covered—but it's about all we can do, at least until there's a new guy in the White House."

"I'm too old for this shit!" Shake punched disconnect and sent his phone skittering across the glass table top.

The television was on as he passed through the living room heading for the kitchen and a news story caught his attention. There was a tight shot of a Cuban flag flying from a pole, waving majestically against a blue sky and scudding white clouds. As he watched, the camera pulled back to reveal that the flag was flying from the roof of a white-washed building on Washington's Embassy Row. A crawl at the bottom of the screen indicated this was the site of the brand new Cuban Embassy soon to be operating in the nation's capital.

Shake stormed out to his new workshop and stood looking around at the tools and materials he'd gathered, sorted, and organized for a new life and new distractions. Then he snatched a length of bamboo and a little saw. He went to work, trying to lose himself in a creative cloud, trying to focus and forget.

An hour later, Chan arrived escorting a tall man that looked like an extra out of a John Wayne western. The guy stood squinting in the bright sunlight outside the workshop door as Shake looked him over. He had all the Texas trappings from a carefully-curled white Stetson to a pair of expensive hand-made riding boots. There was a suspicious bulge under the cowboy-cut jacket that indicated the man was packing a pistol on his right hip. Shake wiped his hands on a shop towel and walked out to see what this character wanted.

"This is Joaquin Sutler," Chan said as the man extended a ham-sized hand toward her husband. "He's a Texas Ranger."

"Retired Texas Ranger," the man corrected her. "But I reckon that's a lot like you and the Marine Corps, Mister Davis. Once in—never out. Can we talk for a spell?"

The stranger was interesting. He had hawk eyes that always seemed to be squinting at things around him and didn't miss much in the effort. In conversation, he tended to speak slowly, looking away until he decided what needed saying.

Then he turned those eyes on his subject like little blue lasers. When Shake escorted him to the wooden benches beneath the live oaks, he noted that the man moved more like a soldier more than a cowpoke. There was something about his steady pace and loose posture that told Shake his visitor was the kind of guy who was ready and willing to draw that iron on his hip instantly. He had the look of a small town sheriff pacing toward a face-off with banditos on the dusty street of some cow town.

"You know," he said when they were all seated and Chan poured iced tea for them. "I reckon the Texas Rangers have got an intelligence outfit that rivals the CIA these days."

"I'm sorry, Joaquin," Shake said trying to figure where this was going. "We just moved down here. I don't really know much about the Texas Rangers."

"Well, sir, there's a few of us—mostly former Marines— who know a thing or two about you." Shake watched the grin form under the man's handlebar mustache and saw sunlight sparkle on the keeper of Joaquin Sutler's bolo tie. It featured a gold Marine Corps emblem.

"I'm part of a little unofficial task force, all Rangers of one stripe or another," he said, "and we're mighty concerned with a situation in the Rio Grande Valley down south of your spread here…"

About the Author

Dale Dye is a Marine officer who rose through the ranks to retire as a Captain after 21 years of service in war and peace. He is a distinguished graduate of Missouri Military Academy who enlisted in the United States Marine Corps shortly after graduation. Sent to war in Southeast Asia, he served in Vietnam in 1965 and 1967 through 1970 surviving 31 major combat operations.

Appointed a Warrant Officer in 1976, he later converted his commission and was a Captain when he deployed to Beirut, Lebanon with the Multinational Force in 1982-83. He served in a variety of assignments around the world  and along the way attained a degree in English Literature from the University of Maryland. Following retirement from active duty in 1984, he spent time in Central America, reporting and training troops for guerrilla warfare in El Salvador, Honduras and Costa Rica.

Upset with Hollywood's treatment of the American military, he went to Hollywood and established Warriors Inc., the preeminent military training and advisory service to the entertainment industry. He has worked on more than 50 movies and TV shows including several Academy Award and Emmy winning productions. He is a novelist, actor, director and show business innovator, who wanders between Los Angeles and Lockhart, Texas.

Gunner Shake Davis, U.S. Marine Corps, might be out of the active ranks, but he's anything but retired. Catch all his adventures by bestselling author Dale Dye in the Shake Davis series of scintillating novels.

Laos File: Searching for American POWs listed as Missing In Action in Southeast Asia, Shake Davis uncovers a conspiracy and some very painful memories from his days as a combat infantryman in Vietnam.

Peleliu File: When a cabal of anti-Western power-players plans to unleash biological warfare, Shake is called on to use his career contacts, historical acumen, and military skills to help special operators in a breathtaking chase through infamous World War II battle sites.

Chosin File: While attempting to rescue his best buddy lost on a covert mission to North Korea, Shake revisits the infamous Chosin Reservoir and discovers a plan to hit the worldwide power grid with a devastating EMP generator.

Beirut File: When his wife disappears on a deep, dark intelligence mission, Shake is desperate to find her. His quest leads him through the tragic Boston Marathon bombing and back to Beirut where Shake served on active duty in the early 1980s.

Contra File: As they investigate gang-bangers running drugs by land and sea, Shake and his best buddy Mike slog through the jungle with Gurkha troops, operate at sea against dopers, and discover the tragedy of human-trafficking that runs rampant in parts of Central America.

For these and other quality military fiction and nonfiction, visit
www.warriorspublishing.com